MURDER, SHE KNIT

"What if selling the yarn by mistake was just a cover story?"

"A cover story for what?" Bettina asked, surprised enough to take her eyes off the road for a second and glance at Pamela.

"What if the yarn has something to do with Amy's murder? She was supposed to deliver it somewhere and the killer intercepted her."

Bettina glanced at Pamela again, a disbelieving smile twisting her lips. "The murderer thought she'd be carrying it around with her?"

Pamela shrugged. "The police never found the knitting bag."

"But you have the yarn now."

"Maybe the murderer's next stop, after discovering the yarn wasn't in the knitting bag, was Amy's apartment. But Dorrie had already cleaned everything out."

"I hope he doesn't find out what Dorrie did with the yarn," Bettina said, still smiling. "Or you're next . . ."

MURDER, SHE KNIT

PEGGY EHRHART

KENSINGTON BOOKS
KENSINGTON PUBLISHING CORP.
http://www.kensingtonbooks.com

KENSINGTON BOOKS are published by

Kensington Publishing Corp.
119 West 40th Street
New York, NY 10018

All Kensington titles, imprints, and distributed lines are available at special quantity discounts for bulk purchases for sales promotion, premiums, fund-raising, educational, or institutional use.

Special book excerpts or customized printings can also be created to fit specific needs. For details, write or phone the office of the Kensington Sales Manager: Attn.: Sales Department. Kensington Publishing Corp., 119 West 40th Street, New York, NY 10018. Phone: 1-800-221-2647.

Kensington and the K logo Reg. U.S. Pat. & TM Off.

First Printing: April 2018
ISBN-13: 978-1-4967-1327-8
ISBN-10: 1-4967-1327-3

eISBN-13: 978-1-4967-1328-5
eISBN-10: 1-4967-1328-1

10 9 8 7 6 5 4 3 2 1

Printed in the United States of America

0 1021 0416484 7

For my mother, who taught me to knit,
and my father, who encouraged me to write

ACKNOWLEDGMENTS

Abundant thanks to my agent, Evan Marshall;
John Scognamiglio at Kensington Books;
and Eileen Watkins, my New Jersey writing friend.

Chapter One

Catrina was nowhere to be seen. Pamela Paterson was not a superstitious person, unless you counted picking up the occasional stray coin on her walks around town. She didn't really think that doing so would bring good luck, though it might, but there was no point in leaving a quarter just lying on the ground.

But for the past few weeks her mornings had begun with a visit from a small black cat. It shied away and bared its tiny teeth if she tried to stroke it, but it readily accepted the dishes of food she'd begun offering after the first few visits. And inevitably it darted across her path as she headed out for her morning walk.

With such regularity had come the need to bestow a name, and the name she had settled on was Catrina. Now she scanned the yard wondering whether Catrina had found a new benefactor or was just a bit late in showing up. But her gaze wandered toward her neighbor's house, and the sunny mood in which she had started the day dimmed. She'd noticed the previous evening that his garbage can had been tipped over and raided, probably by the neighborhood's raccoons. The raccoons were energetic, but her neighbors were usually equally energetic in cleaning up after them. This neighbor's mess still lay exactly as it had lain many hours ago: a black plastic garbage bag with a jagged hole ripped in it, and shreds of paper, orange peelings, empty food containers, and mystery items spread along the side of his house all the way into the front lawn. She wondered whether she should talk to him, but he was new, and she didn't want to start off on the wrong foot.

She'd been good friends with the previous owners, the Bonhams, and had been sorry to see them go, especially when she learned that their replacement would be a divorced man who wanted, for some unfathomable reason, to settle in a house in the suburbs. She had wondered whether a man living alone would keep the house and yard up as tidily as the Bonhams had. And she had been almost positive that Miranda Bonham's flower beds wouldn't receive the loving care they deserved.

She proceeded down her front walk, scanning the yard and bushes for a glimpse of Catrina. Life had been very good lately, despite the daily visits from an omen of misfortune. So if a black cat actually brought good luck, what would it mean if the cat disappeared? That a run of bad luck would follow? Nonsense, she told herself. Don't be silly.

As associate editor of the magazine *Fiber Craft*, Pamela had the luxury of working from home most days, and Arborville, New Jersey, was small enough that most errands could be done on foot. Pamela's destination this morning was the Co-Op Grocery on the town's main street, Arborville Avenue. She was the founder and a mainstay of the Arborville knitting club, nicknamed Knit and Nibble. The group was meeting at her house the following night, and it would be her responsibility to provide the nibbles. In keeping with the season—fall—she was thinking of homemade apple cake. The Co-Op had offered a grand selection of local apples on her most recent visit, and she was hoping a good assortment would still be available.

As she headed up the street, she enjoyed the way the red and yellow leaves on the trees in the yards she passed gave the morning sun a mellow golden glow. November had always been a favorite month of hers, and this year it was particularly special, because she'd be welcoming her daughter home from her first year of college for Thanksgiving.

At the upper corner of her street, Pamela crossed to detour through the parking lot of the stately brick apartment building that faced Arborville Avenue. She was by no means a hoarder, but having cherished her hundred-year-old wood-frame house for two decades, she had an eye for cast-off treasures. Along the back of the building, the trash cans were discreetly tucked behind a length of wooden fencing, and Pamela had carried home various chairs, tables, lamps, and even a large potted plant. Today, however, there was nothing worth pausing over.

Arborville's commercial district was a pleasant jumble of narrow storefronts—some with awnings, some without—shops, Hyler's Luncheonette, a hair salon, three banks, a liquor store, a Chinese takeout, and When in Rome Pizza. It was anchored at one end by the Co-Op Grocery, whose wooden floors and crowded aisles evoked an earlier era. Part of the Co-Op's facade was dedicated to a bulletin board, which announced town council doings, scouting activities, and programs at the Arborville Library. It also welcomed flyers from anyone who had an event to publicize. And in fact, as Pamela drew near, someone was doing just that.

A slender, dark-haired woman in an unusual sweater was tacking up a colorful sheet of paper. Over her shoulder Pamela read the heading, "Wendelstaff College Winter Lecture Series." Then the woman turned, and Pamela recognized her with a pang. It had been five years since that sad, sad time, and seeing Amy Morgan's beautiful face, puckered in sympathy even now, awakened memories Pamela would have preferred remain asleep.

"Pamela Paterson," Amy Morgan exclaimed, reaching out to offer a hug despite the sheaf of flyers in one hand and the box of tacks in the other. She gazed at Pamela intently. "It really *is* you, isn't it?" Pamela nodded. Amy went on. "I had an odd experience this morning—I thought I recognized someone else from the past, but when I spoke with her, she acted like I was hallucinating and practically ran away."

"Well, I'm really me," Pamela said, "and it's great to see you." Amy had seemed too young for the demands of her job back then, and she scarcely looked older now, though her face seemed shadowed by some care that even the smile she offered didn't banish.

"You stayed in Arborville."

Pamela shrugged. "The house *is* too big, but I love it."

"And Penny? How is she doing?"

"Fine—in college now, up in Massachusetts."

Five years earlier Pamela's architect husband had been killed in an accident on a construction site. Amy Morgan had been one of his colleagues, a fellow partner in the architecture and design firm of Paterson, Morgan, Stout, and Crenshaw. Amy had taken time from her demanding schedule to help Pamela with everything from funeral arrangements to legal issues after Michael Paterson's death, as well as offering a shoulder to cry on day or night. Pamela had kept the Arborville house she and her husband had lovingly restored, enjoying the soothing rhythms of the tiny town and wanting her daughter to feel that in most respects her life was still the same, even though her father was gone.

"And you?" Pamela asked. "What are you doing in Arborville?"

"I live here now," Amy said. "I've left the hustle and bustle of the business world for a job at Wendelstaff College." She displayed the sheaf of flyers in her hand and continued, "I'm teaching interior design and I'm the head of the School of Professional Arts." She fingered her sweater. "Trying to become less driven though. I've taken up knitting."

"I thought that sweater looked handmade," Pamela said. "I'm a longtime knitter too."

"I remember that from . . . before." Amy hesitated as if reluctant to bring up memories of the accident.

Sensing her discomfort, Pamela smiled. "It's okay," she said. "I still think about him, of course, but life goes on. And on a more cheerful note, how would you like to get together every week with a congenial group of fellow knitters here in town? We call ourselves

Knit and Nibble and we meet every Tuesday night at seven. We take turns hosting. Tomorrow night we'll be at my house."

"I'd love to get acquainted with some people in town," Amy said. "I'll be there, knitting bag in hand. I live right up your street, in that big apartment building."

"We can catch up on things," Pamela said. "And I know Penny will want to see you when she's here for Thanksgiving. She remembers how kind you were to us—and she's thinking about going into your field."

A slight frown lodged between Amy's smooth brows. "I wouldn't mind being a college student again," she said. "As time goes on, you have to do more and more things you don't want to do. I thought leaving the business world for academia would make me less stressed, but the opposite has turned out to be true."

Pamela bid her goodbye, and Amy headed down the sidewalk, flyers in hand. In the Co-Op, Pamela filled a plastic bag with apples for her apple cake.

"Why the extra cup?" Bettina Fraser asked, surveying the arrangement on Pamela's kitchen table. Atop a pink cloth with a cheery print of deep red cherries and bright green leaves, Pamela had arranged her homemade apple cake on a cake stand from the thrift store. Seven cups and saucers from her wedding china flanked it in two neat rows. Bettina lived right across the street from Pamela and was always the first to show up for Knit and Nibble.

"We have a new member," Pamela said, and described her encounter with Amy at the Co-Op. "She's moved to Arborville now because she's taken a job at Wendelstaff. She was putting up a flyer for a lecture series they're doing."

"I'll get the information and put it in the *Advocate*," Bettina said. "Remind me to ask her about it if I forget." The *Arborville Advocate*, jokingly described by its readers as covering "all the news that fits," was the town's weekly newspaper.

Pamela busied herself at the counter grinding coffee beans and measuring tea leaves into her best teapot, pausing when the doorbell rang. Hurrying through the entry, she opened the door to admit Nell Bascomb and Jean Worthington. "Chilly out there," Nell said, her white hair floating around her face. "Fall is definitely in the air." She unwrapped her obviously handknit scarf from her neck and shrugged her way out of her ostentatiously unstylish gray wool coat, which she threw on a chair in the entry. "The kids at the shelter loved the elephants," she said. "But there weren't enough to go around, so I've got to get busy." She turned to Jean. "Would you like to knit some elephants? They're the perfect way to use leftover yarn. Knitting can be very wasteful otherwise."

Jean touched Nell's shoulder. "You're a dear to be so involved, but I'm a terribly slow knitter. Could I donate some money?" Jean was the owner, with her husband Douglas Worthington, of the second-grandest house in Arborville, and she looked the part. Neither her subtle makeup nor her smooth blond hair called attention to itself, but the overall effect was so harmonious as to suggest great calculation, as well as expense. Jean slipped out of her coat, pale blue and made of the softest, smoothest wool, and carefully laid it atop Nell's coat.

The doorbell rang again, and Bettina came bustling from the kitchen to help greet people as Pamela headed for the door.

Roland DeCamp stepped in, frowning. "There's a cat on your porch," he said.

Karen Dowling followed, chiming in. "And the poor little thing looks hungry and cold. Is it yours?" Her pretty face twisted in sympathy.

"Catrina!" Pamela exclaimed. "I feed her when she comes to the door, but she won't let me get near her otherwise. I thought she'd disappeared."

Bettina collected coats and got people settled while Pamela hurried to the kitchen. She took half a can of cat food out of the refrigerator and scraped it into a plastic dish. On the porch she moved gently toward the tiny ball of black fur huddling against the railing. "Here you go," she cooed. "Dinnertime." The cat bared its teeth, which gleamed in the light from the fixture above. A sound like a faint hiss accompanied the threatening expression.

Pamela put the dish down and turned toward the house. But then she changed her mind and tiptoed past the cat to descend the porch steps and venture down the front walk. Perhaps after five years Amy was confused about which house was Pamela's. But there was no sign of anyone heading down the sidewalk, at least as far as could be seen in the light from the streetlamp. Pamela tiptoed up the steps and past the cat again. Once inside, she peeked through the pane of oval glass in the front door to see it daintily sampling a morsel of cat food.

Nell was already at work. The fuzzy green oval that

was emerging from her busy needles didn't in any way resemble an elephant at the moment, but over the two years Knit and Nibble had existed Pamela had watched in amazement as Nell turned out toy after toy, lately elephants. Ovals sprouted legs and heads and were sewn together and stuffed. Ears and trunks were knitted and grafted on, and little braids became tails. The beneficiaries were the children of women temporarily residing at the women's shelter in Haversack.

Jean was busy too, her needles clicking in an even rhythm as the expensive cashmere yarn she was working with passed through her carefully manicured fingers.

Roland had settled at one end of the sofa and was paging through a booklet of knitting patterns. His project rested in his lap. He tossed the book aside in frustration and scanned the room, fixing on Karen, who had settled at the other end of the sofa and was casting on a new project. "What happened to the scarf?" he said suddenly, his lean face as intense as if he'd just discovered his wallet was missing.

"What?" Karen looked up, alarmed.

"The scarf. You were making a scarf. You'd only done a few inches. Now you're starting something else."

Jean looked over at Karen. "The other yarn was so pretty," she said. "Is that acrylic?"

Karen blinked in confusion. Her cheeks had become noticeably red. She looked down at the plastic needles in her lap, one of which sported a series of even loops fashioned from the bulky navy blue yarn she had cast on for the new project. She murmured something inaudible and her cheeks became even redder.

"What was that, dear?" Nell asked kindly.

"My husband is allergic to wool," Karen said unhappily. "I should have asked him first, before I spent so much on the other yarn. And those skinny metal needles are impossible to work with. So slippery."

Karen had joined Knit and Nibble only recently and was much younger than everyone else in the group, looking barely out of her teens with her pale, silky hair and wide blue eyes. She and her husband owned an old house in Arborville and were renovating it as finances allowed.

"I'll take the metal needles," Roland said. "I can handle them."

"Are you sure?" Bettina said, looking up from the pink granny square her crochet hook was busily shaping. She wasn't actually a knitter, but, as everyone agreed when she asked to join, yarn is yarn. "You're not doing so great with that cable sweater."

"I can handle metal needles," Roland said. "I assure you."

Karen pulled her knitting bag onto her lap and dipped into it, pulling out several skeins of navy blue yarn and tossing them onto the sofa. "They're in here, I know," Karen said, bringing up more yarn, a scissors, and a giant plastic knitting needle. She continued to dig until the space between her and Roland was piled with enough yarn and knitting supplies to stock a small shop.

At last she raised her empty hands and sighed. "No luck. And I keep everything in this bag. I have no idea where those needles could have gone."

Roland picked up the booklet of knitting patterns he had tossed aside and resumed paging through it.

Pamela was soon engrossed in her own project, an

Icelandic-style sweater in natural brown wool with a white snowflake pattern. Snowflakes gradually took shape under her needles, and conversation swirled around her in a pleasant hum.

"I hope you and Penny have plans for Thanksgiving, dear." Nell beamed a kindly smile in Pamela's direction. "If not, please join Harold and me. We've got the whole family coming, but we can easily set two more places."

Pamela looked up from a snowflake. "You're absolutely sweet," she said. "And I'd love to see your family again, but we're invited to eat with old friends in Timberley." The old friends were the Nordlings, who had invited Pamela and Penny for Thanksgiving turkey every year since Pamela became a widow.

Discussions of people's plans for Thanksgiving—which was coming up soon—segued into recommendations for landscapers to handle fall leaf cleanup and observations that Christmas decorations would be up on Arborville Avenue before anyone knew it. The conversation moved on to the town's recent decision to replace all the street signs, leading Roland to snort, "Your tax dollars at work."

"You can afford it," Nell observed mildly. Roland was a high-powered corporate lawyer whose doctor had recommended knitting to lower his blood pressure. He certainly fit the lawyerly mold, with his close-cropped salt-and-pepper hair, his crisp white shirt, and his expensive tie, knotted as firmly for the knitting club as for a court appearance.

An hour had passed, and it was time for apple cake. In the kitchen, confronting the cups and saucers arrayed on the cheerful tablecloth, Pamela realized she had forgotten all about Amy Morgan.

"Where's our new member?" Bettina said as if reading her mind. She stepped through the door and busied herself at the counter, pouring the ground beans from the coffee grinder into a paper cone and setting a kettle of water to boil. Then she began arranging Pamela's cut-glass sugar bowl and creamer on a tray, along with napkins, forks, and spoons.

"She's probably very busy at Wendelstaff," Pamela said. "She's the head of the School of Professional Arts and has a full teaching schedule besides. I suppose she couldn't get away from her office."

Pamela began to slice the apple cake, which she had baked in a ring pan and dusted with powdered sugar instead of making icing. The seductive smell of brewing coffee began to fill the kitchen.

"Roland says only a small slice for him," Bettina said. "I'll take a big slice. It looks heavenly. I don't understand how someone who's such a good cook as you are can stay so thin." Pamela *was* thin, and tall, though in her customary uniform of jeans the effect was more boyish than glamorous. She and Bettina were an unlikely pair. Bettina was neither thin nor tall, but she loved to shop, and she dressed for her life in Arborville with great enthusiasm and flair.

"I was grating apples forever," Pamela said, slipping a slice of cake onto a small plate from her wedding china. She continued until five servings had been delivered to the living room by Bettina. "Three teas and two coffees," Bettina said upon her return.

Soon everyone was settled with their cake and coffee or tea. Conversation returned to the topic of the upcoming holidays. Nell mentioned that she was recruiting volunteers to work on knitted animals for the children at the shelter, and Pamela and Karen offered to make one elephant each. Bettina asked if the elephants could be crocheted. Jean offered again to donate money, saying she could hardly imagine the difficulties faced by women who had to take refuge in the shelter. Roland wondered aloud how much it cost the town to put up and take down Christmas decorations every year.

Dishes were cleared away and projects resumed. Roland picked up his knitting, which had sat untouched through the first half of the evening as he paged through his booklet of knitting patterns. He observed to Karen that the pattern he was trying to follow made no sense and there was no guidance to be found elsewhere in the pattern booklet. So far he'd produced a piece of knitting about twenty inches wide and four inches long, with a twisted ridge of raised stitches snaking through at an odd angle.

"Maybe a cable-knit sweater is a little ambitious for somebody who's just starting to knit," Karen observed, the mild expression on her sweet face making it clear that she intended no irony.

There was no reply. Karen asked Pamela when her daughter would be arriving for Thanksgiving. Pamela's answer and the smile that accompanied it brought forth a smile from Nell and a sympathetic "You must miss her." Conversation slowed, lapsing into occasional comments and then silence. A few people yawned.

"I should have drunk more coffee," Roland said. His four-inch swatch had grown to five inches, and the ridge of raised stitches had changed direction.

Bettina jumped up, saying, "There's more out there."

"Do you want to give me insomnia?" he asked with a frown.

"I'm a little tired too," Jean said. She laid one needle parallel with the other, carefully folded the smooth expanse of knitting that hung from the second, and slipped needles, knitting, and yarn into the large knitting basket she stored her supplies in. She looked over at Bettina. "You're really making progress with those squares. How many did you do tonight?"

"Seven," Bettina said, smiling with pleasure. "Only about ten more to go."

"And when's the baby due?" Nell asked.

"Just next month." Bettina's second son and his wife were expecting their first child, and Bettina was making a pink granny-square blanket to greet the new arrival. She scooped the small pile of pink squares into her knitting bag.

The others tucked their work away too. Roland reminded Karen that he'd take her metal needles off her hands if they turned up. Bettina helped with coats, and soon she was bidding Pamela good night and heading across the street to her own house. Catrina was long gone, returned to whatever makeshift shelter she'd discovered when she took up residence in Pamela's neighborhood. Pamela glanced around for the cat-food dish. It was nowhere to be seen on the porch. Reluctant to have a plastic dish littering her yard as early risers passed on the way to bus stops or school, she headed down the steps.

Between the full moon and the streetlamp, the yard could be seen clearly. The front walk was a silver ribbon of concrete, with a few fallen leaves scattered here and there. The lawn was a soft gray, mottled with more leaves. That soft gray darkened into the shadows along the hedge that divided Pamela's yard from the property of the church next door.

Pamela ventured onto the lawn, puzzled about where the dish could have gotten to. Catrina was often so enthusiastic about her food that Pamela had watched through the oval window in the front door as the cat nudged the dish across the porch floor and down the steps. Well, she decided, the dish clearly wasn't littering the lawn. It would turn up in daylight, and if not, a plastic dish was no great loss.

But as she turned toward the house to go back in, she noticed a flash of white among the shadows under the hedge. Pamela's porch spanned the front of her house, and between the porch and hedge there was only a narrow corridor leading past the side of the house and into the backyard. Had Catrina pushed the cat-food dish all that way in search of a private place to enjoy her meal?

Pamela hurried across the lawn toward the white spot, laughing to herself about the proclivities of this wild little creature that had come into her life. But as she got closer, she stopped. She wasn't looking at a plastic dish, but at a human hand, palm slightly cupped and facing upward. Too shocked to feel frightened, she bent to look closer. The hand emerged from a sleeve whose dark fabric blended with the shadows.

She pushed the unruly branches of the hedge aside, and moonlight illuminated the motionless face of Amy Morgan, still beautiful even in what was quite obviously death. Amy's coat had been unbuttoned and peeled back, revealing a pale sweater whose distinctive texture showed it to have been knit by hand. But its pale color had been stained by a large, dark patch centered to the left of the buttons that marched down its front. Protruding from the center of the stain was what looked like a knitting needle. Pamela bent closer. Yes, it was undoubtedly a knitting needle, its metal surface gleaming in the moonlight. She pushed more branches aside, and Amy's legs and feet came into view.

She'd have to call the police. But just then she couldn't move.

Chapter Two

At last Pamela let go of the branch she was holding, and it fell into place with a shiver of leaves. She backed up. The scene seemed both unreal and all too real, as if she was floating and observing herself from above. She felt a tingle of sweat on her brow, though it was a cold November night and she'd stepped out without a coat, expecting only to retrieve the cat-food dish and hurry back inside.

She staggered. Her head was full of buzzing, leaving no space for coherent thoughts, and a commotion in her chest was invading her throat. She continued backing up, half staggering, until she reached the steps leading up to the porch, where she grabbed the railing to steady herself. The wooden railing was cold in her hand, but its coldness was comforting, a familiar sensation tugging her back to reality.

She climbed the steps, leaning on the railing, then paused as a small streak of black fur dashed past her.

Her hands were shaking so much that it took three tries to punch 911 into the phone's keypad, and when a voice responded, the buzzing in her head made her speechless. Finally she blurted out her address and said, "There's a body in my yard."

Not sure what to do next, and somehow nervous in the empty house, she shakily returned to the porch, still coatless, and lowered herself onto the top step. The porch chairs had been put away the day after the first frost.

From blocks away came a faint high whine. It rose in volume, cutting through the chilly silence. Flashing lights appeared at the top of the street, coming closer, as the siren competed for attention with the buzzing in her head. A police car glided up to the curb, and the siren broke off with a guttural snarl. The lights remained though, more blinding than a camera flash, and illuminating first the church, then Bettina's house, then Pamela's yard, around and around, as they blinked in succession.

A police officer emerged from the car, running, a small officer but speedy. Surprised, Pamela realized it was the young woman officer whose usual assignment was watching over the children crossing Arborville Avenue on their way to the grammar school.

"I'm Officer Sanchez," she said, stopping when she was a few feet from Pamela. Pamela stood up and walked down the steps, a little less shaky now. Out in the yard another officer, a man, was standing in the middle of the lawn. "Are you the homeowner?" Officer Sanchez asked.

Pamela nodded and gave her name.

"And where is the body?" Officer Sanchez raised a foot as if to start up the steps.

"Not inside," Pamela said. "There—in the hedge." She pointed toward the church. "Back by the edge of the porch."

Officer Sanchez turned toward the officer on the lawn. "In the hedge," she called. "Back by the edge of the porch."

A flashlight beam zigzagged along the hedge, dancing over the glossy dark-green leaves.

"Here," the other officer called, and Officer Sanchez hurried toward him.

Now Pamela could see two flashlight beams intermingling as the two officers bent toward the hedge. Leaves rustled as they pushed branches aside. After a few minutes, the male officer took off at a trot, flashlight beam leading the way, heading into Pamela's backyard.

Officer Sanchez returned. "Do you know this individual?" she asked.

Pamela nodded. "She's Amy Morgan. I knew her several years ago, but she just recently moved to Arborville. We were about to get reacquainted. I was expecting her at my house tonight for a meeting, but she didn't show up. I came out here afterward to look for the dish I feed the cat in. And there she was." Now Pamela could see glimpses of the other officer's flashlight through gaps in the hedge, as if he was searching the grounds of the church.

"Did you notice the murder weapon?"

"A knitting needle."

"Do you have any idea why?"

"We're all knitters," Pamela said miserably, and she started to tell Officer Sanchez about Knit and Nibble. But just then Pamela heard Bettina's voice.

"Pamela," she cried from the curb. "What on earth is going on?" Pamela looked toward the direction of the voice, flinching and blinking as the lights on top of the police car blinded her. In the glare, she could barely make out Bettina's figure until she was halfway up the front walk.

"This is my neighbor, Bettina Fraser," Pamela said. "She was here tonight too."

Officer Sanchez stepped aside and intercepted Bettina. From her pocket she took a small notebook. Pamela could hear her confirming Bettina's name and address. Then she said, "We'd like to talk to you in a little while, if you can wait at home for now."

Meanwhile, the other officer had returned to the front lawn and was talking on the phone. Pamela became aware that she was shivering. "We can go inside if you like," Officer Sanchez said gently.

Sitting on the sofa, Pamela explained about Knit and Nibble as Officer Sanchez perched on a chair. It wasn't a comfortable chair, Pamela knew. She had found it at a rummage sale and bought it more for its looks—carved wooden back and needlepoint seat—than its utility. But Officer Sanchez was small and light. She looked young to Pamela, very young to be doing this job, with a sweet, heart-shaped face and dark hair pulled into a neat twist at the back of her head.

"I've heard of the group," Officer Sanchez said with a half smile. "Sometimes the *Advocate* reports on your activities."

"Bettina writes for the *Advocate*," Pamela said, twisting her head toward the door. "She's the person who came across the street before. We don't usually get much excitement on this block." Pamela tried to give a little laugh but her throat twisted painfully and it came out more like a sob.

Officer Sanchez wrote down the names of all the

Knit and Nibble members and then led Pamela through the events of the evening, starting with the first arrivals for the meeting and ending with the moment Pamela came upon Amy's body in the hedge. Then she asked about Amy, pausing to make a note in her little notebook when Pamela mentioned that she'd met Amy as a colleague of her husband's.

Officer Sanchez returned to the front yard. Pamela followed her onto the porch and watched as the other officer strung crime-scene tape between stakes driven into the lawn. Two more vehicles had appeared at the curb, one of them an ambulance. The lights on top of the police car no longer flashed, but bright lights on metal poles illuminated a large patch of Pamela's lawn, several feet of the hedge, and Amy's body. Some branches of the hedge had been tied back so Amy's entire body was visible. Pamela stared at the knitting needle protruding from the handknit sweater and then looked away. But the sight of the needle jogged something in her mind, and a thought struggled to take form.

Someone else, someone in a white coverall, knelt by Amy's body, bowing low as if to examine the site where the knitting needle emerged from the sweater. That person stood up and said something to the male officer. Then another person, also in a white coverall, began to take photographs, darting this way and that in the bright patch created by the lights on metal poles.

Pamela went back in the house and stood at the sink to fill a glass with water. Officer Sanchez's voice called to her from the front door. Pamela stepped into the entry, where Officer Sanchez introduced her to a middle-aged man shrugging his way out of a nondescript winter coat to reveal a nondescript sports jacket. He introduced himself as Detective Clayborn and offered his hand.

"Shall we sit in here?" he asked, heading for the living room before Pamela could answer. She followed obediently and took a seat on the sofa.

"I'll be going over some of the things you told Officer Sanchez," he said, facing her in the same chair Officer Sanchez had occupied, notebook and pen at the ready. In fact, "some of the things" were "all of the things," asked with more of an edge than Officer Sanchez had mustered. He seemed especially interested in the fact that Amy had been a colleague of Pamela's husband. "Are you and your husband still together?" he asked sharply.

"My husband died five years ago," Pamela said, and the detective's homely face softened.

Pamela revisited that sad time, describing her shock at her husband's death and Amy's kindness. Her husband's death was a subject she'd long been able to discuss without tears, but tonight the tears came from somewhere, perhaps as much for Amy. As she dabbed at her eyes, the detective murmured, "You know, we have to ask these things." He shifted in the rummage-sale chair, and it squeaked. "Now," he said, "about this knitting group."

Pamela nodded.

"You all knit, I guess." Again, a thought struggled to take form in Pamela's mind.

"One of us crochets," Pamela said. "Crocheting uses hooks, not needles."

"Did anyone in the group, except for the person

who crochets, have any reason to want Amy Morgan dead?" The chair squeaked alarmingly, and Pamela wondered if she should offer him another. He had a face that she thought could be kind, in circumstances other than this one.

"Nobody else knew her," Pamela said, and explained again that Amy had only recently moved to Arborville and had been recruited for the knitting club only the previous day.

"Okay," the detective said. "Let me double check the names and contact information of the other people in the group." He flipped back through his little notebook, adding, "Even the person who crochets."

As he read the names and phone numbers out, Pamela nodded to confirm them. At last he thanked her, stood up, and turned to head for the door.

"Wait!" Pamela said suddenly, jumping to her feet. The idea she'd been struggling with had finally taken form. She'd been so shocked at the sight of Amy's body that she hadn't remembered the most obvious thing a person would bring to a meeting of a knitting club. And even if she had remembered, what would she have done in her dazed and shaky state?

"Amy's knitting bag!" she said. "Did they find her knitting bag?"

Detective Clayborn stood in the arch between the living room and the entry, brows drawn together and head tilted in puzzlement as words tumbled out of Pamela's mouth.

"She'd have brought a knitting project to the club meeting, yarn and needles at least. So if there's just one needle in the bag and it matches the one in . . . in Amy, it could mean the killer wasn't a knitter at all—just somebody who ransacked the bag for a weapon and used what was handy. And if the bag isn't out there somewhere, it means he made off with the bag. It could have been some kind of mugging."

"Do you know when the last time was that we had a mugging in Arborville?" Detective Clayborn asked with a hint of a smile.

"Well . . . I *have* always felt very safe," Pamela said.

"The answer is never," Detective Clayborn said. "We have never had a mugging. Ninety-nine percent of murders in the suburbs are committed by someone known to the victim." He reached the front door in two large steps and pulled it open. "Did anyone find a knitting bag out there?" Pamela heard him yell.

The answer appeared to be no. Standing on the porch again, Pamela watched as he conferred with Officer Sanchez and the male officer, as well as the two men in white coveralls. Everyone was empty-handed. Then the lights on metal poles were suddenly extinguished. The yard plunged into darkness as Pamela's eyes gradually adjusted to the gentler illumination of the streetlamp and the moon.

From the side of the porch by the hedge, two more people, a man and a woman, emerged bearing a stretcher that held a large white bag the size of a person. The bag seemed to glow in the moonlight. They crossed the lawn, one at each end of the stretcher. The back of the ambulance was already open, and Pamela watched as the stretcher slid into place bearing the bag that contained what was left of Amy. Lights were still on in Bettina's house.

The ambulance pulled away. When everyone else was gone too, Bettina's front door opened and she came hurrying across the street, followed closely by her shelter dog, Woofus. "Wouldn't you know it?" she exclaimed as they rushed up the porch steps, "Wilfred is a hundred miles away in a fishing cabin with his cousin, and here we are with a murderer in the neighborhood." Woofus regarded Pamela nervously. He was a huge, shaggy creature of indeterminate breed who reached nearly to Bettina's hip.

"Whoever it was probably won't come after *us*," Pamela said. "That detective told me almost all murders in the suburbs are done by someone the victim knows."

"Do you want me to stay here tonight?" Bettina asked, her forehead puckering with worry. "Woofus can sleep by the door and keep an eye on things." The dog retreated a few steps and pressed close to Bettina's leg.

"I'll be okay," Pamela said.

"You're sure?"

"Positive."

Bettina insisted on making tea. Then, acting more like a mother than a friend, she tucked Pamela into bed and assured her she'd make sure all the lights were out and lock the door. Downstairs, Woofus gave a mournful whine, and Bettina was on her way down the stairs.

I don't think I'll sleep, Pamela thought. Maybe I should have asked Bettina to stay. The sheets were cool and comforting though, and the pillow yielded to her head. But she only realized she'd been asleep when suddenly she wasn't. The glowing numerals on the bedside clock read twenty after four. A disturbing image had woken her up—the metal knitting needle protruding from the front of Amy's handknit sweater. The image was accompanied by an even more disturbing thought. Sweet little Karen Dowling had been unable to locate the metal knitting needles she'd been using for the project she abandoned.

Chapter Three

Pamela opened her eyes. Early-morning sunlight brightened the white eyelet curtains at her bedroom windows. Normally she welcomed this cheerful start to her day and preferred waking up naturally to being buzzed awake by an alarm clock. But today her burning eyes and the heaviness in her head made her roll over to face the wall, willing her mind back to the blankness that would lure sleep to return.

But it was hopeless. Pulling the comforter over her head only created a dark screen on which her mind projected scenes from the previous night. Nerves throbbing, she flopped onto her back and threw the covers off, staring at the ceiling. Then she sat up and swiveled, toes landing on the small hooked rug at her bedside. Her morning ritual usually involved a shower, followed by coffee, toast, and newspaper at her kitchen table. Today she simply pulled on a robe and slid her feet into slippers. Coffee wouldn't make up for the hours of sleep she'd lost, but it might ease the throbbing that had started up behind her eyes as soon as she was upright. And the routine of carrying out the same motions she'd carried out every morning for two decades would put at least a bit of her life back in her control.

One duty would intrude on her morning ritual, however. She'd have to call Penny. They talked once a week, at least, and many emails passed back and forth in between. But Pamela certainly didn't want Penny to stumble upon the news of Amy's murder before she herself could tell her.

Downstairs she shakily filled her kettle and set it going on the stove while she poured already-ground coffee left from Knit and Nibble into a paper cone. Waiting for the kettle to boil, she stared moodily out the window, noting that her neighbor still hadn't done anything about the trail of garbage that led from his tipped-over garbage can into his front lawn. If anything, the spectacle was worse, as if the raccoons had returned to the can and pulled out more treasures to investigate.

The coffee was welcome; it was too hot for more than tiny sips, but richly bitter. She settled at the table, wondering if she should fetch the paper or whether the drama at hand was enough for now, without reading about the whole world's troubles—and not looking forward to what the *County Register* might have already done with the story of Amy's murder.

The thought of having to field her Arborville neighbors' questions sent her into a moody reverie. When the ringing phone suddenly interrupted her thoughts, she started violently, setting off a miniature tsunami in her coffee cup.

It was Penny on the other end of the line, but a barely recognizable version of her usual cheerful self.

"Mom?" she asked, as if afraid of the answer to even that basic question. "Are you okay?"

"You know, then," Pamela said. "I was just about to call you."

"Lots of the kids up here are from New Jersey," Penny said. "News travels fast."

"Well," Pamela said, "I'm fine, and Bettina and Wilfred are right across the street, and the police say it was probably someone Amy knew, not some random Arborville murderer. So please don't worry about me."

They talked for a few more minutes, Pamela sketching in a few details that Penny asked about, but not the ones that she herself wished she could erase from her memory, like the vision of the knitting needle protruding from Amy's bloody sweater. Before the call ended she turned the conversation to Thanksgiving and Penny's upcoming visit. By the time they said goodbye, Penny sounded a bit more like herself, and she signed off with her usual "Love you, Mom," her voice almost as cheerful as if the whole conversation had been about nothing more pressing than holiday plans.

Pamela had no sooner returned to her coffee than the phone rang again. This time it was Bettina. Pamela assured her that she'd slept fine and mentioned that she'd talked to Penny. Bettina said she had a busy day ahead of her but would drop everything if Pamela didn't want to be alone. "I'm really fine," Pamela said, wondering how many times she'd be repeating that phrase in the days to come.

She went back to nursing her coffee, feeling less shaky. After a few sips, she heard a faint sound coming from the direction of the front door, something like peeping, or meowing.

Could it be Catrina? She'd never actually *asked* for food, as if trusting that the very sight of her would make a meal appear.

Pamela rose and peeked out into the entry. Through the lace that curtained the glass oval in the front door, she could see a tiny dark shape bobbing into view and then disappearing. She crept forward a few yards, then a few more, stooped in front of the door, and drew the lace aside. The shape bobbed up, and two angry yellow eyes met Pamela's.

"Okay, you're hungry. I understand," she murmured. Amusement that this little creature had the nerve to be so demanding momentarily distracted her from the sad business of the night before. In a few minutes she stepped out onto the porch, plastic dish half-full of cat food in hand. "Here you go," she cooed, and the tiny fur ball bent to the dish, pausing to cast a suspicious glance upward.

"Might as well bring in the paper," Pamela murmured to herself and headed down the steps. It was another bright fall day, and despite herself, she felt her spirits lifting slightly.

The yellow crime-scene tape was still up, draped between the stakes that fenced off the section of her lawn that skirted the hedge. As she gazed, the hedge began to tremble, though the day was perfectly still. Then, from the corridor between the hedge and the side of her front porch, a crawling figure emerged.

Pamela stifled a shriek and backed up toward the porch. But the day was bright; most evildoers wreaked their evil under cover of darkness, and besides, she was curious.

"Hello," she called. "Can I help you?"

The crawling figure looked up and then stood up, grasping at the hedge to keep her balance. It was a young woman, dark-haired and stocky, dressed in baggy jeans and a down jacket.

"Can I help you?" Pamela repeated. "This is my house." As if the fact that she was standing on the lawn in her robe and slippers wouldn't make that clear.

"Oh, hello." The woman bent to dust off her knees. "I didn't think to ring the bell." She advanced toward Pamela. "Dorrie Morgan, Amy's sister."

"I'm so sorry," Pamela said. "So terribly sorry. I guess the police . . ."

Dorrie nodded. "They called last night—called my parents, that is, and my parents called me. They were devastated, as you can imagine. And this morning the cops were at my door at eight a.m."

Was *she* devastated? Pamela wondered, scrutinizing Dorrie's face to see if her eyes looked like eyes that had recently cried. She couldn't tell, but she knew different people processed grief differently. She continued studying Dorrie, looking for a resemblance to Amy that went beyond Dorrie's dark, glossy hair. She could see it, she guessed, if everything about Dorrie had been elongated. Amy had been tall and willowy, with a delicate, oval face, graceful nose, wide eyes, and a sweet mouth. Dorrie was stocky, and her face was more round than oval, with a nose like a carelessly molded lump of dough.

"I wanted to see where it happened," Dorrie said, shrugging and lifting her hands with open palms.

"Would you like some coffee?" Pamela said suddenly. "I just made a pot." A battered van was parked at the curb. Pamela had never seen it on Arborville Avenue before and figured it must be Dorrie's.

Catrina had vanished by the time Pamela climbed back up the steps, Dorrie at her heels. The plastic cat-food dish, now licked clean, remained exactly where Pamela had placed it, as if Catrina had felt trusting enough to eat her breakfast in the open.

Pamela poured a cup of coffee for Dorrie and freshened her own, repeating again how sorry she was about Amy's death. Then she added, "Did the police say whether they have any leads?"

Dorrie gave an inconclusive shake of the head. "Lots more people to talk to, they said. Lots and lots. I'm not sure they'll get very far—at least in some circles."

"Oh?" Pamela frowned.

"Amy had struggles at Wendelstaff, trying to get things organized. I'm not sure the job was turning out like she expected."

"The police will certainly talk to her colleagues at the college," Pamela said.

Dorrie nodded. "I told them they should. They're probably on their way there now. But people can be protective of each other in an atmosphere like that. They have their little cliques, and of course they're afraid of bad press for the college. Besides, the police might not ask the right questions."

She shrugged and gave the inconclusive head shake again. "But Wendelstaff probably doesn't have anything to do with it. If the killer was someone from there, why would Amy's body have ended up in your hedge? And with a knitting needle as the murder weapon?"

The image of Karen Dowling searching in vain for her metal knitting needles entered Pamela's mind like an unwelcome visitor pushing through an unlatched door. Even more unwelcome was the sudden recollection that Karen's husband taught at Wendelstaff. Pamela started to say something but bit her tongue. Anyway, Dorrie had tilted her coffee cup to her lips at an angle that suggested she was draining the last drop, and soon Pamela was ushering her through the entry to send her on her way.

"Looks like you've got more company," Dorrie said as she stepped out onto the porch.

A truck from the local TV station was parked at the curb, and a young woman was just climbing out of a car parked behind Dorrie's van. It was too late to pretend that no one was home, so Pamela sighed and waited in the doorway.

"Marcy Brewer, from the *County Register*," the young woman announced as she bounded up the porch steps. "Just a few questions, please." She barely reached Pamela's chin, despite the extra-high heels on her chic boots, but her confident voice implied that refusal would be pointless. "Finding your old friend murdered in your front yard must have been quite a shock," Marcy Brewer said, shaping her brightly colored lips into a sympathetic smile. Her eyes sparkled with encouragement.

"Of course it was," Pamela said. "And it sounds like you already know pretty much everything you need to know." She looked toward the curb, where another fashionably dressed young woman holding a microphone was talking to a man carrying a camera mounted on a three-legged stand. "I'll give you two minutes," she added, "and then I'm going inside. I refuse to be on television wearing my robe and pajamas." She hurriedly sketched out the history of Knit and Nibble and explained why she had invited Amy Morgan to join, and then she excused herself and closed the door. Through the door's oval window she watched as Marcy Brewer conveyed her message to the small crew from the TV station.

Their trip had not been totally in vain, however. As Pamela continued watching, the cameraman set up his camera on the sidewalk. The fashionably dressed young woman stationed herself at the edge of the area marked off by the crime-scene tape and began to speak into her microphone.

Pamela had never been one to use working from home as an excuse to lounge about in robe and pajamas. Her brain functioned better when she was dressed, she believed, and her customary morning walk provided another impetus to face the day in jeans and a shirt or sweater. But everything was different today—everything except a pending deadline for the magazine. Perhaps the distraction would be welcome, she decided, and she climbed the stairs to her office, tugging her robe around her more securely and retying the belt.

As Pamela sat at her computer waiting for the screen to brighten, another recollection came unbidden. She was standing in front of the Co-Op Grocery talking to Amy. Amy had seemed so tense, and she'd talked about having to do things she didn't want to do. She hadn't mentioned Wendelstaff specifically. But now—with what Dorrie had said about Amy struggling to get things organized at the college—that must have been what she meant. Did she do something that made someone at Wendelstaff angry enough to kill her? Dorrie had dismissed the idea that Wendelstaff was involved. But maybe it shouldn't be dismissed.

The article she was editing for the magazine—a description of the author's trip to Mongolia to study native felting techniques—was fascinating, and Pamela sank gratefully into her work. She only realized she'd been staring at the computer for at least three hours when she heard the clunk on the porch that announced the arrival of the mail. She thrust her shoulders back, straightened her spine, and rolled her head from side to side, realizing too that it was way past time for some nourishment other than coffee.

The pile of mail was larger than usual. Sorting it at the kitchen table, she soon discovered why. The carrier, perhaps a sub unfamiliar with the route, had left mail for several of her neighbors, including someone named Richard Larkin at the address right next door. She wrote "Not at this address" on the envelopes that had gone astray and tucked them under the hinged cover of her mailbox. She gazed at the garbage scattered along the side of the neighboring house. Richard Larkin's garbage. What could such an oblivious and inconsiderate person be like? Someone totally unaware of how civilized people lived? Flouting the normal conventions of daily life?

She decided to get dressed.

Pamela was standing at the kitchen counter making a sandwich when she glanced out the kitchen window and noticed someone heading along the sidewalk, just passing Richard Larkin's house. The someone was a stocky, dark-haired woman wearing baggy jeans and a down jacket and carrying a large plastic bin. She looked familiar. It took Pamela a second to

Peggy Ehrhart

realize she had met the woman only that morning. It was Dorrie Morgan, Amy's sister.

She hesitated, uncertain whether to continue spreading mayonnaise or not, but she was starving. She was just layering slices of roast beef on her mayonnaise-covered whole-grain bread when the doorbell rang. She rinsed her hands, fingered the dish towel in a quick drying motion, and hurried through the entry.

Dorrie Morgan entered without being invited, headed for the kitchen, and triumphantly set the plastic bin on the kitchen table. "Well," she said, dusting off her hands, "I've found a home for one thing." She glanced at Pamela. "At least I hope I have."

She flung the lid off the bin, and it bounced to the floor. Pamela got a glimpse of a confused jumble of yarn, knitting needles, and pattern books.

"Amy's knitting supplies," Dorrie announced. "I hope you'll take them."

Pamela opened her mouth, but all that came out was, "I . . . uh . . ."

"The police are done up there already." She nodded in the direction of Amy's apartment building at the top of Pamela's street. "Speedy. Now it's time to clear all her stuff out. That's my job. My parents can't handle it. You don't know anybody who'd like a pile of interior decorating books, do you? Or ten years' worth of *Architectural Digest*?"

Dorrie seemed awfully cheerful for someone whose sister had just been murdered. But Pamela reminded herself again that different people process grief differently. Perhaps this bustling energy was Dorrie's attempt to keep herself from succumbing to the sorrow she really felt.

"You wouldn't have any extra food?" Dorrie said suddenly, her glance straying to the slices of bread on the counter, one piled with roast beef. "Amy didn't eat much. The refrigerator's bare, and I've been up there working all morning."

Pamela assembled the partly made sandwich, wrapped it in a napkin, handed it to Dorrie, and sent her on her way. Then she made another sandwich for herself.

She was very curious about the contents of the plastic bin, always interested in paging through other people's pattern books and seeing what kinds of yarn they had collected. But she had a looming deadline and four more articles to edit, so she retrieved the bin's cover from the floor, clicked it resolutely into place, and ate her sandwich.

Chapter Four

It was already dark outside when Pamela rolled her desk chair back and raised her eyes from her computer screen. She arched her back and raised her arms in a welcome stretch, pleased with the amount of editing she'd been able to manage on so little sleep. She was just in the act of sending her day's work off to *Fiber Craft* when a chime downstairs announced that she had a visitor. She hurried down the stairs, flipped on the porch light, and pushed aside the lace curtain over the door's oval window. After the previous night, she certainly wasn't going to open her front door to just anyone. But the eyes that peered back at her were the guileless hazel eyes of her friend and neighbor Bettina.

Bettina slipped in, exclaiming, "That little cat ran away when she saw me climbing up the steps. I hope she doesn't go hungry tonight."

"She's become quite demanding," Pamela said. "I'm sure she'll let me know that she expects to be fed."

"But more important than the cat," Bettina continued, scrutinizing Pamela's face, "how are *you*? I had babysitting duty all afternoon with the Arborville grandchildren or I'd have been over much sooner. Did you sleep okay last night? Have you been eating?"

"I had a roast beef sandwich. Come on in." Pamela turned and headed for the kitchen.

"I can't stay long," Bettina said, following her through the entry. "Wilfred's back from fishing, and then I've got to do some writing for the *Advocate*. That was my morning, covering a program at the library for the senior citizens. Some local author is teaching them how to write memoirs. And of course I talked to the police about last night."

Pamela slid into one of the wooden chairs that flanked the kitchen table. "Anything interesting?" she asked in voice that suddenly felt quavery.

Bettina took the other chair. "They've been busy little beavers. Clayborn's been talking to everybody he can find, and that industrious county medical examiner has already done the autopsy. She's a woman, you know. Very competent. But Clayborn has no leads whatsoever, and there's no way to pinpoint the time of death exactly. Obviously it happened after dark though. And before other people started showing up for the meeting."

"It would have been Amy's first meeting," Pamela said, "and she probably wanted to make sure she wasn't late, even though she lived in that apartment building right up the street." A sudden thought occurred to her. "But wait—couldn't she have been killed somewhere else and then the killer brought the body here? The church parking lot goes all the way around the church, and in the back, the hedge is the only thing between the parking lot and my yard. Her body wouldn't have had to be carried in from the curb. The killer could have driven into the lot and pushed the body through the hedge."

"She was killed here," Bettina said. "They found blood all along the hedge, and scuff marks as if she was knocked down in the yard and then dragged."

"Killed right in front of my house . . ." Pamela put her hands to her face and regarded Bettina over her fingertips.

"Looks like." Bettina nodded.

"This is just terrible," Pamela said suddenly. Her day at the computer had distracted her so that for long stretches she'd forgotten all about the previous night. But now, as she talked to Bettina, the realization of what she'd been through less than twenty-four hours earlier made her sag in her chair. Bettina reached for Pamela's hand, cradling it in both of her own. "It was my fault," Pamela sighed. She left her hand in Bettina's comforting grip but lowered her head to the table and rested her forehead on her other arm. "If I hadn't invited Amy to join Knit and Nibble, she'd never have come here, and she'd still be alive."

Bettina stroked her hand. "Don't tell yourself that. You had no way of knowing what would happen. If someone was after her, they were after her."

Pamela looked up. "No leads at all? What about the knitting needle she was killed with? Wouldn't there have been fingerprints? Especially on a metal needle like that."

"I thought about fingerprints," Bettina said, "and so did they. But they said the knitting needle was too skinny to get enough of a print to be useful."

"What if they never figure out who did it?"

"I have an idea," Bettina said. "But I'm not sure if I should mention it. I didn't say anything to Clayborn."

"Karen Dowling?" Pamela whispered.

"The missing metal needles," Bettina whispered back. "And she got so flustered when she couldn't find them—or maybe she just *pretended* she didn't know where they were."

"But she wouldn't. She couldn't. A sweet little person like that?"

Bettina shrugged and widened her eyes. "Maybe she's not so sweet."

"Her husband teaches at Wendelstaff," Pamela said. "Amy was having some problems there. She hinted at it when I first ran into her up at the Co-Op. She seemed stressed. And today her sister—"

Bettina looked puzzled.

"Oh, we got started talking about other things and I forgot to tell you," Pamela said. She described her conversation with Dorrie Morgan after Dorrie crawled out of the hedge, and then Dorrie's return with the plastic bin of knitting supplies. "And speaking of that—"

Pamela bounced up from the chair, suddenly ener-gized, and fetched the plastic bin from where she'd stashed it on top of her washing machine.

"What interesting goodies." Bettina lifted out a skein of soft, fine yarn in a subtle, glowing shade of gold. "Feel this." She stroked the yarn and offered the skein to Pamela.

"Wow—I've never seen anything like this," Pamela said. "It's gorgeous." She stroked it too, relishing the smooth silkiness under her fingers. "And it's apparently mystery yarn." The skein had become separated from its identifying label, if it had ever even had one.

Bettina rummaged among the contents of the bin and brought up three more skeins of what was clearly the same unusual yarn. But each of these was circled by a wide band of paper with the words "That Bedford Shop" printed on it in curly letters. Pamela examined a label more closely. Smaller letters identified "That Bedford Shop" as a "Purveyor of All Things Natural" and gave its location as "Brooklyn, NY," but otherwise the label was strikingly uninformative.

Bettina returned to the bin. "That's all there is of that yarn," she said, "but she had a good collection of knitting needles." A handful of needles clattered onto the table, including a set of wooden ones big enough to handle yarn the thickness of rope. A few needles rolled onto the floor, where they chimed against Pamela's glazed tile floor.

"And—hello—what's this?" Bettina flourished a small bright yellow card. "'Dorrie Morgan,'" she read. "'Fantasies.'" And she read off an address in Haversack.

Pamela reached for it. "It must be her business card," she said. "I guess she wanted me to be able to get in touch." She studied the card. "This address is right near one of my favorite thrift stores—Railroad Avenue, that street that runs along the tracks. Kind of a seedy area." She looked up. "I wonder what the fantasies are."

"To each his own." Bettina pulled up a few balls of yarn in random colors and then lifted out a magazine-sized booklet. Its cover featured a wholesome-looking woman wearing a red turtleneck sweater and posing under a tree with red and yellow leaves. Her satisfied smile implied that she herself was responsible for the sweater's existence. The words "Classic Patterns" were printed across the tree's upper branches.

Pamela picked up the booklet and began to page through it. "These really are classic," she said, displaying a page that showed a handsome middle-aged man wearing a V-necked cardigan and petting a cocker spaniel. She turned the page to reveal a picture of a young woman in a 1950s-style sweater set and a pleated plaid skirt. "Complicated pattern," she murmured, skimming the written instructions and flipping the page for the continuation.

Bettina had gotten up and was standing at Pamela's shoulder. "Whoa," she said. "How cute!" In the white space left where the instructions ended was a delicate drawing in black ink. The drawing showed another young woman, not model-pretty like the woman in the photo, but rendered in charming detail—detail that was almost photographic. Amy had been a talented artist. Below the drawing were a few lines of writing in the bold hand that Pamela recognized as Amy's. (Of course someone as artistic as Amy would show her flair in her handwriting as well.) Bettina read them aloud. "'Perfect fit. I hope she thinks of her cousin every time she wears it.'"

"Let's see what else is in here," Pamela said as successive pages showed variations on the sweater theme—a woman's V-neck, a shrug, a sleeveless shell. She paused when she turned a page to find another sketch and comment, this one showing an elderly woman in a dressy sweater with a lacy pattern knit into it, an exact replica in black ink of the sweater in the photo on the previous page. "For Grandma Rogers," the comment read. "A big hit—Christmas 2015."

"Is it all sweaters?" Bettina asked.

"Looks like." Pamela turned more pages. "And it looks like those were the only two she made. Or at least the only two she gave as gifts and then recorded."

Bettina leaned past Pamela to peer into the bin. She lifted out a few more skeins of yarn, not the mysteriously glowing Brooklyn yarn, but ordinary yarn with a label Pamela recognized from the hobby shop. Then she lifted out another pattern booklet.

"Socks!" Pamela exclaimed, as Bettina lowered the booklet to the table. "Challenging. Let's see if she made any of these."

They both leaned over the table as Pamela slowly turned the pages of the booklet. The patterns seemed arranged in the order of their difficulty, starting with a basic one-color sock. Each was illustrated with a colorful photo of feet posed to show off the socks to best effect.

"Making socks seems like an awful lot of work," Bettina said, running a finger down a page filled with the coded instructions for a pair of socks with a contrasting band at the top, "considering how cheaply you can buy them. I think I'll stick with crocheting baby blankets."

"Mostly people do it for the challenge and the fun," Pamela said. "It's fascinating when you realize you've just created a heel."

They had nearly reached the end of the booklet, with no evidence that Amy had ventured into the realm of sock-making. But on the very last page, suddenly there was Amy's bold handwriting again. "Love's labor's lost!!! Never again!!!" The words filled the margin above a photo of an elegant pair of argyle socks, the pattern divided into variously colored diamonds intersected by lines that formed diamonds of their own.

"Argyles," Pamela whispered, barely able to keep the awe out of her voice. "That's the hardest pattern in the world to knit. You have to have separate bobbins, one for each color, and you have to count stitches like mad to make everything come out even."

"She must have really loved the guy," Bettina said. "At least for a while. I wonder what happened." Pamela turned the page, curious whether they'd find a sketch of the heartthrob who'd inspired so much knitting effort—and so much disappointment. But in the white space after the instructions left off was only a repetition of those sad words: "Never again!!!!"

They stacked the pattern books back in the bin, added the heap of needles from the table and the stray needles from the floor, and piled all the yarn on top.

Bettina glanced at the clock and sighed, "Look at the time. I've got to get started on dinner. Do you want to eat with us? If it's Wednesday, it must be meatloaf." Bettina had a repertoire of seven dishes, though the week's schedule was occasionally interrupted when Wilfred was in the mood to make his special chili.

"I'm fading," Pamela said. "I'll have some more roast beef and go to bed early."

"You're sure?" She squeezed Pamela's hand. "I'm just across the street if you need anything."

Pamela led Bettina into the entry but paused halfway to the door. "Catrina might be out there," she said. "Just let me check so we don't scare her away."

She crept further, knelt, and pushed the lace curtain aside. There was no sign of the cat, but something white was sticking out from under the edge of the doormat. It looked like a folded piece of paper. Normally she'd dismiss a flyer left on the porch as an offer for chimney-sweeping or gutter-cleaning. But now she felt her throat tighten.

"Something's out there," she called to Bettina, still on her knees.

"What?" Bettina hurried to her side.

"Under the doormat. I'll get it." She grabbed the doorknob, pulled herself to her feet, and stepped out onto the porch, trying to dismiss the idea that a piece of paper under the doormat could represent a threat. A few seconds later she and Bettina were studying the paper at the kitchen table.

The message appeared to have been written in haste, with a not-too-sharp pencil. "Hope you can read this," it said. "Wanted to let you know the funeral is tomorrow at eleven a.m., Maple Branch Presbyterian. Parents are hosting a reception afterward." It was signed, "Her sister, Dorrie."

"Weird to just leave a note," Bettina said.

"She's kind of weird," Pamela said. "But I'm glad to know about the funeral." She folded the paper and tucked it near her calendar.

Catrina was cowering against the porch railing when Pamela stepped onto the porch to bid Bettina goodnight. Pamela fed her, fed herself, and went to bed.

Chapter Five

The next morning found Pamela sitting at her kitchen table finishing up her usual breakfast of coffee and toast. Normally she would have been reading the *County Register,* but the paper remained tightly folded and encased in its flimsy plastic bag. Today wasn't a normal, leisurely morning. Pamela had a funeral to attend.

She swallowed the last few inches of coffee, gave the cup a quick rinse, and headed upstairs to study the contents of her closet. She'd given away her special-occasion suit because she couldn't bear to put it on again after her husband's funeral, and her wardrobe reflected the fact that she lived in a small New Jersey town and had a job she could do at home. A few pairs of slacks were intermingled with her wardrobe staple, jeans. And a few jackets hung side by side with casual shirts of cotton or flannel. None of the shirts looked very crisp, however, so she pulled a brown wool turtleneck, one of her few store-bought sweaters, from the closet's upper shelf. Brown slacks would be okay, she thought, and one of the jackets was a sedate brown and black stripe. She recalled buying it long ago for a job interview.

In the bathroom, she studied her hair. Too long to hang loose at a funeral, she decided, and gathered it into a wide barrette at the nape of her neck. She added a bit of lipstick and a pair of silver earrings.

Not expecting visitors, she almost lost her footing on the stairs when the doorbell chimed unexpectedly. She steadied herself by grabbing the railing and hurried down the last few steps. Bettina was standing on the porch, peering through the lace that curtained the door's oval window. Bettina was wearing a dressy wool coat in a deep lavender shade instead of her usual cold-weather wrap, which was a down coat the color of a pumpkin.

"I saw your car in the driveway, so I knew you were still here," she said as the door swung back. "Why don't we ride out there together?"

"Ride out where?" Pamela said.

"The funeral, of course." Bettina stepped inside. She'd topped off the lavender coat with an olive-green scarf. The effect was particularly striking with her bright red hair, described by Bettina herself as a color not found in nature.

"You're going?"

"I was planning to. She was a fellow knitter, after all, and I thought you might want company."

"You're too sweet," Pamela said. "I'd love company. I almost wonder if her parents will blame me. I'm not sure what I'd think if I were them."

"Someone wanted Amy to be dead," Bettina said. "That person would have found a way to kill her no matter where she was. It just happened to be your yard, and it wasn't your fault."

"I hope you're right," Pamela said. "I'd feel better if the police had found someone to arrest."

"We should get going," Bettina said. "Maple Branch is about an hour's drive. We'll take my car."

Maple Branch was west of Arborville. Pamela and Bettina headed for Route 80, and Pamela counted off the exits till it was time to take the winding exit ramp and cruise along a sparsely traveled road. Soon a wooden sign told them, in elegant gold letters, that they were entering Maple Branch and that it had been founded in 1791. It was a pleasant town with old houses, some wood, some brick, situated on big rambling lots.

"What a pretty church," Pamela said as Bettina pulled into the parking lot. "So simple, but just perfect." The church was gray stone, set in the middle of a still-green lawn and surrounded by mostly bare trees hanging on to a few yellow leaves.

"Wilfred grew up Presbyterian," Bettina said. "Plenty of money, of course, and everything is done just right, but it's considered bad form to show off."

About twenty cars were already lined up in the parking lot, and another had pulled in behind them. A door opened on one of the parked cars, a white Porsche, and a familiar figure climbed out.

"Is that Roland?" Pamela asked. "What on earth is he doing here?"

"I emailed him and told him about it," Bettina said. "I emailed all the Knit and Nibble people. I thought they'd like to know, since Amy would have been a member."

Roland hurried along the slate walk that led from the parking lot to the church steps and disappeared through the heavy wooden doors.

"Isn't Roland awfully busy at work?" Pamela said.

"Trying to ease up a bit, I guess. Doctor's orders. That's where the knitting comes in. He's supposed to stop and smell the roses."

"By going to funerals?"

Inside there were white roses in the foyer, just a few, in subdued arrangements that seemed to fit the understated style of the old church. But as they waited for an usher to return from seating the couple that had climbed the steps ahead of them, one of the heavy doors behind them opened and light poured into the shadowy space. "Can you help me with this door?" an irritated voice said. "I've got my hands full."

Pamela turned, blinking at the sudden brightness, to see a young man balancing a giant flower arrangement on his hip while his free hand held the door at bay. "I've got it," she said, leaning her back against the door as he edged past.

The usher had returned. "The service is just about to start," he said with a flustered glance at the arrangement.

"Maple Branch is further away than I thought," the young man said, shrugging. He was inside now, and the giant arrangement was resting on the floor. It reached nearly to the young man's waist.

"I'll take care of it," the usher said, not too happily. The young man pushed one of the doors open and started to leave as a few people came in the other door. The usher looked despairingly at the arrangement and finally hefted it onto a table, moving aside a pile of funeral programs. He turned to Pamela and Bettina. "People usually ask if there's a charity they can donate to. This congregation is very practical."

Pamela reached for the card nestled among the greenery that framed a profusion of white flowers, some blooms so exotic that Pamela didn't know if she'd ever seen anything like them before. Embossed black letters at the top of the card read, "Florimania." Below was a handwritten message: "In deepest sympathy. Jean and Douglas Worthington."

Inside, the church smelled like old wood and lemon oil. The usher led Pamela and Bettina to an empty pew halfway down the aisle. They slid into place along the polished wooden seat and opened their copies of the funeral program.

A simple coffin of dark wood stood at the head of the aisle, closed, with a small spray of white roses on top. Subdued arrangements of white roses, like those in the foyer, flanked the altar. Pamela had never met Amy's parents, but she suspected the elegant black-clad couple in the front row were probably them. And she thought she recognized Dorrie in the same row. Roland was seated several rows back, and with him were Nell Bascomb, in her ancient gray wool coat, and Karen Dowling, in navy blue that made her fragile blondness look all the more fragile.

"How nice of them to come," Pamela whispered to Bettina, touched that the bond among the members

of Knit and Nibble was so strong that it extended
even to a member the others had never had a chance
to meet.

The service began with a welcome and a prayer
delivered by the minister, a courtly gentleman with
thick white hair, who was draped in lustrous dark
green. Then, "Lord, you have been our dwelling
place," he intoned, gazing upward. More words,
comforting in their biblical cadence, followed. After
a pause, he looked directly at the congregation and
his voice became more conversational. He mentioned Amy's youth in Maple Branch, the accom-
plishments that had led to a satisfying career in
New York City, and the decision to devote herself to
educating another generation. He himself seemed
moved, and he paused a few times to compose himself. Muffled sobs echoed from here and there in the
sanctuary.

Pamela felt herself growing more serene, soothed
by the church's pale walls and stained glass windows.
More prayers followed. The minister's voice filled the
room, quietly insistent, his words almost secondary
to the comforting effect of their rhythms. He paused,
and from the back of the church came a voice singing
"Amazing Grace."

After final words of blessing, the coffin was borne
down the aisle by six men in dark suits, one not yet
out of his teens—a cousin, perhaps, or a nephew?
The couple Pamela had guessed were Amy's parents
followed. Pamela could see the echoes of Amy's
beauty in her mother's beautiful face, now frozen as
if in a stoic attempt not to cry. Behind them came
Dorrie, in dark pants not much dressier than the
baggy jeans she'd worn when Pamela first met her,

and a black leather jacket. She was followed by a muscular man with blond hair cut so short he almost looked bald. He had apparently made no attempt to stifle his emotions. His eyes were rimmed with red, and he dabbed at his wet cheeks with the fingers of both hands.

Out in the autumn sun people stood uncertainly, a few talking in muted voices, as the coffin was slipped into the gleaming black hearse. Several approached Amy's parents, who had formed a makeshift receiving line along with the minister just outside the church doors.

"Coming to the cemetery?" said a voice behind Pamela, and she turned to face Dorrie, who offered a copy of the funeral program. "In case you didn't keep yours," she said. "There's a reception afterward, at the Old Stone Inn." She nodded toward the three-some by the church doors. "So you don't have to talk to them now." She flipped the program over to show a neatly drawn map. "Directions are on the back. It will be very posh, of course."

The mournful procession, cars with headlights on following the hearse, made its way along the road Pamela and Bettina had taken into town, past the wooden sign that welcomed visitors to Maple Branch and advised that it was founded in 1791. After a few more minutes, a graveyard came into view, an uneven, grassy field with tombstones so worn by weather and arranged so haphazardly as to suggest they marked graves dating from the early days of Maple Branch, if not before.

The procession turned onto a narrower road that

skirted the far edge of the graveyard and followed an ancient gray stone wall that rambled up gentle slopes and down gentle valleys. As they drove, the ancient tombstones gave way to more modern ones, gleaming marble and granite, and arranged in more regular rows. The narrow road ended in a parking lot, separated from the nearest graves by a stretch of grass and a small grove of tall, slender evergreens.

Pamela and Bettina had been nearly the last in the procession of cars. They had stopped at the church to talk to Roland, who said he was going back to his office, and Nell and Karen, who were heading back to Arborville. All three said they had exchanged a few words with Amy's parents, who seemed touched that the members of the knitting group wanted to pay their respects.

Now most people had left their cars and were making their way toward where the coffin rested on the grass next to a freshly dug grave. Pamela and Bettina had parked at the far edge of the lot, and the shortest route to the grave lay through the evergreens.

"Cypress, I think," Bettina observed as they stepped into the shadowy grove. "Appropriate for a cemetery."

They made their way among the dark trees, enjoying the rich, spicy smell, crunching on the small cones underfoot. Suddenly they heard voices coming from nearby. The owners of the voices were hidden by the thick, needle-like foliage of the trees, but Pamela thought one of them belonged to Dorrie Morgan. The voice was higher-pitched though, as if twisted by some recent misery, strikingly unlike the matter-of-fact tone Dorrie had used so far in speaking of her sister's murder.

Pamela couldn't make out the exact words, and

anyway the voice was soon cut off by another voice, deeper, but sounding equally miserable. In fact, after a few unintelligible syllables, any attempt at words gave way to violent sobs.

The Dorrie voice returned, sounding more angry than sad now, and talking loud enough for the words to carry through the grove. "I'll bet you wouldn't cry if it was *me* that was dead," the voice said. "I'll bet you'd even be glad—especially if *she* was still alive."

The sobs continued, uninterrupted by any words of contradiction.

"You *would* be glad, wouldn't you?" the Dorrie voice continued. "Glad, glad, glad, glad." More sobs. "I'm going now, crybaby. I'm going to watch them put her in the ground." Feet, probably Dorrie's, crunched on cypress cones.

Once the voices started, Pamela and Bettina had paused and slipped behind the nearest cypress, putting the tree between them and the spot the voices seemed to be coming from. Now they looked at each other in amazement, Bettina's hazel eyes open wide. "Wow!" she mouthed silently.

Pamela took her arm and stepped in the direction of the grave, though it wasn't visible from where they stood. "They may want to get started," she said. As they emerged from the grove, Dorrie strode ahead of them, hands in the pockets of her black leather jacket.

The minister watched as the three of them advanced across the grass, waiting until they had joined the small group gathered respectfully at the far end of the open grave. "Let us pray," he said as heads bowed, and he concluded a few minutes later to whispered "amens."

The coffin was lowered into the grave, and people watched reverently as a few shovels of dirt landed with gentle thumps on its polished surface. The minister skirted the edge of the grave and joined Amy's parents, shaking their hands and touching each of them on the shoulder. Then people began moving back toward the parking lot. Dorrie followed her parents, who were walking with the minister. The rest of the people straggled along in pairs or small groups, some chatting quietly. Pamela and Bettina, trailing at the very end, were the last to reach the parking lot.

As they approached the car, Pamela stopped and grabbed Bettina's arm. "Look," she said, "over there. The woman standing by the little Fiat."

"The one with the curly brown hair?"

"Yes—and the green coat."

"What about her?" Bettina murmured as she rummaged in her purse for her keys.

"It's Amy's cousin—I'm sure."

"Well, you knew Amy longer than I did. In fact I never actually knew her at all, so I certainly never met her relatives." She jingled the keys and set about unlocking the car.

"The knitting booklet in the plastic bin," Pamela said. "The little sketches of the people Amy had knit things for. They were so detailed they were like photographs. I'm sure this is the cousin that she made the vintage-looking sweater set for, the pattern where she wrote, 'I hope she thinks of her cousin every time she wears it.'"

Bettina paused, her hand on the open car door. "It does look like her," she said, studying the young woman in the green coat. She turned her gaze to Pamela, who was now staring vacantly into space.

"Shall we go now?" she asked. "People are heading over to the reception."

"I'm thinking about argyle socks," Pamela said. "Remember the other knitting pattern booklet in Amy's plastic bin? The one with that pattern for argyle socks? And on the page with the pattern, she had written 'Love's labor's lost!!! Never again!!!' I wonder if the Love's Labor's Lost man was at the funeral. Did you notice anyone wearing argyle socks?"

"He wouldn't come, would he? If he broke up with her."

Pamela started to answer, to say that love can be complicated—though her love for her husband had never been—but she was interrupted by Dorrie. Dorrie was strolling across the asphalt with her hands in the pockets of her black leather jacket, squinting in the sunlight. "Are you guys coming to the reception?" she asked. "There's going to be lots of good food and booze."

But instead of answering the question, Pamela asked one of her own, blurting out with no preamble, "Did Amy have a boyfriend?"

Dorrie didn't seem surprised though. "Lots of them, I imagine," she said. "With her looks. What do *you* think?"

"Did the police inquire about boyfriends?"

"*Duh.* Yes, obviously. But I didn't have anything to tell them." She turned toward where her mother was standing near the hearse with her husband and the minister. "Hey, Ma," she called, "did the cops ask you about Amy's boyfriends?"

Pamela glanced at Bettina and saw her own distress

mirrored on her friend's face. "Please don't bother your mother," Pamela said, touching Dorrie's shoulder. But it was too late. In a few seconds Mrs. Morgan was at her daughter's side, a head taller than her stocky offspring.

The tension in Mrs. Morgan's face had eased a bit since the funeral, perhaps soothed by the minister's attentions and the simple gravity of the burial ceremony. With her willowy figure, wrapped in a stylish black coat, and her dramatic coloring—pale skin and dark hair—she could almost have been Amy, except for the faint lines in her forehead and around her eyes. And Dorrie looks like her mother too, but somehow . . . so homely, Pamela thought. As if reading her mind, Amy's mother reached toward Dorrie and drew her closer.

"I'm so sorry for your loss," Pamela said, imagining how devastated she'd be to lose her own daughter. She introduced herself and Bettina and explained her connection with Amy from that long-ago time.

"The knitting club," Amy's mother said, her face twisting with fresh grief but still beautiful.

"I'm so sorry," Pamela said again. "I'd give anything if I'd never invited—"

"It wasn't your fault," Amy's mother said.

Dorrie squirmed out of her mother's grasp. "They want to know if the cops asked you about Amy's boyfriends," she said.

Pamela raised her hands and spread her fingers as if to push the question back to Dorrie. "Please," she said, looking from Dorrie to Mrs. Morgan and back, "this isn't the time or the place . . ."

"No," Bettina echoed, "definitely not the time or place."

But Mrs. Morgan's expression didn't change. "Amy didn't share details of her love life with her parents," she said in a quiet voice. "So I didn't have anything to tell the police." She bent her head slightly to gaze into Dorrie's face. "Did you?"

"Why would she tell me things like that?" Dorrie asked, sounding irritated. "We weren't that close, you know."

Since Mrs. Morgan hadn't seemed surprised by Pamela's curiosity and was still lingering at Dorrie's side, Pamela decided maybe it was okay to pursue the topic. "There was a blond man at the funeral who seemed really upset," she said, watching their faces. "His eyes were red, like he'd been crying."

"Allergies," Dorrie said. "Ragweed. It's everywhere this time of year."

"But, Dor—" Mrs. Morgan glanced quickly at Dorrie, a tiny frown deepening the faint lines in her pale forehead.

"Allergies," Dorrie said again.

"Darling?" It was Amy's father, arriving at his wife's side. He was tall and thin too, with a face that was distinguished without being exactly handsome. "Shall we drive over to the Old Stone Inn?" he said, taking Mrs. Morgan's arm. "The caterers might not start serving until we get there, and a lot of people are already on their way."

"These are friends of Amy's," Mrs. Morgan said, and Pamela and Bettina supplied their own names.

"Thank you for coming," Amy's father said, and led his wife away. Dorrie trailed along after them.

"Allergies?" Bettina asked, raising her eyebrows in disbelief. "Did you notice if the blond man was wearing argyle socks?"

"He didn't look like the argyle-sock type," Pamela said, "and this *is* a bad time of year for people who are bothered by ragweed."

"She could have had other boyfriends," Bettina said. "Maybe she broke up with someone else when she met argyle-sock man, and that someone else decided he could only forget her if she was dead. Maybe the blond man was the someone else." She opened the car door again and slid into the driver's seat.

"We have a lot to think about," Pamela said. "Can you unlock this door for me?"

Chapter Six

The Old Stone Inn was a rambling structure set on a grassy rise along the main road heading back into town. The central portion was indeed old stones, as old and random as the stones in the wall along the edge of the graveyard. A long clapboard addition had been grafted on, looking scarcely newer than the original building.

The reception was being held in a spacious room with deep, many-paned windows and a floor of broad wooden planks, obviously polished by generations of faithful housekeepers. The windows looked out at a garden that was impressive even in its late-autumn state, with shrubbery in contrasting shades of green and vines bearing purple berries.

A long table at the end of the room offered trays of little sandwiches, a cheese platter with tastefully arranged crackers, and bite-sized raw vegetables piled in artful patterns, all displayed on a smooth white cloth. Next to the table was a bar with a handsome young man in a white shirt and black bow tie at work pouring champagne into champagne flutes.

Amy's parents and Dorrie stood along the wall that faced the windows, talking to a middle-aged couple whose concerned expressions made their sympathy clear. An informal line of people stretched along the wall chatting, even laughing occasionally, waiting for their turn to offer their condolences.

Pamela and Bettina stood uncertainly near the entrance to the room. They didn't know anyone except Dorrie. "Nice-looking food," Bettina whispered. "Shall we have a bite to eat and a glass of champagne while people who actually know the Morgans have a chance to talk to them?"

As if reading their minds, a young woman, also in white shirt and black bow tie, approached and offered a tray covered with delicate bite-sized pies. "Fabulous," Bettina murmured, reaching for one. From the other direction came another young woman miraculously keeping a tray covered with full champagne flutes steady.

Champagne in hand, Pamela felt brave enough to nod and smile at a woman who glanced over and caught her eye.

"Terribly sad occasion," the woman observed, a little pucker of sympathy appearing between her brows. She looked about the same age as Amy's parents and was wearing a simple black dress with a matching jacket. She had accented the outfit with a double string of pearls—real ones, Pamela was sure. As the woman stepped closer, Pamela sensed a faint hint of expensive perfume. "I'm June Seegrave," she added.

"Pamela Paterson," Pamela responded. "And this is Bettina Fraser."

"Have you known the Morgans long?" June Seegrave asked.

"Actually, we don't know them at all," Pamela said, and she explained her connection with Amy.

"Lovely young woman," June said. "And a terrible blow to her parents. They're such good people, and so involved in the community. Always looking for someone to help." She sighed. "It just doesn't seem right."

"June! How are you?" said a voice behind Pamela. She stepped back, and a fourth woman joined the group, dressed like June in chic but sedate black, with pearls. "It's been years."

"Maple Branch has missed you," June said.

"I've missed Maple Branch, but Andy's job, you know. The offer was just too good to turn down."

More introductions—the woman's name was Lydia Bostock—and everyone again agreed what a sad occasion it was. "It was sweet of you to come back for this," June said.

"I felt so bad when I heard."

The young woman who had offered the miniature pies reappeared with another tray, this time piled with miniature puff pastries, sliced in half and filled with something that looked very tempting. "Crab," the server informed them.

More champagne followed and no one said anything for a few minutes except to exclaim about the tastiness of the crab puffs.

Lydia began to scan the room. "The crab puffs went that way," June said with a wink, gesturing toward the retreating server.

"Is that Katherine Waring?" Lydia asked, nodding toward a much older but also very elegant woman chatting with a group of women about her age and equally elegant.

"Yes. She looks great, doesn't she?" June said. "Widowed now, and thinking about following her children to the West Coast."

"Nate Waring was such a sweet man. I'm sorry to hear he's gone. What else is new in town?" Lydia smiled at Pamela. "Excuse us just a minute," she said. "I have a bit of catching up to do."

"Well," June said, "the new middle school finally got built, and after four terms, Marlys Grover decided not to run for mayor again, and lots of people have been up to no good. Jim Steiner ran off with Elward Koster's wife, and Tracy-Jean Slade disappeared with a quarter of a million dollars of the taxpayers' money."

Lydia raised a tastefully manicured hand to her mouth. "Oh my gosh," she said.

June nodded. "And after Jeff Morgan got her that job too." She turned to Pamela and said quietly, "Tracy-Jean Slade was the Maple Branch borough clerk. Jeff Morgan is Amy's father." She turned back to Lydia. "A fabulous new restaurant opened in town, Fontani di Fiorenza, but then the chef at Taste of Tuscany accused the new place of stealing all his recipes."

"Taste of Tuscany was always so good," Lydia said. "I miss it. Perhaps we'll move back to Maple Branch when Andy retires."

The champagne server returned to claim empty champagne flutes, and June said, "Shall we pay our respects now?"

"We should tell the Morgans goodbye and thank them," Pamela said to Bettina as June and Lydia joined the receiving line, which had dwindled to just two young women about Amy's age. Amy's mother accepted a hug from the older woman she'd been talking to, the woman stepped away, and the two young women took her place. Now the older woman was talking to Dorrie, then suddenly there were four people in the receiving line. Dorrie and her parents had been joined by the muscular blond man who had been at the funeral. The older woman took both his hands in hers and pulled him away with her. The two young women moved on to talk to Dorrie.

"It was a lovely funeral and reception," Pamela said, taking Mrs. Morgan's hand. "I wish we'd met under other circumstances." Next to her she could hear Bettina murmuring something similar to Amy's father.

"Thank you for coming," said Mrs. Morgan. "I wish the circumstances had been different too." Her eyes strayed to Dorrie, who was looking fixedly at the blond man and the older woman who had claimed his attention. "At least we still have Dorrie," she said. "The girls were so close—as close as sisters could be. Nary a fight the whole time they were growing up."

Dorrie frowned slightly and did a strange thing with her eyes. "Nice of you to come," she said without looking at either Pamela or Bettina.

Pamela was longing to ask who the blond man actually was, but before she had a chance to, Dorrie slipped away.

Chapter Seven

The young woman looked about the same age as Penny. That's what made it especially shameful. She was wearing skinny jeans, fashionable wedge-heeled boots, and a striking plaid jacket cinched at the waist and flaring over her slender hips. She carried a roomy leather satchel.

She came planning to spend the night, Pamela reflected grumpily. It was Friday morning and she hadn't had her coffee yet. Richard Larkin had time for girlfriends—girlfriends much younger than he was, she was sure—but no time to clean up his spilled garbage. The trail of orange peelings, plastic yogurt containers, used coffee filters, and who knew what else still stretched from the remains of the black plastic garbage bag at the mouth of the tipped-over bin all the way to the front lawn. And while she was on the subject of Richard Larkin's failings, judging from the buildup of fallen leaves, the lawn apparently hadn't been raked in at least a week.

Pamela watched the young woman hurry down Richard Larkin's front walk and turn in the direction of Arborville Avenue. Probably catching the bus at the corner, Pamela decided. He can't even be bothered to give his paramours a ride home?

The whistling of the kettle brought Pamela's thoughts back to her own concerns, and she set about making coffee and toasting a slice of the whole-grain bread that was a Co-Op specialty. Only a few scoops of coffee beans had remained in the can after she ground what she needed for breakfast, and so she added coffee to the grocery list fastened to the refrigerator door with a tiny magnetized mitten.

Catrina had already been fed—the little creature had been peering through the oval window in the front door as Pamela came down the stairs that morning—and the newspaper brought in. She settled at the kitchen table with her coffee and toast and turned to the Arts and Lifestyle section of the paper. More serious news would have to wait until the coffee had done its work.

Half an hour later Pamela was dressed in her cool-weather uniform of jeans and a sweater. She tucked her grocery list into her purse and retrieved a few canvas bags from her supply—long ago Nell had prevailed upon her to renounce paper and plastic. Then she grabbed her jacket and her favorite scarf, a recent knitting project she'd done with violet mohair yarn, and headed out the door. Her front walk was nearly hidden under a layer of newly fallen leaves in an intricate pattern of gold, orange, and rust. She'd have to do some raking of her own, she reflected, but the work would be a pleasure on such a bright, crisp day.

She navigated the narrow aisles of the Co-Op, pushing her cart over the ancient wooden floors, picking up a loaf of whole-grain bread at the bakery counter, a tempting wedge of blue cheese at the cheese counter, and a new supply of coffee beans before turning into the produce section. As she paused over a bin of acorn squash, fingering the glossy dark green and gold ridges, a pleasant voice behind her said, "Excuse me." The Co-Op's aisles had been laid out in an era before people bought so many groceries at once that they needed large carts to accommodate all their selections. Traffic jams often occurred. Pamela had left her cart in mid-aisle as she pondered the squash. Now she turned to see a strikingly handsome man gesturing at the obstructing cart, but smiling as he did so.

Too young for me, she thought, and was surprised at her reaction. She'd resolved not to date again until Penny was out of the house and off at school. Now Penny *was* out of the house and off at school, though she'd barely been away three months. Are you getting interested in men again so soon? she wondered. Perhaps, but this man really was too young, barely thirty, with carefully groomed dark hair, smooth olive skin, and unexpectedly bright green eyes.

"Oh, I'm sorry," she said, and steered the offending cart closer to the squash-bin side of the aisle.

"No problem." He smiled (lovely teeth too) and moved on. She contemplated the flattering way his buttery suede jacket fit his obviously well-toned torso. Nicely put-together outfit, she reflected as her gaze traveled downward. Then something about the outfit caught her special attention.

She turned back to the acorn squash, selecting the smallest one she could find, and moved on to the apples. She'd eaten all the apples left over from making the apple cake for Knit and Nibble, so she tore a plastic bag from the roll hanging over the apples and began to fill it.

As she asked herself whether she'd really seen what she thought she saw, she distractedly added apple after apple to the bag until it was bulging. Drawn back to the present by the weight of the bag in her hands, she laughed and hefted it into her cart. She'd be eating an apple a day for the foreseeable future.

Pamela browsed along the produce aisle, adding salad greens, cucumbers, and tomatoes to her cart. The handsome man was still shopping for produce too, working his way through root vegetables. He paused to weigh a bunch of carrots in the old-fashioned scale that dangled from chains near the end of the aisle, slid the carrots into a plastic bag, and dropped the bag into his cart. Then, apparently ready to move on to the meat department, he wheeled his cart purposefully forward.

Pamela watched him carefully, and as she watched, his long strides lifted his pants cuffs to expose his socks. Yes, they were argyle socks, with intricate diamond patterns intersected by lines that formed diamond patterns of their own. They had been knitted in a rich combination of maroon, dark green, and a buttery amber that matched the color of his elegant suede jacket. He turned the corner and was lost from view.

There had been no one wearing argyle socks at the funeral, at least that she and Bettina had noticed, but here were argyle socks, right in the Arborville Co-Op. Were these the socks Amy had knitted from the pattern in the knitting booklet she and Bettina had pored over? And was this the man about whom she had written, "Love's labor's lost!!! Never again!!!"

Pamela hastened past the root vegetables and lingered near the section of the meat department that offered freshly made sausage. The handsome man was looking at chicken. She waited, willing him to take a step, edging closer as he picked up a package of chicken thighs and deposited it in his cart. He was on the move again. She followed, eyes fixed on his ankles, as his long strides once again lifted his pants cuffs and the elaborate socks came into view. Yes, the socks had definitely been knit by hand, though very skillfully. The deep, rich colors made it clear that the yarn was wool, and high quality, not the synthetic yarn used in commercially produced argyles.

Pamela added some chicken thighs to her own cart too, and headed for the front of the store to check out. Two bags of groceries were the most she could manage on a walking errand.

Fifteen minutes later she was striding along Arborville Avenue, one of her reusable canvas bags dangling from each hand. She turned onto her own street and glanced over at the trash cans marshaled behind the stately brick apartment building where Amy had lived. Someone was just climbing out of a sleek silver Audi parked in one of the spaces behind the building—a familiar someone. It was the handsome man from the Co-Op Grocery. As Pamela watched, he opened the trunk of the car and lifted out two bags of groceries.

He must live here, she realized with a quiver of excitement. Amy lived here. And she knit a pair of argyle socks. And he's wearing a pair of argyle socks. But her note in the knitting pattern book suggested that whatever motive prompted her to put all that effort into her gift, she later wished she hadn't made the effort. "Love's labor's lost!!! Never again!!!"

The handsome man disappeared through a door in the back of the building, and Pamela stepped closer to the fencing that hid the trash from view, just in case someone had put out something interesting. She'd have to come back for it, of course. Her two bags of groceries were already weighing heavy on her arms.

"Well, hello there! Haven't seen you in a while." It was Mr. Gilly, the building's super, at work using a rake to scour the last of the fall leaves out from under the shrubbery. He was an easygoing man in his fifties, tall and wiry, and Pamela had heard from people in the building that he could fix anything. He also loved to talk. Pamela usually picked up her pace when she saw him working outside, but today she greeted him with a smile. He dropped his rake and strolled over.

"Nice-looking car," she said, nodding toward the Audi.

"Belongs to Dr. Randolph," he said.

"The man who was just unloading groceries?"

Mr. Gilly nodded. "That's him."

"He's a doctor?"

"Emergency room. Englewood Hospital. Works the night shift. That's why he's around during the day."

Pamela stepped closer to him and lowered her voice. "I knew Amy Morgan," she said. "So sad."

"Oh, cops all over the place." Mr. Gilly felt around in his jacket pocket and pulled out a pack of cigarettes. "The residents didn't know what to make of it."

"She hadn't lived here very long," Pamela said. "I

wonder if many of the other people in the building had gotten to know her."

"He had." Mr. Gilly nodded toward the Audi.

Pamela continued on her way, musing on what she had just learned. Two attractive young people with professional careers—definitely well-suited to each other in that regard. Living in the same apartment building, of course they would catch each other's eye. Romance blooms, she knits him a pair of argyle socks, but then something goes sour, very sour.

An idea struck her with the force of a physical blow. She stopped suddenly, halfway down the block, and stood blinking in the autumn sunlight. The handsome man in the argyle socks was a doctor. A doctor would know everything there was to know about the human anatomy—definitely enough to wield a metal knitting needle as a deadly weapon. And if you worked in an emergency room you'd probably see crimes committed with unlikely murder weapons all the time. You'd get ideas.

But he looked like such a pleasant man. He had spoken to her so pleasantly in the produce aisle. And didn't doctors take an oath to do no harm? But love was a powerful and dangerous force, and broken hearts could turn otherwise nice people into savages. Pamela knew this more from literature than from life. Still . . .

Pamela resumed walking, but she didn't go home, at least not right away. She stopped off at Bettina's house to report what she had discovered. Bettina lived in the oldest house on the street, a Dutch Colonial that had already been standing for fifty years when Pamela's hundred-year-old house was built. It had housed the owners of an apple orchard that had provided the name for Pamela's street, Orchard Street. Then developers had come and the land had been divided into lots and more and more people had moved in. But a few apple trees still hung on in backyards here and there, grown up from the old root stock and yielding sour apples only good for pies.

Wilfred Fraser answered the door. "Pamela!" he greeted her. "You're just in time. She's gotten herself into quite a state." Pamela stepped into Bettina's living room with its comfy make-yourself-at-home style.

Wilfred was a genial bearlike man with ruddy cheeks. Since his retirement he'd adopted a uniform of plaid shirts and bib overalls. He spent his days building dollhouses in his basement workshop.

"Is she okay?" Pamela said, alarmed.

"It's the blanket," he said. "For the baby."

"They don't want it to be gender-specific." Bettina hurried into the room. "And I've already crocheted a mountain of pink granny squares." Bettina had started the blanket as soon as her second son and his wife announced that their baby was to be a girl.

"Not gender-specific?"

"In other words, just because she's going to be a girl they don't want her to be automatically associated with pink."

"It's just fun though, isn't it? Little girls in pink. It doesn't mean she has to act a certain way or think a certain way."

Bettina sighed. "In their minds it does. Modern, I

guess. Boston. Not like backward little Arborville. If they'd told me sooner, I'd have made it any color they wanted. Or just white. I can see a sweet little face peering out of a white blanket."

"Can you start over with white?" Pamela said.

"I don't know if there's time," Bettina said. "And what will I do with all those pink squares?"

"Turn them into a blanket for the women's shelter in Haversack? I'm sure Nell would love something like that to pass along to them."

"Good idea," Wilfred said. "It's an ill wind that blows nobody good."

"Umm." Bettina nodded and chewed on her lip. "Nell would like that, wouldn't she? And maybe I won't make the Boston people any blanket at all. I thought I was doing something nice."

She looked so downcast that Pamela reached out and patted her shoulder.

"I suppose I won't be able to buy pink dresses either," Bettina said. "Maybe not dresses at all. I suppose they won't even let her have one of Wilfred's dollhouses."

"I could build her a firehouse," Wilfred said.

"You could, sweetie," Bettina said, giving his waist a squeeze. She sighed. "The Arborville grandchildren are boys. Their mother never told me they couldn't wear blue." She turned to Pamela. "How would you feel if Penny told you she didn't want you to knit her any more sweaters?"

"I guess I'd be making a lot more elephants for the women's shelter."

"Well, it's not the end of the world," Bettina said,

mustering a smile. "Maybe I'll learn to make elephants too. Want some coffee?"

In the kitchen, they settled at Bettina's well-scrubbed pine table. Bettina poured coffee into handmade mugs from the craft shop and set out a few slices of crumb cake. "I found the argyle-sock man," Pamela said. She described following the handsome man through the Co-Op to get a closer look at his socks and her conversation with Mr. Gilly. "Mr. Gilly called him 'Dr. Randolph,'" she said. "I don't know what his first name is."

"He knew Amy, and she made him socks, and he knows anatomy," Bettina said, gazing at Pamela with wide eyes.

Pamela nodded in agreement. "So maybe Karen Dowling is off the hook." And to herself she added that if the murder was the result of a romance gone sour, it would have happened anyway, and it could have happened anywhere. So she hadn't invited Amy to her death when she invited her to join Knit and Nibble.

"He could have an alibi though." Bettina reached for a piece of cake and gestured for Pamela to take the other.

"You've got a point." Pamela grimaced in disappointment. "Mr. Gilly said he's on the night shift."

"But he can't work *every* night. They must get some time off. Maybe he gets Tuesday nights off. Weekends are probably busy in an emergency room. And we don't know what time his shift starts. He could be free every night until eight or ten or later."

Pamela nodded. "Amy was killed before seven. After dark, but before seven."

"I have a friend." Bettina wiped her fingers on a

napkin and nodded toward the second piece of crumb cake. "You don't want this?"

"I just had breakfast. What about the friend?"

"She's a nurse at Englewood Hospital. I'll ask her if she can find out what his schedule has been lately."

Chapter Eight

The Icelandic sweater was almost finished. All that remained was the top of one sleeve, and then to sew the whole thing together. Pamela had returned home after her morning grocery errand and her visit with Bettina, eaten a quick lunch of lentil soup, and settled at her computer for an afternoon of work on the magazine. Now it was evening and she was rewarding herself for such a productive day by lounging on the sofa with her knitting. With great satisfaction, she watched the intricate white snowflakes take shape under her persistent needles, admiring the way the paler yarn contrasted with the warm brown of the background. She'd splurged on Icelandic wool for the project, from real Icelandic sheep, and the colors were natural—white wool from white sheep and brown wool from brown sheep.

She was pleased that the sweater would be finished in time to wear during the coming winter. But that meant she had to find a new project, lest her hands be idle for long. Perhaps a sweater for Penny. If she worked really hard she could have something ready by Christmas. Penny had appreciated the handknit sweaters, scarves, hats, and mittens that had flowed from Pamela's hands over the years. Hopefully going away to college wouldn't make her scornful of clothes that showed a mother's love.

Her mind wandered to the plastic bin of Amy's knitting supplies and the mysterious silky yarn with its subtle golden glow. Would it be ghoulish to knit the yarn into a sweater for Penny? There couldn't possibly be enough anyway—or could there?

She carefully laid her knitting aside, making sure that no stitches were near enough the end of a needle to slip off. She retrieved the plastic bin from the top of her washing machine and set it on the kitchen table where the light was good. Just as she recalled, there were only four skeins of the yarn. One had no label, and the other three were circled by the wide bands of paper printed with the words "That Bedford Shop" in curly letters, and the added information that the shop was a "Purveyor of All Things Natural" in "Brooklyn, NY." She fingered the yarn, admiring again its curious silkiness. It was so delicate and soft that thin needles would be required to do it justice. The result would be a fine, tight knit, but many many more skeins would be required if a sweater was to result.

Pamela carried the skeins out to the living room and set them on the coffee table. As she studied them, an interesting thought came to her. A visit to the shop could serve another purpose as well—kill two birds with one stone, as Wilfred would say. Perhaps Amy had made frequent purchases from the shop; perhaps she had friends in Brooklyn, even a secret life. Before Pamela picked her knitting up again, she went to the door and looked out toward Bettina's house. All the windows were dark. She'd have to wait until the next day to enlist her friend in the excursion she planned.

"No, I don't think it would be ghoulish," Bettina said. They sat at Pamela's kitchen table, sipping coffee from Pamela's wedding china. She'd decided long ago that there was no point in having nice things if a person didn't use them. A skein of the mystery yarn sat between them, along with a plate containing two blueberry muffins.

"It could be a way of remembering Amy," Pamela said. "I'd want someone making nice things from my yarn if I was gone."

"No word, by the way, from my nurse friend," Bettina said. Pamela had already fed Catrina and walked uptown, where she'd picked up the muffins from the Co-Op's bakery counter. Bettina reached for one and peeled off the crinkled paper. Pamela reached for the other. "What if we find out he wasn't at work at the time she was killed?" Bettina added. "That would mean he has no alibi. What do we do then?"

"We'll think of something. Did you say anything to the police?"

"I told them about the argyle socks and they just laughed."

"I sort of hope it wasn't him," Pamela said. "He seemed so nice."

"Who would it be then? Karen Dowling?" Bettina took a bite of the muffin.

"I hope it wasn't her too. But I don't want it to just be . . . *unsolved* . . . forever."

"So—'That Bedford Store.'" Bettina put the muffin down, picked up the skein of yarn, and studied the label.

"On Bedford Street. I never knew Amy had a Brooklyn connection."

"So you're thinking . . ."

"If we go to this shop where she got the yarn we might learn something about her that we don't already know. Maybe she had a secret life."

"With enemies." Bettina put the yarn down and picked up the muffin.

Pamela nodded. "With enemies. And I'll get more of the yarn and make the not-ghoulish sweater for Penny. Don't you think this color will be pretty on her?" Something about the yarn seemed to invite stroking. She reached toward the skein.

"Do you feel ancient?" Bettina said as she braked at a red light. It was as if they'd wandered into an alternate universe where no one aged. None of the people hurrying along the crowded sidewalks looked older than thirty.

"I do," Pamela said. She was scanning the storefronts for the address she'd looked up on the Internet. "I think it's the next block," she said, "but where on earth will we park?" A skein of the mystery yarn was tucked in the canvas bag on her lap.

Cars lined the curb, snugged up bumper to hood with barely an inch between. "We'll have to turn up one of these side streets." Bettina clicked on her turn signal, then braked again as a bicycle swerved in front of her car. Pamela suppressed a scream.

She made the turn and they cruised past compact

row houses, some freshly painted, others wearing ancient, faded siding. The row houses were interrupted by an auto body shop and then a weedlot with a chain-link fence between it and the sidewalk. In the next block they found a parking spot in front of a narrow two-story stucco building. Next to it, on a much wider lot, a construction project was rising and a sign advertised condominiums already for sale.

Back on Bedford Avenue they strolled past narrow storefronts displaying vintage clothing, antique furniture, jars of pickles and rich purple jam, and crusty bread in fanciful shapes. Tall curtained windows gazed down from apartments above the shops. Pamela imagined that a century or more ago, when the structures were new and the shops served a different clientele, the goods for sale might not have been all that different. Around them surged slender women in boots and skinny jeans, their flowing hair topped by close-fitting knitted caps, and slender men dressed as if on holiday from a lumberjack camp.

That Bedford Shop was indeed on the next block. Pamela twisted an ancient brass knob, and the weathered wooden door swung back. A bell rang out with a sweet jingle. Inside, the air was heavy with a rich, waxy scent. A table displayed neatly arranged stacks of soap, jars and bottles of various sizes, and a basket containing candles tied in pairs with ribbons. And then, of course, there was yarn, skeins and balls of all colors and textures, piled in profusion on the floor-to-ceiling shelves that lined the room.

"Hello?" A woman looked up from a book nestled in her lap. She was seated on a high stool behind a wooden counter that could have been part of the shop's original décor. "Everything in here is natural," she said. "From our farm upstate—beeswax for the candles, tallow for the artisanal soap, and lanolin for the lotions. All the fragrances are made from pesticide-free flowers and herbs. And the yarn, of course"—she waved a proprietary hand—"is from our sheep."

She was older than the people thronging the sidewalks. Her wavy brown hair was threaded with strands of gray, and faint lines interrupted the smooth expanse of her pale forehead. Her eyes looked tired.

"Yarn is what I'm looking for," Pamela said.

"Browse away." She bent toward the book as if eager to get back to it.

"I'm trying to match some particular yarn that came from here." Pamela reached into the canvas bag. She had barely lifted the skein of yarn beyond the rim of the bag when a most amazing transformation came over the woman behind the counter. She slid off the stool, ignoring the plop as her book landed on the floor, and leaned toward Pamela. Any trace of tiredness vanished from her eyes. She gestured eagerly as Pamela moved closer to the counter, the skein resting on her outstretched hand. Pamela laid it on the counter where, even in the dimness of the little shop, it seemed to glow.

"Where did you get this?" the woman cried.

Taken aback at her excitement, Pamela retreated. "A . . . a friend had it. And it was given to me. I only have four skeins, and I want enough to make a sweater." Pamela turned and began scanning the shelves of yarn, searching for the same glowing gold color and silky texture.

"It came from here," the woman said. "But it won't be on those shelves. We don't have it now." She extended her hand and let it hover a few inches above the skein. "In fact"—she leaned across the counter—"I want to buy this back from you."

"I . . . I'd just as soon keep it," Pamela said. The woman's shoulders sagged. The hand that had been hovering over the skein of yarn retreated. "Did you know Amy Morgan?" Pamela asked.

"Amy Morgan?" The woman squinted and tilted her head as if searching her memory for the name. "No, the name doesn't ring a bell." She continued to squint, and she bit her lips in puzzlement. The effect was somewhat theatrical, and Pamela wondered if she was faking.

"I got the yarn from Amy Morgan," Pamela said. "From her sister, really. Amy was murdered."

The woman's hands came together as if she was about to pray. "Oh my God, that's horrible," she said. Then, "Wait—it was in the *Times*, wasn't it? Quite a story. New Jersey. People don't expect those things to happen in the suburbs." She let her hand hover over the yarn again. "But, no. I didn't know her. Are you sure you won't sell the yarn back?" The look in her eyes was so desperate that Pamela almost relented. But Amy had meant so much to her. And there was something very special about the yarn.

"Why do you want the yarn back?" Pamela asked.

"It wasn't supposed to be sold," the woman said. She lowered her hovering hand and began to stroke the skein of yarn.

"Why was it in the shop if it wasn't for sale?"

"It wasn't actually for sale," the woman said. "It was sitting on the counter while I went out for lunch and my assistant sold it while I was gone." She continued to stroke the yarn and reluctantly pulled her hand away as Pamela tugged the yarn free and slipped it back in her canvas bag. Then the woman seemed to remember that she was actually the proprietress of a shop that sold yarn. "We develop interesting yarns all the time," she said. "If you'll leave your email address and phone number, I'll call you if something similar turns up."

Pamela was sure Bettina was bursting with the same obvious question that she herself was longing to ask. But she held her tongue until Bettina had maneuvered through the Saturday-afternoon traffic bustle of fashionable Brooklyn—more pedestrians and bicycles than cars—and they were speeding toward the Triborough Bridge.

Then she half turned in her seat and addressed Bettina's profile. "Why on earth do you think she was so anxious to get that yarn back?"

"I was just about to ask the same thing," Bettina said, changing lanes as a menacing truck rose up behind them. Pamela waited for it to roar past.

"It could be some really valuable kind of yarn, and the assistant didn't know and sold it for much less than it was worth," she said.

"Alpaca," Bettina said. "Or what's that other one?"

"Vicuña?"

"That's it. Vicuña. Those little creatures that live in the Andes."

"They haven't been domesticated," Pamela said. "They have to be captured to be shorn. Somebody wrote an article about them for *Fiber Craft*. She went to Peru for the research. The Incas knew about vicuñas, but only royalty was allowed to wear their wool."

Pamela studied the passing scene for a few minutes. The expressway arched over a patchwork of old brick warehouses and factories scrawled with graffiti, interspersed with sleek new multi-story apartment and condo buildings. Then a vast cemetery stretched to the left, with the Manhattan skyline as a backdrop. She turned to Bettina again. "What if selling the yarn by mistake was just a cover story?"

"A cover story for what?" Bettina asked, surprised enough to take her eyes off the road for a second and glance at Pamela.

"What if the yarn has something to do with Amy's murder? She was supposed to deliver it somewhere and the killer intercepted her."

Bettina glanced at Pamela again, a disbelieving smile twisting her lips. "The murderer thought she'd be carrying it around with her?"

Pamela shrugged. "The police never found the knitting bag."

"But you have the yarn now."

"Maybe the murderer's next stop, after discovering the yarn wasn't in the knitting bag, was Amy's apartment. But Dorrie had already cleaned everything out."

"I hope he doesn't find out what Dorrie did with the yarn," Bettina said, still smiling. "Or you're next."

"It's not funny," Pamela said, turning away. They were approaching the Triborough Bridge, its cables swooping down from its angular towers and gleaming in the late-afternoon sun. To the right was the blue expanse of the Long Island Sound.

"I'm sorry," Bettina said. "I'd never say something like that if I thought it could really be true." Neither talked for a few minutes, then Bettina drew her breath in suddenly.

"What?" Pamela said, startled.

"Now that woman in the store knows you have it. And you gave her your phone number, your landline. Anybody who has the phone number for a landline can find the address where it's located. Why didn't you just give her your cell phone number?"

"Habit," Pamela said. "I've had a landline longer than I've had a cell phone." She paused. "Anyway, this is silly. There were only four skeins of that yarn. No matter what it might be worth, even a hundred dollars a skein, *five hundred* dollars a skein, nobody would kill a person for that."

"Probably not," Bettina said. "Nobody *here*. But two thousand dollars could be a lot of money for somebody from somewhere else."

"What if the yarn was being used to smuggle something into the US?" Pamela said. "Something from Peru."

"Or Colombia," Bettina said. "The Andes are in Colombia too."

"You're not thinking it could be drugs, are you?" Pamela looked at Bettina in amazement. The bridge curved upward as it crossed the water. They were reaching its crest, and Bettina's eyes were fixed on the asphalt ahead. "Amy would never have been involved with drugs."

"You're probably right," Bettina said. They were on the down side of the crest now, gazing at the gray ribbon of the expressway as it curved toward a cluster of high-rise apartment buildings, reddish-brown, with the George Washington Bridge coming into view beyond.

"But here's an idea," Pamela said, suddenly excited.

"Hang on!" The driver of a giant semi speeding past on the left had apparently realized that the exit he wanted was actually coming up on the right. He swerved in front of Bettina with inches to spare as she pumped her brakes. The driver in the van behind her honked frantically. The semi changed lanes again, and Bettina sighed in relief.

"Good reflexes," Pamela said.

Bettina sighed again and laid a hand over her heart. "Can you hear it thumping?" she asked. Both hands back on the steering wheel, she glanced over at Pamela. "So—what's the idea?"

"Maybe something else is wrapped up in the skeins," Pamela said.

Headlights were coming on in the lanes of oncoming traffic as the sun set to the left of them. The Manhattan skyline was silhouetted against a sky streaked with orange and pink and yellow.

"Like what?"

Pamela gazed past Bettina's profile at the dramatic view. "Have you ever looked around Nell's house when Knit and Nibble met there?"

"Sure," Bettina said. "She and Harold have lots and lots of stuff."

"From their trips, starting right out of college when they'd hitchhike around Europe. Souvenirs of all kinds."

"What does this have to do with the yarn?"

"She told me that one time when they were in Peru building a school for some village she bought a little silver llama from a booth on the village market day. All the luggage is x-rayed on the way out of the country and it turned out the llama was a valuable antiquity. She had to leave it behind. The locals sneak into archeological sites and dig up things that should really go to museums."

"Something would have to be awfully small to be hidden in a skein of yarn, and awfully valuable to make it worthwhile."

"It was tiny, according to Nell. The Incas buried them in graves, lots of them. So their kings would have plenty of llamas in the next life. And collectors pay a lot for things like that, because they're hard to get ahold of if you're not a museum."

"Well," Bettina said, "I know what we're going to be doing tonight."

"You're right," Pamela said. "I can't wait to see what's inside those skeins."

"Let me just run in and tell Wilfred we're back," Bettina said as they pulled into her driveway. "I'll be over in a couple of minutes."

Pamela hurried across the street to her own house, averting her eyes from the trail of garbage that still stretched along the side of her neighbor's yard. It was completely dark now, but the streetlamp gave enough light to reveal that the arrangement of orange peelings, yogurt containers, and crumpled paper was undisturbed. At least he seems to eat healthily, Pamela said to herself—no evidence of fast food, or even take-out pizza.

She fumbled at the lock, at first unable to find the keyhole on the dark porch. Once inside, she switched on the porch light for Bettina and started to push the door shut. But then she noticed Catrina poised against the railing, gazing at her as if unsure even after all this time whether the better choice might be to flee.

"It's okay," Pamela whispered soothingly. "I won't hurt you, and I'll be right back with food."

She tossed the canvas bag on the sofa, and the skein of yarn slipped out. In the kitchen she opened a fresh can of cat food and retrieved the plastic container she'd designated the official cat-food dish. The doorbell interrupted her preparations, and she stepped into the entry. Through the lace curtain on the door she recognized Bettina.

"You're still feeding that little cat?" Bettina said as she slipped inside.

"Trying to," Pamela said. "Is she out there?"

"Something furry tore down the steps as I was coming up. I didn't mean to scare her away." Bettina glanced toward the sofa, where the yarn glowed brightly against the teal blue of the sofa's upholstery.

Pamela spooned half a can of cat food into the plastic dish and set it against the railing where Catrina had last been seen. "Would *you* like something to eat?" she asked as she stepped back inside. "I'm starving."

"I never say no to food," Bettina said. "But just a bite. Tonight is sausage and sauerkraut night, and Wilfred is looking forward to it."

"I have some interesting cheese from the Co-Op and a loaf of their good whole-grain bread."

They ate at the kitchen table, quickly, because they were anxious to pursue the idea they'd hatched on the drive back to New Jersey. Then Pamela went to fetch the rest of the Brooklyn yarn from the bin on top of the washing machine.

When she got back, Bettina was sitting on the sofa

squeezing the skein of yarn they'd taken to Brooklyn. "I don't really feel anything," she said. "And the yarn is so soft I'd think a lump inside would be really obvious." She continued squeezing, then slipped the skein out of the wide band of paper that encircled it. The yarn held together, an intricately twisted mass the shape of a very large cruller.

"Give me the end," Pamela said. Bettina tugged it loose, and Pamela seated herself in a rummage-sale chair with a carved wooden back and needlepoint seat. As Bettina turned the skein this way and that, Pamela pulled at the yarn, which stretched between them like a thin golden cord. She wound it around her fingers until she had a small nubbin, and then she began to wind it around itself, forming a ball that grew larger and larger. But the process revealed nothing in the skein of yarn except yarn and yet more yarn.

She smoothed the tail end of the yarn from the first skein onto the ball and placed the ball between them on the coffee table. They repeated the process with skeins two, three, and four, finding nothing hidden in them at all.

"Well," Bettina sighed, and she slumped against the sofa back. "It was an idea."

Pamela nodded. "It was an idea." She added the fourth ball to the three already lined up on the coffee table. "Do you want more cheese and bread?"

"I really have to get back home," Bettina said. "And I hope you'll have more for dinner than just cheese and bread."

Pamela leaned forward in the chair. "Don't leave quite yet," she said. "Some more details in that article about vicuñas are coming back to me, details that could explain the yarn—"

She was interrupted by a mournful howl from the front porch. Bettina sat upright, startled.

"It's the cat," Pamela said. "Sometimes she wants seconds." She hurried to the kitchen and emerged with an open can of cat food and a spoon.

Settling back in the rummage-sale chair, she said, "Back to the vicuñas. The local Andean people use them in fertility rituals."

"Interesting, but what does that have to do with the yarn?"

"That woman in the yarn store looked like her biological clock might be running out."

"And she's trying to get pregnant by doing some ritual with special yarn?" Bettina laughed.

"People believe all kinds of things. That shop was full of strange potions."

"Well," Bettina said, pushing herself up off the sofa. "I hope she doesn't show up here wanting to take the yarn back—and not willing to acccpt no for an answer."

"How could she even find mc?" Pamela asked.

"You gave her your landline number. Remember?"

Chapter Nine

"Well, this is just the end." Pamela said it aloud. She didn't usually talk to herself, but the spectacle she was viewing through her kitchen window that Sunday morning called for more than silent disapproval. The sound of her kettle whistling called her back to her own tidy domain, and she quickly measured freshly ground coffee beans into a paper cone and added boiling water. As the rich coffee smell wafted up from the pot, she returned to contemplation of the sight that had provoked her irritation. Not only had the garbage mess she'd been studying for several days not been cleaned up, but some animal— probably a raccoon—had tipped over a second garbage can, torn open another plastic garbage bag, and added an assortment of vegetable trimmings, Styrofoam trays, and wadded-up paper towels to the original mess.

"Richard Larkin actually came outside to put more trash in the second can and never even noticed what had happened to the first." She said that aloud too. Then she put a piece of whole-grain bread in the toaster, poured a cup of coffee, and sat down at the kitchen table, in the chair that faced away from the window.

I'll write him a note. She said this to herself and began to read the newspaper.

Toast eaten, coffeepot drained, and newspaper perused, she rummaged among her stock of the free notepads that arrived with solicitations from various charities. She chose one with a border of flowers. "Dear Neighbor," she wrote. "You may not have noticed, but raccoons have tipped over your garbage cans and made quite a mess. I hope you will clean it up soon since it is the view from my kitchen window." She signed it, "Your neighbor to the west, Pamela Paterson." She would drop it in his mailbox when she went out for her walk.

She stepped toward the counter, coffee cup and toast plate in hand. Her eyes strayed toward her neighbor's house just in time to see an attractive young woman stepping out onto his porch. The girlfriend. She clucked disapprovingly. Time for girlfriends but no time to keep his yard clean. And . . . Pamela studied the young woman. She wasn't even the same girlfriend. The first girlfriend had worn a chic ensemble of skinny jeans and a belted jacket, her hair in a shiny blond bob. This young woman was dressed in a flowing skirt, topped with a knitted poncho. Her blond hair was long and tousled.

Richard Larkin was a complete lothario.

In the living room Pamela released her irritation by grabbing the throw pillows that had gotten bunched up at one end of the sofa as she'd lounged with her knitting the previous night. She fluffed each one into shape and distributed them in a neat row, making sure the one with the needlepoint cat wasn't deployed so that the cat was standing on its head. As she tucked it into place, a gleam of metal caught her eye. She leaned closer to discover a knitting needle nestled in the groove formed by the welting on the middle sofa cushion.

It had to be one of Karen Dowling's needles, gone astray the night she rummaged in her bag to hand them over to Roland. She plucked it out and set it on the coffee table. Surely the other one could not be far away. Finding it would put to rest once and for all the terrible fear that sweet little Karen Dowling was Amy's murderer.

Pamela tossed all the throw pillows on the rug and ran her finger along the welting on all three sofa cushions. No knitting needles emerged. Then she pulled the cushions free and tossed them on the floor. Under the cushions were a few stray coins and many dust balls and crumbs, but no knitting needles. She examined the welting on the cushions that made up the back of the sofa and probed between the cushions with her fingers. Finally, for good measure, she examined each throw pillow carefully, just in case she hadn't noticed a knitting needle partly embedded in their fabric.

But in the end there was only one knitting needle. What could it mean if Karen had arrived at the meeting with one of the metal needles already missing?

She needed a destination for her walk, aside from delivering her "Dear Neighbor" note. She decided to pay a visit to Karen Dowling. She'd drop off the lone knitting needle and maybe have a little chat.

Fifteen minutes later, Pamela had slipped the "Dear Neighbor" note into Richard Larkin's mailbox and was striding up Orchard Street enjoying the crisp fall day. There had been a frost the night before. The remains of the black-eyed Susans in several yards were shriveled and brown. Flower beds that had held on even into November with bits of greenery or at least spots of fading rust and gold were bleak jumbles of broken stems. She grasped the ends of the violet mohair scarf that had been her project before she started the Icelandic sweater and snugged it up more securely against her throat.

Karen and Dave Dowling lived a few blocks above Arborville Avenue, up a slight hill, on a street that paralleled Orchard. Their house was wood frame, like Pamela's. It was nearly as old, and in just about the same state of disrepair that Pamela's had been, that long-ago time when she and her husband had taken on the task of making it beautiful again.

As she turned the corner onto the Dowlings' block she could see a figure kneeling on the sidewalk. As she got closer she realized it was Karen. Karen was bundled in a down jacket that had definitely seen better days, and she was digging industriously at a patch of dirt around a tree between the sidewalk and the curb. Beside her was a cluster of misshapen brown and ivory knobs—tulip bulbs, Pamela guessed.

"I admire your ambition," Pamela said when she was a few steps away.

Karen looked up with a startled expression. "I didn't hear you coming," she said and rocked back into a sitting position.

"Those will be beautiful in the spring," Pamela said. "Tulips, I think."

"Tulips." Karen nodded. "I always dreamed of having a yard where I could plant things . . . and a house to fix up." She twisted and gazed back at the house. Its porch sagged alarmingly, and the paint on its narrow clapboards was the faded blue of much-washed denim. But Pamela could see its potential, and she said so.

Instead of answering, Karen turned back toward the street and lowered her head. She wiped her cheek with a grubby hand, and when she looked up again, it was with a smudge of dirt under one eye. A tear dripped from the other.

"We might not even be here when these come up," she said, her mouth twisting and the words barely squeezing out. "It all seemed so wonderful. Dave's job offer. The chance to put down roots in a nice town like this." She made a sound like a cross between a laugh and a sob. "Wendelstaff College. I wish we'd never heard of it." She plunged her garden trowel into the soil, excavated a narrow hole, sighed deeply, and sniffed. "I hate to waste the bulbs," she said, her voice calmer. "Someone will enjoy the flowers."

Pamela lifted the knitting needle out of her bag. "I found this hidden in my sofa," she said. Karen looked up. The needle glinted in the sun. "I couldn't find the other one though."

Karen shrugged and reached for the knitting needle. "I can't stand these metal things, but I guess one of them won't do Roland much good." She stared at it as if wondering what to do next, then stuck it in the ground next to the hole she'd just dug.

"So your husband isn't staying at Wendelstaff?"

Karen nodded. "Not past the end of the year." She was still on her knees, face turned up toward Pamela.

"Had you met Amy Morgan?"

The tears that had been held in abeyance returned with a gasp and a wail. Karen covered her face with one hand, rose clumsily to her feet, and retreated toward her house. She almost tripped as she hurried up the steps that led to the sagging porch, but she regained her balance, pushed through the front door, and vanished.

Pamela extracted the knitting needle from the ground and tucked it back in her bag. Perhaps the police would want to compare it with the one that had been found in Amy's chest.

On her way down the hill Pamela decided a visit to the Wendelstaff campus might be useful. She'd say she was researching interior design programs for her daughter. That way she could get in front of some of the people Amy had worked with as head of the School of Professional Arts. Amy herself had implied she was having problems there—and Dorrie had confirmed it. Maybe Dave Dowling was one of the problems. Today was Sunday though. The next stage of her sleuthing would have to wait until Monday morning.

At the corner of Orchard Street and Arborville Avenue she hesitated. There was plenty of food at home, but a crisp fall day like this one called out for something roasting in the oven. She'd roast a chicken, with sage stuffing from her own sage plant, and the leftovers would provide many more meals.

Pamela had always cooked, a real dinner every night, even after she and Penny were the only ones to eat it. And she'd set the table with her wedding china and cloth napkins. With Penny in college now, some meals were simpler and the china didn't always come out, but cooking was rather like knitting—though it could get repetitious, even the repetition was soothing, and the result was so satisfying.

She turned right instead of heading straight down Orchard. Even though it was Sunday, she had resolved to put in several hours of work for the magazine—she'd spent too much time away from her desk in the aftermath of Amy's murder. But a roast chicken for dinner would provide a nice reward after a long editing session.

The door to the Co-Op Grocery swung open, and Jean Worthington emerged. She was pushing a cart piled high with Co-Op Grocery bags. Pamela recognized Jean's Volvo at the curb. Its subtle gray sheen had always struck her as exactly the sort of finish Jean would pick.

"Why, Pamela," Jean said with one of her gracious smiles. "I see you're on foot. I do so admire your devotion to exercise." The smile faded. "How tragic about Amy! I just can't believe that would happen in our little town—and on our very street."

"The funeral was terribly sad," Pamela said. "Almost everyone from Knit and Nibble was there. I was the only one who really knew her, but Bettina and I rode out to Maple Branch together. And Nell and Karen came, and even Roland. So nice of all of them." Jean seemed on the point of speaking but Pamela went on. "The flowers you sent were amazing. I didn't know so many kinds of flowers came in white."

"I wanted very much to be there," Jean said. "But we needed some work on the koi pond and that was the only time the man could come. You have to be there to tell them things, you know, or it's hopeless." She pushed her cart a few feet along the sidewalk. "Don't forget we're at my house Tuesday night," she added. "I'm not a baker like you, but I've ordered some very cute cookies from a bakery in Timberley."

The Co-Op stocked chickens from a local farm. Soon Pamela was on her way home, with a shopping bag containing a fresh chicken, an onion, and a supply of celery. She was looking forward to a pleasant cooking session later that day. She'd make cornbread from scratch to crumble for the stuffing and harvest some leaves from the sage plant in her backyard.

There was an errand to do, though, before she settled down in front of her computer.

She dropped the food off at home and crossed the street. Wilfred Fraser was apparently in the mood for cooking too. He answered the door with an apron tied over his bib overalls. Bettina's comfortable house smelled delicious. "Five-alarm chili," Wilfred said, licking his lips. "Have a seat. I'll call Bettina."

"Look what I found," Pamela said as Bettina came down the stairs. She flourished the metal knitting needle. "It was lost in my sofa, I guess from when Karen was pulling everything out of her knitting bag."

"So that means . . ." Bettina raised her eyebrows.

"I'm not sure. I couldn't find the other one."

"But this one could match the one in Amy's chest."

Pamela nodded. "Would your police friends be interested in checking?"

"No guarantee, but they certainly *should* be," Bettina said. "I'll hand it over."

At home, Pamela ate a quick cheese sandwich and then climbed the stairs to her office. An article on free-form yarn sculptures held her interest, but the next one, on the evolution of the spindle, required a break to make a pot of coffee halfway through. Four articles later, she looked away from the computer screen to realize the room had grown dark except for the puddle of light her desk lamp cast on her keyboard. It was time to harvest some sage and get a batch of cornbread going.

The sage grew in a wooden barrel at the edge of the driveway. It had started life twenty years earlier as a tiny seedling from the garden store and had outgrown container after container. Now it resembled a good-sized shrub—a very fragrant shrub.

Catrina was waiting on the porch when Pamela stepped outside. Pamela heard a sound coming from behind the hedge that separated her yard from Richard Larkin's. As she watched, a large man bobbed up and down, making his way from the side door to the front yard. A black plastic garbage bag trailed along at his side. Despite the streetlamp, it was hard to make out his features.

In the morning, the garbage trail was gone and an upright garbage can sat at the curb.

Chapter Ten

Wendelstaff College was a pastoral enclave along the river that separated Arborville and its equally suburban neighbors from grittier Haversack to the west, the county seat and locus of the courthouse and the jail. Pamela found a spot in the parking lot labeled "Visitors" and followed a path that cut between buildings variously constructed of stone and brick and garnished with ivy until she reached the central quadrangle. Students hurried to and fro, laden with backpacks, on paths that crisscrossed the yellowing grass.

She'd been on the campus for lectures and films, but had no idea which building housed the School of Professional Arts. A young man was walking just ahead, backpack flopping against his down jacket. "Excuse me," she called, noticing that it was chilly enough today that the phrase produced a little puff of steam.

"I'm late," he called back. "Can't stop." He sped up. As if to punctuate his words, a bell began to toll. She paused and pushed the cuff of her glove down to check her watch. It was just nine a.m.

She had more luck with an older woman heading toward her. "Professional Arts?" the woman asked. "There are several departments, not all in the same building—fashion design, interior design, photography, and landscape architecture. That one's by the gardens at the edge of the campus. Which one do you want?"

"Interior design," Pamela said. On reflection she'd decided that the ruse of researching programs for her daughter was a very good idea.

"Through there." The woman pointed across the quadrangle. "It's in the building behind that big brick one with the white columns." She looked Pamela up and down and added. "You're not connected with Wendelstaff, are you? I suppose they'll let you through. And anyway, they're not usually very awake this early in the morning. If they give you any trouble, assure them you're not trying to attend a class and you're not even part of the college."

Pamela continued on across the quadrangle. She heard them before she saw them, the sound echoing as she bore left to cut around the brick building with the columns. "NO FAIR. NO FAIR. IT'S NOT FAIR," came the chant, male voices mixing with female voices in a ragged harmony. "NO FAIR. NO FAIR. WENDELSTAFF IS NOT FAIR," came a variation.

Once behind the brick building she could see where the sound was coming from. A dozen students were marching in a circle in front of the steps that led into a strikingly modern building with a dramatic glass-and-steel facade. They carried large signs that read, "PROMOTE WENDELSTAFF." The marching stopped as Pamela drew closer. A dozen pairs of eyes examined her, some from beneath woolly caps pulled down low, others from above mufflers snugged up cozily around necks.

"I . . . I have an errand inside the building," Pamela volunteered. "I'm not connected with Wendelstaff."

The neat circle parted, six people in a semicircle on either side of the steps, and Pamela entered the building as they stared at her.

Inside, the halls were eerily empty. As Pamela passed closed door after closed door, glances through windows revealed empty lecture rooms. At last, after turning this way and that as if in a maze, she came to a door with a plaque that read, "Interior Design." She tapped on the door and then opened it cautiously. A voice from an inner room called, "If you want Olivia Wiggens, she's back here."

Pamela ventured toward the sound of the voice. In the inner room, a striking woman in her thirties rose from behind a desk and extended her hand. Her expertly lipsticked mouth shaped an embarrassed smile. "Olivia Wiggens," she said. "How did you get them to let you in?"

"I told them I wasn't connected with Wendelstaff," Pamela said.

"Please don't judge us by this. Wendelstaff is not one of those places where the students are always protesting something." She gestured toward the chair that faced her desk and took her own seat again. She was dressed in an austere black-and-gray ensemble that seemed chosen to harmonize with the avant-garde style of the building she inhabited. "What can I do for you?"

"My daughter is interested in interior design," Pamela said. "She's a freshman up in Massachusetts now, but she didn't have a major in mind yet when she picked that college." She paused. "What *are* the students picketing about?"

"Me," Olivia said, and the embarrassed smile appeared again. "In support of me, I should say. I was passed over for a promotion to head the School of Professional Arts. My degree is from here and the students think Wendelstaff should have more confidence in its own graduates. The person who got the promotion had an MFA from Parsons."

"I noticed you said 'had,'" Pamela said. Olivia nodded. "Amy Morgan? Very sad. It's been in all the papers."

"The police have been all over the place, of course."

"Of course." Pamela recalled Dorrie saying the police might not ask the right questions. She quickly added, "Do you by any chance knit?"

"Oh, please! Yes, I know she was killed with a knitting needle. I was in a studio class from six to ten that night, and the police checked my alibi. One of the students in the class backed me up."

"What will happen now? With the job? Wendelstaff still needs someone to head the School of Professional Arts."

"They'll find someone else from Parsons, I suppose." Olivia frowned at Pamela. "Why did you come here? Do you even really have a daughter?" She rose again and extended her hand across the desk. Pamela had been dismissed.

* * *

Pamela had hurried through the crowd of picketing students and up the steps of the building so quickly that she hadn't looked closely at them. Now, leaving the building, she paused just outside the heavy glass doors and watched as the marchers slowly traced their ragged circle on the concrete below. The chant was the same as before: "NO FAIR. NO FAIR. IT'S NOT FAIR," as was the variation: "WENDELSTAFF IS NOT FAIR."

Her eye was drawn to one of the young women, bundled in an oversized coat cinched at the waist with a wide leather belt. The young woman's face was tense with excitement and her voice carried above the others. She strode forward rhythmically, emphasizing every second syllable with a decisive stamp of her right foot. The other students kept time by bobbing their picket signs, but this young woman's hands were otherwise occupied. She was knitting.

Pamela made her way down the steps, one hand on the elegant steel handrail that bisected them. Her gaze was fixed on the knitter. As she got closer she could see that the leather belt was actually an ingenious harness that anchored one of the knitting needles. A strand of yarn emerged from a leather pouch that dangled from rings attached to the belt, and a sleeve appeared to be taking shape, fashioned from yarn in a bright fuchsia shade.

Pamela had read about such devices, perhaps in an article submitted to *Fiber Craft*, but she'd never seen one. They stemmed from an era in which women's hands were never idle, and an hour spent walking to market to sell eggs or vegetables was an hour that couldn't be devoted solely to daydreaming.

A sitting knitter could rest the left-hand needle in her lap as she handled the yarn to form each stich, but a walking knitter had no lap. Thus the harness.

The marchers parted as before, leaving a path flanked by two semicircles. A few were silent, then more, and the chanting trailed away on the word "WENDELSTAFF." The knitter took a deep breath and looked up from her knitting. Her face was quite red, from the shouting Pamela imagined.

She looked right at Pamela and took a few steps to close up the gap that would have allowed Pamela to leave the marchers behind her. "Do you support our cause?" she asked.

"I was a friend of Amy Morgan's," Pamela said. "We'd been out of touch, but she'd recently moved to my town. I know she was excited about the job. When she accepted it, I'm sure she had no idea that such complicated campus politics were involved."

The young woman frowned. "Olivia was in line to be head of the School of Professional Arts, and she deserved it. There was no reason at all for the search committee to look any further. There were students on the committee, but that's always just window dressing. The higher-ups do exactly what they want no matter how the votes turn out." Her voice rose and began to crack. Whether from overuse or because she was on the verge of tears, Pamela wasn't sure. She went on, "Olivia has an MFA from Wendelstaff. It's like they're happy to recruit students and take our money, but then they might as well just come out and say, 'Your Wendelstaff degree isn't really worth very much—not like a degree from someplace like *Parsons.*'" She punctuated the sentence with a sarcastic twist of the lips.

"I see you're a knitter," Pamela said, nodding toward the partially finished fuchsia sleeve that dangled from the young woman's needles.

"Well, *duh.*"

"I've read about those knitting harnesses," Pamela went on pleasantly, ignoring the young woman's scorn. "I guess you must be quite devoted to your hobby."

"Knitting is not a *hobby.*" Her smooth forehead creased. "It's a way of life."

"Amy was a knitter, you know," Pamela said. "You probably saw in the papers that the murder weapon was a knitting needle."

"Well, *I* didn't do it." She locked eyes with Pamela as if not to do so would suggest she was lying.

"I guess the police talked to a lot of people on campus."

"I was in a studio class from six to ten that night, and the police checked my alibi. Olivia backed me up."

Something sounded very familiar about that wording. As Pamela recalled, Olivia Wiggens had said basically the same thing, except that one of the students had backed her up. What if the studio class only had one student in it? So only two people were present, Olivia and this young woman? The young woman stepped aside and looped the strand of fuchsia yarn around the fingers of her left hand. She was ready to begin knitting again. Around her the other students picked up their signs. A few took tentative steps.

Pamela had discovered a whole new reason for Amy's murder and at least two suspects to go with it. But she'd come to Wendelstaff College with a particular question in mind, and she asked it now.

"Dave Dowling lives in my town too," she said. "Is he connected with the School of Professional Arts?"

The young woman nodded. "Photography." She finished the stitch and looped the yarn around her finger for another. "He's a good guy," the student said. "No reason for his contract not to be renewed—except people from *Parsons* have fancy ideas." Her lips twisted in another sarcastic smile.

Pamela's heart sank. Karen certainly did have a motive to want Amy dead. She could hardly wait to hear from Bettina whether the knitting needle from the sofa cushion matched the one from Amy's chest.

Pamela preferred to use her walking time for daydreaming. She had never understood why people would want to broadcast their half of a phone conversation to the world at large—or at least the casual passerby. She'd heard many intimate and even incriminating details divulged by people with their phones glued to their ears, and she didn't want to join that cohort. So she waited until she was back in her car to take out her cell phone, place a call to Bettina, and ask, "Did the knitting needle I found in my sofa match the murder weapon?"

Bettina sighed. "I tracked Clayborn down first thing this morning and gave it to him, but there's no word yet. And I don't know if he even understands why it could be important. He was rushing to his car and I handed the needle to him and tried to explain. He just grabbed it and grunted at me."

At home, Pamela opened a can of lentil soup. She'd wait till dinnertime to bring out more of the roast chicken and cornbread stuffing from the previous night. After her lunch, she climbed the stairs to her office and poked the button that brought the computer to life. Several emails from her boss at *Fiber Craft* popped up, with the attachments that she knew meant more articles to edit. She was always happy to know that *Fiber Craft* had plenty of work for her, but it was the last email that made her smile. She opened it first.

"So anxious to see you, Mom," it read. "I'm getting a ride instead of taking the bus, but the guy I'm riding with has class until three Wednesday. So I'll be home at seven or eight." It was signed, "Love, Penny."

Then she opened the first email, brought the attachment up in Word, and got to work.

Chapter Eleven

Perhaps Catrina had been especially excited—or disgusted—by the new brand of cat food Pamela had decided to try. Responding to the feline eyes meeting hers through the oval window in the front door, Pamela had filled the cat-food dish the previous evening and set it in the customary spot near the porch railing.

But as she stepped onto the porch this morning to retrieve it and bring in the daily paper, there was no cat-food dish to be found. She scanned the yard, trying to suppress the memory of what she'd discovered the last time she went searching for an errant cat-food dish. The last few fallen leaves speckled the fading lawn, but there was no cat-food dish to be seen. Out near the end of the driveway, however, lay something else that needed to be retrieved—the weekly *Arborville Advocate*, encased in its customary green plastic sleeve. It had rained a bit the previous night. The grass glistened with moisture, and the leaves that had fallen since the last raking were wet and shiny.

No one subscribed to the *Advocate*—it arrived unbidden. But Bettina's post as chief writer in charge of almost everything gave her access to the police. Interest in the paper's content waxed and waned depending on what was going on in town and whether or not it was garage-sale season. Pamela imagined this issue of the *Advocate* wouldn't be left languishing on too many driveways. She knew through the grapevine that Amy's murder had caused quite a stir.

Heading back up the walk, she caught sight of the cat-food dish under the azalea bush next to the porch steps and bent to collect it. She made her coffee and toast and spread out both newspapers on the kitchen table. But she didn't need to read the *Advocate* to know that the police had made no progress in figuring out who killed Amy.

Breakfast finished and papers read, Pamela dressed in her customary jeans and sweater. In the entry she pulled on her jacket, snuggled the violet mohair scarf around her neck, and set out. She was deep in a pleasant daydream involving Penny and a holiday baking project, eyes focused on the sidewalk to avoid slipping on the wet leaves, when a voice said, "Whoa there!" She jumped back and teetered. A strong hand wrapped around her arm. She looked up to discover that the hand belonged to Dr. Randolph.

She'd reached the stately brick apartment building at the corner of her block.

"Are you okay?" he asked, his handsome face puckering with concern.

"You startled me."

"It was either that or have you run me down."

"Sorry," Pamela said. "These leaves are wet and I didn't want to slip."

"Well, no harm done." He took a step toward the parking lot, then paused. "I understand we have a friend in common," he said, looking into her eyes. "Amy Morgan—and I should say 'had.'"

Pamela blinked. How would he know she'd been a friend of Amy's? Had Amy mentioned that she was on her way to a knitting club at Pamela Paterson's that fateful night? So he knew right where to find her when he went after her with a knitting needle?

Her mouth wasn't sure what words it wanted to form so she found herself stuttering. Dr. Randolph continued staring into her eyes. Finally he spoke again. "Mr. Gilly," he said. "It's never a good idea to discuss anything with him unless you want the world to know it."

With a nod that Pamela wasn't sure would be called friendly, he continued on to the parking lot. A few steps further, he turned to add, "Is it you who's been wondering about my schedule at the hospital?" Pamela felt her mouth drop open. "Too many people in the world have nothing to do but mind other people's business," he called before heading for his car.

With no pressing errand in Arborville's commercial district, Pamela turned right on Arborville Avenue instead of left. The day was bright and brisk, and the air fresh after the previous night's rain. The trees' bare branches traced delicate patterns against the clear sky. But her pleasant daydream involving Penny and a Thanksgiving pie that she had just about decided would be pecan had been driven from her mind. In its place was the image of something

like a board game in which Dr. Randolph and Karen
Dowling were advancing toward a final square labeled
"MURDERER." Trailing them, but not too far
behind, were Olivia Wiggens and the unnamed knitting protester. In the middle of the board sat a large
ball of soft wool that glowed with a strange golden
light.

Pamela usually enjoyed her strolls along this stretch
of Arborville Avenue. It featured some of the town's
older and grander houses, with landscaping that
evoked an earlier time and featured birdbaths, garden
statuary, and in one case a fountain. But today she
was oblivious. When she reached the sign that, with a
flourish of gold and an elegant script, welcomed
people to the neighboring town, she crossed the
street and headed back the way she had come.

She was indeed preoccupied, but not too preoccupied to slow down as she turned onto Orchard
Street. The encounter with Dr. Randolph had rattled
her. She'd neglected to make her usual detour to inspect the trash cans hidden behind the wooden fencing at the edge of the stately brick apartment
building's parking lot. As she made her way across
the asphalt, she noticed that indeed there were
castoffs today. Some had even escaped their corral.
A rich orange casserole dish, like one of those expensive Le Creuset ones, sat atop a lamp table. A sleek
leather armchair sidled up next to a bookcase.

Pamela stepped closer. She absolutely did not
need another chair, but leather armchairs bought
new went for hundreds of dollars. Maybe Penny
would be able to use it someday . . . But as she stroked
the smooth leather, bending this way and that to

inspect for scratches, her eye strayed to the bookcase, and then beyond.

Something was tucked between the bookcase and the last trash can, something large and flat, like a painting. A strip of canvas about as tall as the bookcase but only a few inches wide was visible. But pictured in that narrow strip were a ball of yarn and a swath of knitted fabric. Pamela tugged at the edge of the painting and succeeded in exposing the hands and knitting needles that were creating the knitted fabric. The hands were slim and graceful, and they came to life in the dabs and swirls of oil paint. The artist was clearly not an amateur.

Pamela tugged again, and the entire painting slid out. Now the owner of the hands was revealed—a young woman poised on an old-fashioned chair, her in-progress knitting trailing over her lap. But someone had slashed the canvas savagely down the middle, focusing particularly on the knitter's face. Despite the disfiguring slash, the knitter looked familiar—the dark hair, the wide eyes, the sweet mouth. Pamela looked closer. It was Amy Morgan!

Mr. Gilly emerged from a door in the back of the building and paused to light a cigarette. "Pretty girl," he said, exhaling at the same time. "It's a shame what happened. And I guess somebody didn't like the painting."

"Why is it out here?" Pamela asked.

"Her sister took away everything anybody in her family wanted. Then she told me to clean out the rest."

"Was it damaged like this when you took it out of the apartment?"

Mr. Gilly took a drag on his cigarette and nodded. "Like I said, I guess somebody didn't like the painting."

"I guess I could take it if I wanted? It's just going to the trash."

"Sure, help yourself. I don't know who else would want it in that condition."

In her excitement about the painting, Pamela forgot all about the leather chair.

Pamela pressed Bettina's doorbell again, harder this time. She waited, but there was still no answer. Both Wilfred's ancient but lovingly cared-for Mercedes and Bettina's solid Toyota Corolla were in the driveway though. And a strange sound was emanating from behind the front door—a low hum. She retreated from the porch and pushed her way between a pair of rhododendron bushes to take a look in the living room window. What she saw revealed that Wilfred, at least, was home, and it also explained the sound. Wilfred was vacuuming the living room rug.

She tapped on the window to no avail, so she returned to the porch, where, instead of ringing the bell again, she pounded on the door. At last it opened a crack as Wilfred peeked out, then wider as he recognized Pamela and smiled.

"Let me make sure my shoes are clean," Pamela said, scuffing her feet against the door mat. "I was creeping through your shrubbery."

"Whatever for?"

"I couldn't get any answer when I rang the bell."

"Come on in." Wilfred stepped back and waved Pamela into the house.

"I do admire the way you and Bettina handle the division of labor," Pamela said.

"A happy wife is a happy life," Wilfred said cheerfully.

"And I guess you're here to see the boss." His eyes shifted from Pamela's face to the painting. "Hey—is that another one of your antique-store finds?"

"Not quite." She swung it around so the front was visible.

"Hmm." A little crease appeared between his brows. "What happened?"

"I'm not sure . . ."

Just then Bettina's voice floated down from the second floor. "Is that Pamela down there, Wilfred? Why didn't you call me?"

"Just about to, love."

Bettina hurried down the stairs. Before she was even at the bottom, she paused to ask, "Have you been hitting the tag sales already this morning?"

"This is a clue," Pamela said. She waited until Bettina stepped into the living room to add, "It's a painting of Amy Morgan, complete with evidence that someone didn't like her very well."

"My, my." Bettina stooped to examine the painting more closely. "She was a *lovely* woman." She turned to look up at Wilfred. "Don't you think so?"

"Only if I liked them that young," Wilfred said loyally. He picked up the vacuum cleaner and moved off toward the dining room.

"I think we should show this to the police," Pamela said, raising her voice over the hum of the vacuum. "A person who'd slash a painting of Amy could easily be a person who'd stick a knitting needle into her heart."

A disgusted puff of air escaped from Bettina's lips. "Clayborn just laughed about the Brooklyn yarn and the argyle socks. As far as the slashed painting goes, he'd probably say it sounds like a clue from one of those British TV mysteries."

"But the knitting needle I found in my sofa," Pamela said eagerly. "That could really mean something if it matches the one that killed Amy."

"He *did* get back to me about that," Bettina said. "Karen Dowling isn't a suspect."

"She isn't!" Pamela's voice rose in amazement. "I don't really want her to be, but how can they say that?"

"Maybe they know things we don't know."

"But maybe *we* know things *they* don't know."

Wilfred reappeared, vacuum cleaner in hand, and headed for the stairs.

"Coffee?" Bettina said. "And how about a slice of that good Co-Op bakery crumb cake? I know you hardly eat anything for breakfast."

In the kitchen, Bettina bent to comfort Woofus the rescue dog, who was hiding under the table.

"Poor thing," Bettina said. "The vacuum terrifies him—not that he's that brave under normal circumstances."

She busied herself pouring coffee into her handmade mugs from the craft shop and set a loaf of crumb cake on a wooden cutting board. As she watched the preparations, Pamela described almost running into Dr. Randolph that morning.

"It's Bob," Bettina said, handing Pamela a cup. She cut two slices of crumb cake and slid them onto napkins. "Bob Randolph. I heard back from my nurse friend at the hospital."

"And?" The cup Pamela had been lifting to her lips paused halfway up.

"She isn't allowed to give out information about

people's schedules. But now we know his first name is Bob."

"He knows we've been asking about him." Pamela set the cup back down on Bettina's pine table without drinking from it. "He didn't seem very happy about it."

"Have some crumb cake." Bettina nudged one of the napkins toward Pamela, but Pamela had other things on her mind. "You may be right about the police not being interested in that painting," she said. "But I certainly am. So many questions—or at least two. Who slashed it, and who painted it? It shouldn't be impossible to answer the second one at least."

Pamela fetched the painting from the living room and balanced it on the kitchen table with the upper edge leaning against the wall. She and Bettina studied it from their chairs. The artist had emphasized Amy's pale skin and her dark hair, contrasting them with a deep garnet background. She was dressed in a simple blouse that could have suited the heroine of a nineteenth-century novel. Part of an ornate chair back was visible over one shoulder. Its curves echoed the rounded blooms arranged casually in a vase nearby. The strand of wool twined around one of the skillfully painted fingers was a rich shade of indigo.

"Does that look like a signature to you?" Pamela pointed to the lower edge of the knitted swatch that flowed from Amy's needles. Barely visible against the indigo, an angular scribble interrupted several rows of neat stitches.

"I think it starts with a 'C.'" Bettina touched the canvas. "Or is the corner of that thing she's knitting just curling up a little?"

"It's definitely a 'C.' And then there's a squiggle,

and then a period." She lined her finger up next to Bettina's. "See where there's kind of a bump."

"Or it says 'Cho.' That squiggle is an 'h.'"

"If it's a period, then the 'Ch' could be short for 'Charles.' Or 'Chet.' Or 'Chad.'"

A deep voice behind them said, "Whatever his first name is, his last name is 'Lawrence.'" They both turned to see Wilfred, vacuum cleaner in hand, staring at the painting. "You're too close," he said. "If you stand back here it kind of comes into focus."

Pamela jumped up and joined Wilfred in the doorway. "He's right," she said excitedly. "It says 'Ch. Lawrence.'"

Bettina pushed her chair away from the table, tilted her head, and stared at the painting. "Yes," she said. "Definitely 'Ch. Lawrence.' This is a job for Google. Let me get my fancy phone."

Five minutes later they had determined that "Ch. Lawrence" was Chad Lawrence and that his work was handled by the Grainger Gallery on Washington Street in Hoboken.

"Do you have anything on your schedule this afternoon?" Pamela asked Bettina.

"Hoboken," Bettina said. "Let's do it."

"How's one p.m.?" Pamela said. "I need to check in with the magazine."

"Perfect! I'll drive if you navigate."

Chapter Twelve

From across the street Pamela could see that her mailbox was overflowing. She collected the box's contents, carried the stack of envelopes, circulars, and catalogues to the kitchen, and spread it all out on her kitchen table. Much of it proved to be intended for her neighbors, suggesting that the usual mail carrier hadn't yet returned from wherever he had gone. The only piece of mail for her, aside from a few items addressed to anyone at her address who answered to "Resident," was a utility bill. Among the mail for her neighbors was a catalogue of expensive lingerie for the house three doors down and a letter in a business-sized envelope addressed to Richard Larkin, AIA.

Pamela's late husband had been Michael Paterson, AIA—an architect. So that was Richard Larkin's profession too. She wasn't sure how that made her feel about him. But he *had* cleaned up the garbage mess, and there had been no repeated raccoon incursions. Perhaps she'd drop the letter in his mailbox when she headed out again instead of handing it over to the substitute mail carrier to misdeliver a second time. The stationery looked expensive. Maybe the letter was important.

Upstairs Pamela checked her email to discover a rush editing job from *Fiber Craft*, an article on hand-made rag dolls. It had been accepted months ago but her editor had decided at the last minute that it fit the holiday crafts theme of the upcoming issue. She set to work and was finished just in time for a quick snack of bread and cheese before hurrying back out to rendezvous with Bettina. The jeans and sweater she'd worn for her morning walk would have to do for the Hoboken outing. She grabbed her jacket and scarf and the letter for Richard Larkin, AIA, and stepped outside.

Pamela raised the flap of Miranda and Joe Bonham's mailbox and dropped the letter for Richard Larkin, AIA, inside, where it joined a batch of envelopes, circulars, and catalogues rather like the pile she had pulled out of her own box. Turning away, she glanced at the ceramic planter Miranda had tended so carefully, with pansies in the spring, marigolds in the summer, chrysanthemums in the fall, and holly boughs in the winter. The Bonhams had left in September, before Miranda had time to plant chrysanthemums. The remains of last summer's marigolds, leaves shriveled and black, flower heads shapeless knobs, made a woeful spectacle.

Well, she said to herself as she stepped off the porch, you couldn't expect a man, even an architect, to take the same interest as a woman would take in details like flowers on the porch. And obviously girl-friends that were replaced every few days wouldn't have time to develop an interest in how Richard Larkin's porch looked.

Bettina waved from across the street. "What are

you doing?" she called when Pamela reached her driveway.

"Mail for my new neighbor," Pamela said. "That sub mail carrier is hopeless."

"You're telling me. Did you know Daryl Roberts gets catalogues where you can buy those pipes people use to smoke marijuana?"

"Shelley Huber buys really expensive lingerie."

"He's quite nice-looking," Bettina said.

"Who?"

"Your new neighbor."

"You've seen him?"

"A couple times," Bettina said. "He's an architect, you know."

"I know," Pamela said.

"Wilfred has talked to him—about the dollhouses. He was very interested. Maybe you should get to know him. Now that Penny is away at college you could—"

Pamela shook her head vigorously. "I'm not even thinking about that." She continued shaking her head. "Besides, he has girlfriends. Lots of them, and they're really young."

"You look young."

"Not interested."

Heading down the Turnpike in Bettina's Toyota, they chatted about the knitting club and the new granddaughter Bettina was expecting in December. When they left the Turnpike at Exit 17, Pamela began to navigate, watching for the Weehawken/Hoboken exit as they headed east, lest they get swept up in the traffic surging toward the Lincoln Tunnel.

"Parking will probably be hopeless on Washington

Street," Pamela said as they skirted the top edge of
the little city. Bettina turned down a residential street,
and they cruised past lovingly tended row houses,
doors and window frames freshly painted in deep,
glowing tones.

"I remember when only starving artists wanted to
live in Hoboken," Bettina said. "Now each of these
little houses is probably worth a few million dollars."

They continued along the narrow street, slowing
down only to discover that a likely parking place was
actually a fire hydrant or that the sign looming from
the curb read "NO STANDING." At last Bettina
pulled up next to a spot near the end of the block.

"Grab it," Pamela said. "I have no idea how far along
Washington Street this gallery's address will turn out
to be, but it's fun to window-shop in Hoboken."

Pamela reached into the back seat for the painting, which they'd wrapped in a plastic garbage bag.
The two women strolled a few blocks to Washington
Street, checked the addresses of the shops near the
corner, and decided the Grainger Gallery must be to
the south. Washington Street was actually a wide
avenue, lined with flat-topped nineteenth-century
buildings, their rooflines and window frames softened with Victorian flourishes. Five or six stories,
each with a row of narrow windows, were stacked atop
sidewalk-level storefronts. Broad awnings shaded bow
windows that displayed each shop's artfully arranged
offerings.

They passed a florist with masses of chrysanthemums braving the chill out on the sidewalk. A bakery
window featured crusty oval loaves in colors ranging
from pale wheat to deepest pumpernickel. Shops offered vintage clothing, antique furniture, handmade
silver jewelry, and clothes for impossibly pampered

babies. A door opened, and a young woman pushing a stroller stepped through it. The smell of fresh-ground coffee wafted toward the street until the door closed behind her. Then, suddenly, they'd reached the Grainger Gallery. Displayed in its window were a series of shadow boxes constructed from what looked like wood rescued from an earlier use. In the boxes, small plastic figures carried out puzzling activities in settings clipped from decorating magazines.

"Quite the up-and-coming talent," said a voice at Pamela's elbow. "Leilo Bildlein. His work was featured at the last Venice Biennale."

Pamela turned in the direction of the voice. A small wiry man with a cup of take-out coffee in one hand was reaching a key toward the gallery door with the other. He wore a black turtleneck and black pants, and glasses with thick red-plastic frames.

"I hope you weren't waiting long," he added. "I would have left a note, but I just popped over to the coffee shop." His mouth formed a shopkeeper's smile. "I'm Gary Grainger."

He pushed the door open and flattened himself against it to let Pamela and Bettina go first. "Are you interested in Leilo's work?" he asked once they were all inside. He backed toward a cluttered desk in the corner and set the coffee down. Curiously, the walls in the room they had just entered were totally bare.

"It's fascinating," Pamela said, "but we're not here to buy, unfortunately. We're trying to solve a puzzle." She shifted the painting, still wrapped in the plastic garbage bag, around so it was leaning against her knees.

Gary Grainger's professionally pleasant smile reappeared. "Now you've got me curious," he said, shifting his gaze from her face to the plastic-wrapped rectangle.

Pamela reached behind the painting, grabbed the edge of the garbage bag's opening, and tugged at the bag so it fell around the painting like a garment being shed. The plastic rustled on its way down. She lifted the painting so the signature at the bottom wasn't hidden by the folds of plastic on the floor.

"Oh, my!" Gary Grainger raised his hand to his mouth. "What has happened to this beautiful work of art?"

"Is this a Chad Lawrence?" Pamela said. "Do you know him?" She lifted the painting higher and leaned around it to point at the signature she and Bettina and Wilfred had deciphered.

"Of course. He's one of my artists. But this particular painting was never handled by this gallery. Where did you get it?"

"I collect antiques," Pamela said. "I acquired it . . . from one of my favorite sources."

Bettina caught her eye and winked.

Looking as squeamish as if he was confronting a human who had suffered the same fate as the painting, Gary Grainger aimed a tentative finger at the slash. "What on earth happened?"

"We don't know." Bettina and Pamela spoke in unison, then Pamela took over. "We thought we'd start with figuring out who the artist was."

"Unquestionably Chad Lawrence. I'd know it even without the signature." He retracted his finger and leaned closer. "Ravishing woman. I never knew her full name, but this isn't his only portrait of her. He called her his muse."

Pamela debated whether to tell Gary Grainger that the picture's subject was now dead. As if she could read Pamela's mind, Bettina tightened her lips. She signaled a subtle negative with a tiny quiver of the head. Bettina was right, Pamela realized. They might be able to learn more if the gallery owner didn't realize that one of his artists was connected with a woman who had just been murdered.

"Chad Lawrence couldn't have done this, could he?" Pamela asked, running a finger along the edge of the slash. "He's not one of those eccentric artists who's never happy with his work?"

"No, no. He's very professional. But I'm puzzled about why he never offered me the painting to sell in the gallery." Gary Grainger's brow puckered, then he smiled. "Perhaps it was a gift though, a gift for her. It seems very intimate, with the knitting and all. None of the other portraits of her showed her knitting."

He gestured at the bare walls. "Chad's actually mounting a new show today. He's coming by midafternoon with the paintings. They'll be hung in here."

"Maybe we'll stop in again later," Pamela said. She tugged the plastic bag back over the painting.

Out on Washington Street, they strolled on past the gallery, pausing to admire a window display a few doors down. Ceramic plates and bowls in muted tones that suggested natural clay were arranged in place settings. Tucked beside them were homespun napkins and knives, forks, and spoons shaped from metal with a dark silvery sheen. "Don't let me go in here," Bettina said. "I ran out of cupboard space long ago."

Right beyond the tempting window was a café. Lace curtains hid the lower half of the windows, but peering above the curtains, they could see small tables set with perky flowers in vases. A counter along one side was crowded with cakes, pies, and trays of pastries. Most of the customers were well-dressed women of various ages, sipping from cups or raising forks from delicate dessert plates to their lips.

"Shall we?" Pamela said. "Then we'll stop by the gallery again. It will definitely be interesting to talk to Chad Lawrence."

Seated at one of the small tables, they ordered coffee and cherry tarts. "We'll be indulging tonight too," Pamela said. "Jean said something about cookies from a fancy bakery."

Bettina laughed. "The knitting may be helping Roland's blood pressure, but I'm not sure his doctor would approve of the extra calories."

They chatted about the knitting group until they were served, and then they lapsed into silence punctuated by appreciative hums as they conveyed forkfuls of pastry and deep red cherries to their mouths. Pamela liked her coffee black, and the rich bitterness of the café's special coffee made the tart taste all the sweeter.

"He must have known Amy well if he did multiple portraits of her," Bettina said suddenly. She rested her fork on the edge of her plate.

Pamela nodded and swallowed a mouthful of tart. "And he wouldn't be the first artist to succumb to the charms of his model."

They continued eating. But when the plates were empty, except for pastry crumbs and streaks of cherry syrup, Pamela gave voice to the idea that Bettina's comment had triggered. "Let's say he *was* in love with her. He gives her the painting as a love of-fering and she rejects it—and him. So he destroys it."

"And then he destroys *her*." Bettina's eyes widened. But then she frowned. "How would it all work though? He lies in wait for her outside your house? How would he even know she was going there? And then he goes back to her place and somehow lets himself in and slashes the painting? Wouldn't it make more sense for him to get away as fast as he could after he stabbed her with the knitting needle?"

Pamela listened, pursing her lips. She shook her head. "It could have happened the other way around. He shows up with the painting, declares his love, and is rejected. He's so miserable that he slashes the painting, bids her farewell, and goes on his way. But the rejection stings, and he decides if he can't have her no one will. And maybe she had mentioned that she was going out later. He lurks outside her building and follows her down the street to my house."

"And the only weapon that's handy is a knitting needle?"

"He used one of her kitchen knives to slash the painting, but he didn't decide to kill her till he got outside, so he didn't take the knife with him."

A hand appeared and collected the plates and forks. "I like those murder shows on TV too," the server commented with a genial smile. "Especially the British ones. The people seem so normal, but then they're killing each other. Not like anything that could happen in real life."

The street door of the gallery was propped open and Gary Grainger was standing on the sidewalk, regarding the scene though his red-framed glasses. He'd added a trim-fitting black leather jacket to his ensemble. Beyond the row of cars parked nose-in along the curb lurked a battered van with its back doors ajar. Something about the van looked familiar. The doors swung back further and a muscular man leaped to the pavement. He leaned back into the opening and was hidden from view by the door nearest the sidewalk.

Pamela had gotten only a fleeting glimpse of the man, but something about him looked familiar too. She leaned the painting of Amy, shrouded in its black plastic garbage bag, against the gallery's front window.

"Cops don't like the double parking," Gary Grainger observed. "But how else can anybody unload anything along here?"

A curious spectacle moved toward them, edging between two parked cars. It appeared to be a vase of flowers, at least a vase of flowers rendered in two dimensions, walking on human legs clad in faded, paint-spattered jeans. When it reached the sidewalk, the vase of flowers dipped to the ground and a male face popped out above its upper edge. It was a rugged face with an irreverent twist to the lips and blond hair cut so short the man almost looked bald.

"Four more to go," the owner of the face said to Gary Grainger.

"Take your time," he responded. "No sign of the cops yet."

Pamela and Bettina looked at each other. It was the man from the funeral; the man who'd seemed so distraught. "Is he Chad Lawrence?" Pamela asked

Gary Grainger after the man had edged through the doorway with the painting.

The gallery owner nodded. His eyes remained fixed on the van.

Pamela and Bettina stepped into the gallery and watched Chad Lawrence lean the painting carefully against one of the walls. Gary Grainger stayed behind on the sidewalk. Twenty or more paintings leaned against the walls, some stacked against one another, waiting to be hung. Most of them were larger than the painting of Amy, and none of them were of humans— at least, none of the visible ones. Chad Lawrence seemed to have been exploring variations on a theme, painting the same vase and the same flowers over and over, the flowers becoming noticeably droopier and then finally dead.

Pamela waited until they were alone in the gallery and then leaned toward Bettina and whispered, "Would he have been so sad at the funeral if he'd been the one who killed her?"

Bettina shrugged. "Feeling guilty?" she whispered back. "Or he realized that if he'd left her alive she might change her mind about him some day. Now it's hopeless."

They waited while Chad Lawrence brought in the remaining paintings and moved his van to a side street. When everyone was back inside the gallery, Pamela introduced herself. She explained that she had come across an interesting painting and had traced its artist to the Grainger Gallery. She reached for the wrapped painting, which had been leaning against Gary Grainger's desk. Chad Lawrence regarded the plastic-swathed parcel with amused condescension, as if humoring its owner.

Pamela loosened the plastic garbage bag and let it fall to the floor. Chad Lawrence's face went blank. As if remembering himself, he twisted his lips back into their former near-smirk.

"Interesting," he said in an offhand way. "Where'd you come across this?"

Pamela repeated her line about acquiring it from one of her favorite antiquing sources. She watched his face closely. If he'd given it to Amy and he was the one who slashed it, he'd know perfectly well it hadn't made its way to an antique store. But he was on guard now, and his expression remained bland, except for the slightly up-tilted lip.

"It *is* one of mine," he said. "An earlier period in my artistic evolution." He stared at it fixedly for a long minute. "Too bad about the damage, but it's not worth much now. What would you take for it?"

"I'd like to hang on to it," Pamela said. "At least for a while." Her fingers tightened on the edge of the canvas. "Did you know the subject?"

"A model." He shrugged in a not very convincing show of offhandedness. Pamela shifted her gaze to Bettina's face. Bettina bit her lips as if suppressing a laugh. "I worked with her for a while. Now I'm into flowers." He waved toward one of the canvases lined up against the walls. It was one in which the flowers still looked reasonably fresh. "I don't know what I'd do with it anyway."

He rearranged a few of the paintings, stepped back from the wall, glanced around the room, and nodded in satisfaction. He reached a hand toward Gary Grainger for a handshake. The contrast between the tall, muscular artist in his grimy jeans and the slight gallery owner in his trim black outfit and his determinedly fashionable red-framed glasses was striking.

"I guess we're all set, then," Chad Lawrence said. "See you at the opening." With a nod toward Pamela and Bettina, he was out the door. They watched through the gallery window as he hurried out of sight. Pamela was just about to suggest that she and Bettina head back to Arborville when Gary Grainger spoke.

Chapter Thirteen

"He was in love with her, you know," he said suddenly, his voice rising. He seemed excited to have someone to share this bit of gossip with. He nodded toward Bettina. "I could tell he wasn't fooling you with that story about how she was just a model. Like I said, I never knew her full name. But his feelings were obvious from the way he talked about her. And for a while there he hardly painted anything else."

He whirled around, took a few quick steps toward the cluttered desk, and began shifting piles of paper here and there. A few loose sheets fluttered to the floor. After a bit he gave a cry of triumph and waved a catalogue in the air.

"Chad's last show," he explained, stepping back toward them and leafing through the catalogue. "Here she is." He pointed to a color photo of a painting in which Amy was stretched out on a sofa in an interior that evoked a Victorian parlor. He flipped from page to page. "Here she is again, and here, and here."

Pamela was glad they'd lingered. She'd suspected the connection between Chad Lawrence and Amy went beyond artist and model—tantalizing as even that connection might be. But learning that he'd been in love with her was very useful. She recalled the crack Bob Randolph had made about too many people in the world having nothing to do but mind other people's business. Gary Grainger certainly had many things to do besides keeping track of which artists were in love with which models, but it was understandable that he would take an interest. He might seem nosy, but nosy people were a great boon to the amateur sleuth.

She was distracted from these reflections by a sound between a gasp and a yelp. It had come from Gary Grainger. "Are you okay?" Bettina said soothingly and reached out a comforting hand.

He was holding the catalogue in both hands, pages spread wide, staring at yet another of the Amy portraits. "This is that woman who was killed last week," he murmured as if to himself. "Amy Morgan." He looked up from the page he was staring at and turned toward Pamela. Through the lenses of the red-framed glasses his eyes looked larger than normal. "I can be a very perceptive guy," he said. "About two minutes after you showed me that painting I realized there was more to your interest than just who painted it. And now I know why. What are you up to, anyway?"

Pamela explained that Amy Morgan had been very kind to her at a difficult time of her life and had recently become a neighbor. She confessed that she'd come upon the painting in the trash outside Amy's apartment building. She had embarked on a quest to figure out who painted it and who might have damaged it, because the answers to those questions might lead to Amy's killer.

"The police aren't looking for her killer?" Gary Grainger said.

"Of course they are," Bettina cut in. "But sometimes the police don't ask the right questions."

"Well." Gary Grainger closed the catalogue with a snap. He was silent for at least a minute, as if processing this new information.

"I feel sorry for anyone who suffers from unrequited love," Pamela said. "Amy was single. And Chad is attractive, in a way—and certainly talented. He seems a little eccentric, but nice enough. Do you think he was too Bohemian for her tastes?"

"*She* may have been single," Gary Grainger said, "but *he* isn't. In fact, we show his wife's work too." He darted toward the cluttered desk and returned with a glossy postcard that he handed to Pamela. "There's a show of her work up in here right now." He continued on toward an adjoining room.

But Pamela stared at the card, too distracted to follow. Bettina lingered at her side. "New work by Dorrie Morgan," the card announced. "Meet the artist 6:00 to 8:00 p.m., Wednesday, November 16, at the Grainger Gallery."

"Dorrie!" Pamela whispered, displaying the card. "Dorrie Morgan is his wife."

"Different last names," Bettina whispered back. "Everyone does that now, including my Boston son and his wife, but it's confusing." They caught up with the gallery owner.

Like the front room of the gallery, the walls in this room were white. Hanging all around were row upon row of striking black-and-white photographs. Each showed a stark shape, like a malformed castle or a rock formation from some alien planet.

"Ice sculptures," Gary Grainger said. "For obvious reasons I can't exhibit the actual works of art, unless I decide to install a walk-in freezer."

Pamela leaned close to the nearest photograph to ponder the signature. "She's Amy Morgan's sister, you know," she said in response to Gary Grainger's puzzled look.

"Oh, my." Gary Grainger's eyes got big behind his glasses. "I didn't make the connection. I never knew Amy's last name when she was just . . . the model. That certainly makes things interesting." Then, as if returning to the role of gallery owner, he said, "Dorrie makes the actual sculptures and then photographs them. So artistic and so perishable. Amazing what you can do with an ice pick."

They strolled from picture to picture, occasionally pausing in front of an especially curious image. In her mind Pamela was comparing ice picks with knitting needles and realizing that Chad Lawrence and Dorrie Morgan probably had equally strong motives for murdering Amy.

Gary Grainger's voice cut through her musings. "It took a long time to get these photographs hung," he said. "Chad did all the work though, because Dorrie had to be somewhere. However in love Chad might have been with his model, he's devoted to his wife too."

"How long has the show been up?" Bettina asked.

"Just a week, since last Wednesday morning. Chad worked here Tuesday till after closing time."

Pamela looked at her watch. It was edging past five, and they'd hit Turnpike traffic for sure. They had to be at Jean Worthington's for Knit and Nibble at seven. "You'll be wanting to close," she said. "You've been very kind to spend all this time with us."

"Oh, no problem," he said. "I stay open till seven."

Outside the sky was darkening and lights were coming on along the street. Bettina waited till they were settled in the car, the painting in its plastic wrapping stowed safely in the back seat. "Well," she sighed. "I guess he's got an alibi."

Pamela smiled a half smile in the dark. "But *she* doesn't."

She wasn't sure Bettina had heard. Bettina had started the engine and was beginning the delicate process of extracting her car from a parking spot that had required all her skill to squeeze into. She eased back, then forward, twisting the steering wheel as far as it would go in each direction. Headlights approached from behind and she paused. The headlights paused too.

"Waiting to claim the spot, I think," Pamela said.

"I hope he stays out of my way." Bettina jerked the steering wheel to the right and pressed on the gas. The car lurched from the space as Pamela cringed, expecting to hear a squeal of metal as fender scraped fender. But they were on their way.

Bettina turned left and then left again, then cruised up Washington Street toward the cross street that would take them away from Hoboken.

Ten minutes later they were heading north on the Turnpike, moving faster than Pamela had expected, multiple lanes of brake lights like glowing red ribbons stretching ahead of them. "We're doing fine," Pamela said after checking the clock on Bettina's dashboard. "We'll have plenty of time to eat before we're due at Jean's. I don't want my only dinner to be gourmet cookies and coffee."

Bettina gave a noncommittal grunt. She braked as the car in front of her slowed. When the traffic picked up again, Pamela spoke.

"You'd have to be very skilled with an ice pick to make those ice sculptures of Dorrie's," she said.

"Very." Bettina nodded.

"Amy had a knitting needle sticking out of her chest."

"That's true," Bettina said. "It wasn't an ice pick, though I see the similarity. And if my husband had been hopelessly in love with my sister, I'd be tempted to look for a remedy too."

The image of the thoroughly domesticated Wilfred pursuing anyone made Pamela smile. And besides, Bettina didn't have a sister.

"Dorrie definitely has a motive," Pamela said. "We don't know where she was last Tuesday night, but we know she *wasn't* at the gallery hanging pictures for her show. A gallery show is kind of a big deal. Wouldn't she be there working unless she had something very very important to do?"

"Like kill her sister"—Bettina paused to maneuver quickly out of the lane that was hastening them toward the exit for Newark Airport—"with an ice pick?" she concluded when the glowing ribbons of brake lights once more stretched ahead.

"She wouldn't have to have *done* it with an ice pick," Pamela said. "But if you were used to handling an ice pick, you could do an awful lot of damage with a metal knitting needle too."

"Possibly so." Silhouetted against the glare of headlights from traffic in the oncoming lanes, Bettina's head nodded slowly. "Possibly so," she repeated.

"What if we *did* have to survive on gourmet cookies and coffee for dinner?" Pamela asked, suddenly excited.

"Because . . . ?"

"Haversack is sort of on the way back to Arborville. Dorrie lives there or has a studio there or something. I remember the address from that business card she left when she gave me Amy's bin of knitting supplies. It's on Railroad Avenue, right near that big thrift store I like."

Chapter Fourteen

"What are we going to say to her?" Bettina asked as they cruised along. "We just thought we'd drop in and ask you if you killed your sister?"

"I'm working on an angle," Pamela said. "I'll start off with the painting. We'll see how she responds."

After they left the Turnpike at its northernmost end, Pamela guided Bettina to Haversack and the stretch of Railroad Avenue where her favorite thrift store was to be found—and nearby, hopefully, Dorrie Morgan. But as they cruised along with railroad tracks on one side and buildings on the other, they saw nothing that looked remotely like a place where a person would live, or even create and photograph ice sculptures. They passed a few low, dark buildings that could have been small factories, a business that offered pool chemicals, another whose impressive sign announced that it supplied and installed commercial plate glass, and one that sold marble and granite, cut to order. But they were all closed.

"Here's the thrift store," Pamela said. Bettina slowed and pulled off the road. The thrift store was dark too, with the neat parking spaces marked off across the building's front occupied by only one lone car. A display, feebly illuminated by a light on a high pole near the street, featured a sofa, a coffee table, and a few jauntily dressed mannequins.

"You're sure it was Railroad Avenue?" Bettina said. "This doesn't look promising at all—and there's nobody around to even ask."

"Let's just drive a little bit further. The address was definitely something in the hundreds, and the thrift store is 102." Pamela leaned past Bettina to squint at the number posted over the thrift store's door.

"You're sure it was Haversack?" Bettina said. "Sometimes numbers start over at the border of a new town."

"It was Haversack." Pamela nodded decisively. "And look—something's going on at this next place. Start the car up again."

The small patch of asphalt that supplied parking for the thrift store merged into a much larger lot. Bettina followed Pamela's instructions, and they joined several nondescript cars parked in a ragged row. A much larger building set further back from Railroad Avenue was bathed in a cheerful fluorescent glow. People laden with bulging plastic bags were making their way through a pair of automatic doors and heading toward cars.

"It's a discount grocery place," Pamela exclaimed. "I forgot it was here. The Haversack Wholesale Food Depot."

"How does it bring us closer to locating Dorrie?" Bettina asked, sounding a bit grumpy.

"At least there are people. I'll find out if there are any apartment buildings along here, or places where

Dorrie could rent a work space." Pamela reached for the door handle. "There's a guy collecting shopping carts. I'll ask him."

As Bettina watched, Pamela hurried toward a bright patch of asphalt where a small man in a puffy jacket was tucking shopping carts into one another to create a long chain. She leaned toward him. He looked up, and there was a quick flash of teeth as he smiled. He pointed toward the automatic doors. Pamela nodded, suggesting she was pleased, though Bettina could see only her back. The man seemed quite entertained by the message he was conveying, even pausing once to laugh. Pamela nodded again.

Bettina rolled down her window when Pamela was a few steps away. "What on earth?" she said. "You certainly made his day—or night."

"She's in here," Pamela said. "They all know her. Come on. And let's grab that painting." She paused when they got to the entrance and pointed to the store hours posted near the automatic doors. "Open till ten p.m. every night," she said. "Alibi—or not?"

Inside, the air smelled spicy. They hurried down a long aisle between crowded shelves, giant bags of rice on one side and cans of fruit and vegetables on the other. Pamela held the painting close at her side. Near the end of the aisle a butcher counter came in sight, with glistening cuts of meat in parallel bins behind a sloping panel of glass. To the left of the butcher counter was a door.

"Behind that door." Pamela stepped forward and reached for the knob.

They entered a small room crowded with wooden crates stacked in towers of various heights and filled with round and oblong produce in shades of green, yellow, purple, and red. The spicy smell had been replaced by the smell of fruit and vegetables, some of them decaying, as witnessed by the trash bins arranged along one wall.

Somehow space had been found for a table. On the table was a large block of ice, and facing the block of ice but with her back to the door stood Dorrie Morgan. Pamela recognized her dark no-style hair and her baggy jeans, complemented this evening by an equally baggy sweatshirt.

"Dorrie?" Pamela whispered it. If Dorrie hadn't heard the door open, she must be deep in thought.

Dorrie whirled around, eyes and mouth both open wide. "You!" she gasped. "What—?" She paused to compose herself. "How did you find me here?"

"You gave me your business card," Pamela said. "'Dorrie Morgan—Fantasies.'"

Dorrie grunted. "Odd time for a social call. I was really concentrating. The ice has to tell me what's locked inside." She flourished the ice pick in her hand.

"It's not really social," Pamela said. She didn't think it was necessary to mention that her first meeting with Dorrie had occurred when Dorrie crawled out of her shrubbery at eight a.m. "I have something for you. To thank you for giving me the bin with Amy's knitting supplies." She swung the wrapped painting around so it faced Dorrie. She loosened the plastic bag and watched Dorrie's face as the bag slipped to the floor.

Dorrie screwed up her face in an expression that seemed almost comic, twisting her lips into a zigzag and wrinkling her lump-of-dough nose. "Yeah?" she said.

"It was in the trash behind Amy's apartment building. Mr. Gilly seems to have been a little too zealous in his cleanout. I was sure you or your parents would want it. It's been damaged somehow. I guess he handled it kind of roughly, but I think a canvas like this can be repaired."

"We don't want it, actually," Dorrie said.

Bettina caught Pamela's eye and tapped the wrist where she wore her watch. But Pamela was only getting started.

"This is an unusual work space," she said.

Dorrie frowned. "*Duh.* Freezer, of course." She pointed at a broad metal door in the side wall. "I pay them for space to work and space to store my creations. It's a win-win. And that other door goes right out to the loading dock. Handy when I've got something to deliver."

"The store stays open late," Pamela said. "Do you often work late?"

"If I have something that needs to be finished."

"Do you have to check out with somebody when you leave, or do you just leave?"

"Why do you care?" Dorrie regarded the block of ice and then the ice pick. "Look," she said, "I'm really busy. I've got a deadline for this." She nodded past them at the door they'd entered. "And please shut that door behind you when you go out. I don't like curious people wandering in while I'm at work."

Pamela took a few steps back and eased the door closed, even though she had no plans to leave quite yet. Dorrie continued to glance back and forth between the block of ice and the ice pick, then she put the ice pick down and picked a larger tool out of a wooden box on the floor. Pamela didn't know very much about tools, but this one looked like a cross between a chisel and a narrow putty knife.

Maybe it hadn't been so wise to close the door that led back into the grocery part of the store. Dorrie could dispatch them both and escape through the loading-dock door. She hefted the new tool in her hand then began to wave it back and forth, pacing in a small circle and humming.

Bettina edged closer to the door. She touched Pamela on the arm and mouthed the word "Go?" raising her eyebrows to emphasize the question.

But now Dorrie seemed more focused on her project than on her visitors. She was still waving the chisel-putty knife, but she'd turned back toward the table. The waving motions were directed at the block of ice as if she was planning where to attack.

Pamela gave Bettina a small smile and waved her fingers in a "don't worry" gesture. She stepped up next to Dorrie. "I guess the ice carving is the 'Fantasies' on your business card."

"Got it in one try," Dorrie said, waving the chisel-putty knife in wider and wider arcs. She paused to take a glossy postcard from a stack in the wooden box and hand it to Pamela. It was the same card Gary Grainger had showed them at the gallery. On one side was the caption "New work by Dorrie Morgan—Meet the artist 6:00 to 8:00 p.m., Wednesday, November 16, at the Grainger Gallery" and on the other a stark black-and-white image of an ice sculpture.

"Art doesn't pay the rent though," Dorrie said with a disgusted laugh. "So I do other stuff too. Party services, basically. I'll get two hundred dollars for this, when it's done." She poked at the block of ice with the chisel-putty knife.

"You must be very good."

"I am," Dorrie said, sounding a little more friendly.

"But that means I'm in demand. Last Tuesday was just murder."

Behind her, Pamela heard Bettina gulp.

Dorrie went on, warming to her subject. "It was a bachelor party and they wanted a stripper, and then to get home and find out my sister had been killed." She paused, screwed up her face in the odd expression again, and then laughed. "Forget I said Tuesday was murder. Freudian, I guess. I mean, it really was murder, for Amy, so I shouldn't have—uh, used that word."

"A stripper?" Pamela said, her eyes unconsciously straying to Dorrie's jeans and sweatshirt. Perhaps the body they enclosed was more shapely than the clothes suggested—or the thrill of watching a stripper lay less in the body being revealed and more in the process of revelation.

Dorrie laughed again, the disgusted laugh this time. "Not all of my work is abstract," she said, snatching the postcard back from Pamela. "Some is quite representational. They wanted a stripper carved out of ice for the centerpiece of the buffet table. Life-sized. I had to order a giant block of ice, and I worked all afternoon, and then I had to ask a couple of those guys who collect the shopping carts to help me load it into my van, and the party was at a catering hall way down in one of those shore towns. I made it there just in the nick of time, seven p.m. on the dot."

"What do you think?" Pamela asked Bettina as they made their way past the neat rows of shopping carts lined up outside the automatic doors. The smiling man who had steered Pamela to the back room where Dorrie worked looked up from a cart he was tucking into another cart and gave a cheerful wave. "Thanks!" Pamela called.

Bettina widened her eyes and stretched her lips into a comical smile. "What do I think? She volunteered the story, so it's not like she knew we were fishing to see if she had an alibi."

"The time fits," Pamela said. "Almost too perfectly." They stepped from the fluorescent brightness of the market's entrance into the darkness of the parking lot. "Knit and Nibble starts at seven. Amy must have been killed shortly before that, early enough that nobody else was walking up my front walk yet. If Dorrie was pulling up outside a catering hall in a town on the Jersey shore at seven p.m., she couldn't have been in my yard fifteen minutes earlier."

"No," Bettina agreed. "She couldn't."

They made their way back along Railroad Avenue, past the thrift store and the small factories, the pool chemical place, the plate glass place, and the marble and granite place, both staring ahead at the darkness past the reach of the car's headlights.

"I kind of like her," Pamela said suddenly.

"I do too," Bettina said.

"I'm glad she didn't do it."

"I am too."

Chapter Fifteen

"How are we doing on time?" Pamela asked as Bettina turned from County Road onto Orchard Street. She raised her wrist and pushed back her jacket sleeve but couldn't make out the tiny numerals on her watch face.

"It's here, on the dashboard." Glowing numerals on the dashboard indicated that they had twenty minutes to get themselves to Jean Worthington's. Bettina pulled up along the curb in front of Pamela's dark house. "I didn't know we'd be out this long or I'd have left a light on," Pamela said, reaching for the door handle.

"I'll wait till you get inside, in case that woman from the yarn shop is waiting to pounce on you from the shrubbery. Then I'll pull into my driveway and tell Wilfred to order himself a pizza from When in Rome. He won't mind. Tuesday is usually rotisserie chicken."

There was time for a quick sandwich, but Pamela wasn't the only one who was hungry for dinner. Catrina had been lurking near the steps as she came up the walk and had actually followed her onto the porch instead of waiting at a distance for food to appear.

Once the cat was fed and she'd eaten a slice of whole-grain toast with peanut butter, Pamela hurried through her kitchen into the hall that led to her laundry room. She tipped the cover back from the plastic bin that sat atop her washing machine and pulled out one of the golden balls of mystery yarn. In the living room she slipped it into her knitting bag, atop the almost-finished sleeve for the Icelandic sweater project. Knit and Nibble sometimes had a "show-and-tell" component. Maybe someone in the group would be able to shed some light on the mystery yarn, and in any event it was so unusual that her fellow knitters would certainly enjoy seeing it and feeling its silky softness. But she didn't think she'd tell them how it actually came into her possession.

Though Jean Worthington's house was the second-grandest in Arborville, it was right up the block from Pamela's, and it coexisted peacefully with its humbler neighbors. Its Victorian designer had undoubtedly created it as a tribute to its owner's status, but since the original owner had lived during the late 1800s, any hint of vulgar new money had long since dissipated. Jean and Douglas Worthington inhabited it as caretakers of a bit of Arborville history, putting their considerable income to good use funding the maintenance an old house inevitably required.

Bettina waved from across the street as Pamela hurried along the sidewalk. Pamela reached Jean's driveway first, just as Roland DeCamp's Porsche rolled up to the curb. "Good evening," he called cheerfully as the car door swung back and he bounced up out of the driver's seat. He darted along the asphalt to join her, swinging the briefcase that contained his knitting supplies. "Ready for some hot needle action?"

Somewhere nearby, a wood fire burned in someone's fireplace. The tang of smoke in the chilly air made Pamela smile with pleasure. Roland smiled in return.

"How are you doing with the cables?" Pamela asked, not wanting to disappoint him by admitting the smile was not actually for him.

"Work has been hectic," Roland said. "That's why the club is good. At least once a week I get in a solid hour or two of knitting." They paused at the end of the driveway to wait for Bettina. "Are you still feeding that cat?" Roland inquired.

"When she comes around."

Bettina joined them, panting a bit from exertion.

"A female?" Roland said. "She'll be a mother before you know it. Too many strays in town as it is."

"They *do* go after the songbirds," Bettina said. "But who could turn away a hungry little kitten?"

"I could," Roland said.

"Well," Bettina said, "it was very thoughtful of you to go to the funeral."

"We knitters have to stick together." He flourished the briefcase. As they walked up the driveway, he scanned the bushes, his actions so exaggerated that it was clear he was joking. "Nothing lurking out here tonight, I hope." He squatted as if to peer under the shrubs that skirted the edge of Jean's front porch. "It's the same street where it happened, after all. You haven't recruited any more new members, have you,

Pamela? I don't have time for another one of those police interviews."

A tasteful arrangement of cornstalks, pumpkins, and chrysanthemums greeted them on Jean's large porch. Pamela had once complimented Jean on the transformation her porch and front yard underwent as the holiday season got going in early fall. It began with harvest themes in late September and culminated with swags of greenery, giant wreaths festooned with red velvet bows, and a galaxy of tiny white lights, a display that lasted until late January. Jean had confessed that her landscaping service was responsible and that she herself was hopelessly inartistic.

Even Jean's doorbell had an elegant sound, a few notes whose echoes formed a pleasant chord. "Come in, come in." Jean greeted them with a warm smile and gestured them into her softly lit hallway. They stepped onto a narrow Persian runner whose colors were faded in a way that suggested great age and great value. Around the rug's edges, well-tended parquet gleamed. Jean was dressed head to toe in creamy white: a heavy silk blouse tucked into slim wool trousers, with elegant, low-heeled shoes in smooth leather that exactly matched the outfit. Chin-length waves of pale gold hair flowed from a side part, not quite hiding the diamond studs in her earlobes.

Coats handed over to Jean, the three of them turned toward the spacious living room, where a low fire burned in the fireplace. Leave it to Jean to create the perfect autumn ambiance, complete with wood smoke wafting through her yard. Nell had settled into a wing chair at one side of the hearth and was already at work. A fat skein of pink yarn was perched on the arm of the chair, and several rows of what Pamela suspected was to be yet another elephant hung from her needles.

"Wait until you see the cookies Jean has for us," Nell said as they entered. "What a treat—and so clever."

"Oh, I can't really take credit," Jean said from the hallway. "All I did was call the bakery." One silk-clad arm reached toward Roland and the other toward Bettina. "Please make yourselves comfortable."

Roland and Bettina found spots on Jean's sofa, one at each end. Between them stretched a row of needlepoint pillows featuring roses, pansies, daisies, hollyhocks, and more—a veritable garden, all rendered in delicate stiches. Roland rested his briefcase on the large coffee table in front of the sofa but made no move to open it. Bettina set to work on a tiny crocheted circle that would grow into another granny square for the baby blanket project.

"Excuse me," Jean murmured from the hall. "Kitchen duties." Her pale shoes glided along the exotically patterned hall runner. Pamela hurried after until they reached Jean's charming kitchen. Its soapstone counters, stainless-steel appliances, and finely crafted cabinets had been installed after Jean and Douglas bought the house, but the kitchen managed an artful compromise between modern convenience and tradition. Jean added a few cups and saucers to a small group on a silver tray. "They're my Limoges," she said. "I love having a chance to use them."

"Beautiful," Pamela observed, quite sincerely. Aside from her wedding china, most of her pretty things were tag-sale finds or thrift-store treasures, but she cherished them just as much as if they were priceless.

"This will be for the coffee." Jean gestured toward a silver coffeepot.

"I have a show-and-tell," Pamela said, "some very interesting yarn I came across. Shall I bring it out when we take our break for refreshments?"

"Yes, yes," Jean said. "That would be perfect. I think people are already getting busy with their knitting."

The elegant chimes sounded again—a much louder sound when heard from inside the house. Jean hurried back down the hall, Pamela trailing behind. The chimes were still echoing as Jean pulled the door open. Her cordial "Come in, come in" rang out.

Karen Dowling handed over her coat and headed for a third wing chair, the one next to Nell. Pamela moved a few needlepoint pillows aside to take a seat between Roland and Bettina. Jean retreated toward the kitchen.

"Did you walk, dear?" Nell asked as Karen opened her knitting bag.

"Hmm?" Karen looked up, puzzled. "It's not far . . ." Then, as if Nell's look of alarm had triggered something, she added hastily, "Oh, I see what you mean, of course. After what happened last week, being out after dark can feel a little creepy."

"They haven't caught him," Nell said. "I took the car tonight, even though I hate to use the gas when I could just as well walk. So wasteful, not to mention the pollution."

Karen pulled out the project she had launched the previous week. The navy blue scarf she was knitting for her husband had grown considerably. A swath at least ten inches long and eight inches wide hung from the plastic needles.

From the dining room came the sounds of china and silverware being arranged, then Jean appeared in the doorway. "It looks like we're all here," she said. "I'll make coffee and tea when the time comes," she said. "And we have the special cookies, of course. And a show-and-tell." She surveyed her attractive living room and busy guests with a contented smile and sank gracefully into the wing chair on the other side of the fireplace. The soft lighting from the strategically placed lamps smoothed out her already smooth complexion. She reached toward the large basket that contained her knitting supplies.

"My goodness," she said as she lifted the cover. "Nell, I really will have to learn how to make those elephants—or maybe something simpler, without so many appendages, like a seal. I have all these odds and ends of yarn left from various projects—each one just enough for a small animal." She set the cover aside and tilted the basket to display its contents. Indeed, she had balls and skeins of yarn in every color of the rainbow: red, blue, gold, green, violet, and more.

"I'll be glad to show you," Nell said. "The elephants aren't that hard, really, but we could get started with a seal."

Roland pulled his knitting project out of his briefcase and smoothed it across his thigh. He was using expensive wool in a natural off-white shade, perfect for a classic cable-knit sweater. So far, though, the sweater consisted of a piece of knitting twenty inches wide and six inches long, with an erratic ridge of lumpy stitches meandering up the middle. He'd left off in mid-row, so half the knitting hung from one needle and half from the other. He reached back into the briefcase to retrieve his yarn.

Bettina leaned across Pamela to finger the piece of work. "Nice even stitches here at the edge," she commented, smiling encouragingly at Roland. "That takes skill."

"Nothing to it." He got busy with his needles, looping a strand of yarn to form a stich.

Bettina frowned. "I think you're going the wrong direction," she said. "You're going back the way you came. That's always a danger when you leave off in the middle of a row."

"It's fine," Roland said, clicking his needles defiantly. "I know what I'm doing."

"Is that the front or the back?" Karen asked from across the room.

"Does it matter?" Roland continued knitting.

"Sometimes. Will it be a cardigan or a pullover?"

"What?" He looked up, and the needles paused in mid-stitch.

Nell joined the conversation. "Are you planning to button it up the front, or pull it over your head?"

"I haven't decided yet." He'd nearly reached the end of the row, and only a few stitches remained on the left-hand needle.

"Aren't you using a pattern?" Bettina's voice rose in amazement.

"I started with one, but once I understood the basic principles, I put it away." Roland finished off the row with a flourish and smoothed the piece of knitting out on his thigh once more. He looked over at Karen. "How about those metal needles you were going to give me? Did you find them yet?"

"Pamela found one . . . at her house," Karen stuttered, and her cheeks grew red. "It was in a sofa cushion. The other one is . . . somewhere. As soon as it turns up, I'll give them to you."

"Just a few days till Thanksgiving," Jean observed from her perch in the wing chair on the other side of the fireplace.

The perfect hostess, Pamela noted to herself. Let poor Karen collect her wits in peace, though the fact that she got so flustered when the topic of the knitting needles came up was troublesome. Bettina had said that the police didn't consider Karen a suspect, and probably there was nothing to worry about. But she hadn't been scared to walk to Jean's alone. If she was the murderer, of course she'd know there was nothing to fear.

"And then it will be Christmas," Nell commented.

"The town already thinks it's Christmas," Roland snorted. "When did those garlands go up downtown? The day after Halloween?"

"Just about," Bettina said. "But I like the holidays."

"Does anyone know whether the Aardvark Alliance will be using the same lot for the Christmas trees this year?" Nell asked. The Aardvarks were the Arborville High School sports teams, and the Alliance sold Christmas trees in town every year to help fund the sports programs.

"I certainly hope so," Bettina said. "They moved it last year, and Wilfred had to drive all over the place looking for it."

"There was a notice in the *Advocate*," Nell said. "Didn't you see it?"

"I guess not."

"But you work for the *Advocate*," Nell observed mildly.

Little side conversations popped up around the room. Bettina described to Pamela the menu planned for Thursday, when her two sons and their wives would be visiting, along with her two grandchildren. "And they're bringing most of the food," she added happily.

Nell was leaning over the arm of her chair toward Karen, whose cheeks had lost their frantic blush. The conversation appeared lively, but only soft whispers reached Pamela's ears.

Jean was smiling tolerantly at Roland, who was holding forth on how little he got from the town in return for his "ruinous" property taxes.

Nell turned away from Karen to remark, "You can afford it, Roland, so calm down."

As if she'd been waiting for a chance to escape, Jean gently laid her work on the edge of her knitting basket, where the pale pewter yarn of her current project contrasted with the brighter colors of the jumbled balls and skeins.

"I'll start the coffee," she said rising. "And who would care for tea?"

"I'll take tea," Karen and Nell said in unison.

"Four people for coffee then?" The others nodded, and Jean left the room.

Soon the smell of freshly brewed coffee signaled that yarn, needles, and crochet hook could be laid aside. Jean appeared in the arch between her living room and dining room. "Please come in and help yourselves," she said.

The table was spread with a starched white linen cloth. The Limoges cups and saucers were lined up in two neat rows, the pale, almost translucent china set off with bands of gold at cup and saucer rims. The silver tray that had held the cups in the kitchen now displayed a silver coffeepot and matching sugar and creamer. A teapot that matched the Limoges was centered on a smaller silver tray.

But it was the cookies that provoked the most admiration. Arranged on two Limoges platters were tiny sweaters, at least two dozen of them. They were cookie-sweaters. No two were the same, and each had been frosted with great skill. A pale pink cardigan sported minuscule silver buttons, and a black-and-white-striped pullover featured bands of green at neck and cuff. A few sweaters had been inspired by Nordic designs, with reindeer the size of fleas dancing across the shoulders. Small Limoges plates sat nearby to receive each person's chosen cookie-sweaters.

"Look at this," Bettina said. "You have outdone yourself, Jean. I know you said you didn't make them, but you were so clever to think of sweaters."

Jean smiled modestly and rearranged a pile of small starched napkins. "Please do help yourselves," she said. "I have a few dozen more in the kitchen."

Soon people were reseated in the living room, cookie plates and cups and saucers distributed around the edge of Jean's grand coffee table, and laps protected by napkins whose starched folds made them resemble low tents.

"I have a show-and-tell," Pamela said after she'd taken a few sips of coffee and eaten the sleeves of a sweater whose dark-brown surface proved to be chocolate.

"I'm just coming," Jean called from the dining room. "Go ahead and start."

Pamela reached into her knitting bag and brought up the ball of golden yarn.

Jean hurried past the fireplace, glancing toward Pamela with a grimace that suggested she was sorry to be interrupting. She set her coffee and cookies on the table, pushed her knitting basket hastily to the side of her chair and replaced the cover, and settled into place.

"It came from a small shop in Brooklyn," Pamela said, reaching into her bag again and pulling out the band of paper that had encircled the original skein. "'That Bedford Shop,'" she read. "'Purveyor of All Things Natural, Brooklyn, NY.'"

"What took you over to Brooklyn?" Roland asked, gesturing with half of a striped cookie-sweater. "I haven't been there in years."

"She has a college-age daughter," Nell said. "College kids know about cool places."

Pamela let that explanation stand. There was no reason to connect the yarn with Amy and remind everyone of last week's tragic event. "The color and texture are so amazing," she said. "I have no idea what animal the wool came from or how it was dyed. I thought you'd all be interested in seeing it, and maybe someone can solve the mystery of its origins." She held the ball of yarn out to Roland, who set it on his lap and continued eating his cookie. He patted at the yarn with his free hand, obviously not used to being in a group of yarn connoisseurs and uncertain how to react.

After a few seconds, he said, "It makes me want to pet it." Satisfied that he'd acquitted himself suitably, he passed it on to Jean.

"Are you going to make something with it?" Nell

asked as Jean placed the ball of yarn on the coffee table and sent it rolling in her direction. "I see you've made a ball."

"I have to figure out what I have enough for," Pamela said. "There were only four skeins."

"Back in the old days making a ball was always the first step in a knitting project," Nell said. "You couldn't just pull a strand out of a skein and start knitting. You'd end up with a big snarled clump. Now so much yarn comes needle-ready, you might say. But the fancy kinds, like the special wool from special sheep, still come in those traditional skeins."

Pamela remembered pictures in her grandmother's knitting books—a docile husband with outstretched hands several inches apart and wreathed in yarn, linked by a strand of yarn to a woman with a 1940s hairstyle busily forming a ball.

Nell studied the ball of yarn for a few seconds. "Could it be goat hair?" she said. "Aren't some goats rather silky?" She passed the ball to Karen.

"It's so soft," Karen murmured, "the way it feels, and the color, and everything. Could the color be from some plant?" She gave it one last fondle and stood up to hand it to Bettina.

"Saffron, perhaps?" Nell said.

"Saffron is expensive." Roland frowned. "And it would take a great deal to dye even as much yarn as is in this ball. There are much cheaper ways to turn something yellow, I'm sure."

"But the color is so special," Nell said. "Really magical."

Jean's voice came from her spot near the fireplace. "Please help yourselves to more cookies—and there's plenty of coffee and tea."

Bettina handed the ball of yarn back to Pamela and stood up. "Maybe one more cookie," she said. "Anyone else? I can bring some."

"I'll come too." Roland stood up and edged past Pamela. "I could go for another one of those striped ones."

Soon everyone was hovering over the dining room table again. Jean darted into the kitchen with one of the cookie platters and returned with a new assortment, as colorful as the others had been.

Ten minutes later knitting was resumed, in silence at first as people reminded themselves where in a complicated stitch-count they had been or what direction they'd been heading if they'd paused while midway through a row. Then there was a burst of renewed praise for the night's refreshments. Bettina looked up from a pale pink granny square to loyally observe that Pamela's apple cake had been quite delicious too.

"Has anyone done an apple-picking excursion?" Karen asked. She added that it seemed a popular autumn thing to do and she and Dave had resolved not to spend every weekend working on the house.

"Too late now," Roland said. "People do it in September and October. It's like leaf-peeping." His tone of voice made it clear that leaf-peeping, and maybe picking one's own apples too, were silly pursuits.

People returned to their own thoughts. After a few minutes, Nell leaned toward Karen. "How is the house coming, then?" she asked. "Such a brave thing, to take on a fixer-upper."

"We actually haven't done much lately . . . since . . ." Karen smiled sadly.

Nell glanced around, apparently to make sure the

other knitters were focused on their work or their own thoughts, or both. In a voice she probably didn't mean to reach the whole group, she said, "How is Dave's job hunt coming?"

"He's leaving Wendelstaff?" Jean looked up in surprise. "What happened?"

Pamela expected Karen to dissolve into blushing confusion. Her cheeks reddened somewhat, but her voice was calm. "His contract wasn't renewed," she said glancing from person to person with the resigned air of someone who has given up keeping a secret. "Amy Morgan had different ideas about how the School of Professional Arts should be staffed."

Nell's kind face sagged. She stretched a hand toward Karen's chair. All she could reach was the partly finished navy blue scarf that trailed over Karen's knees, so she stroked the scarf comfortingly. "I shouldn't have brought it up," she said, half to herself.

From across the room came Roland's voice. "But Amy Morgan is dead. Maybe that will help him."

The blush Pamela had been expecting arrived now. Karen looked down at her knitting in red-cheeked confusion.

No one was allowed to leave that evening without agreeing to accept a sandwich bag full of cookies. "For your grandchildren," Jean insisted when Bettina balked. "You mentioned that you'll be seeing them on Thanksgiving."

Bettina accepted the cookies with a resigned smile. "They may not last till Thanksgiving," she said. "I don't have much willpower when there are cookies in the house."

Chapter Sixteen

Pies had once come in tin pie pans that could be returned to the bakery for a refill. Anyone prodigal enough to keep the pan would forfeit ten cents. Among the many pie pans in Pamela's collection was an amusing garage-sale find, a battered tin one with this legend stamped onto its bottom:

Brooklyn Pie Company
10-Cent Deposit

But this was not the one she chose for today's baking project. A Thanksgiving pecan pie to be shared with her daughter and old and dear friends required a more elegant presentation. She chose a mottled brown-and-cream stoneware pan that looked as if it might have been at home on a pilgrim's table.

Today would be a day of useful effort, effort that would distract her from thinking about Karen Dowling—especially Karen's blushing confusion the previous night when Roland observed that with Amy dead Dave's job might not be lost after all.

Pamela was not hosting the Thanksgiving feast. Ever since her husband's death, she and Penny had spent Thanksgiving Day with old family friends dating from the era when Pamela was half of a married couple. Michael Paterson had known the male half of that couple since his days as an architecture student, and he had collaborated with him on projects in the city.

But Penny would be arriving that evening, and Pamela wanted her to find a clean and welcoming house, with fresh sheets on her bed and food in the cupboards and refrigerator. And there were pie ingredients to shop for as well.

Pamela had barely looked inside Penny's room since the day the two of them loaded Pamela's car with suitcases and boxes and set off for Massachusetts. Now she opened a window to let the chilly breeze stir the stale air and peeled the bedding off the twin bed that had been Penny's ever since she graduated from her crib.

This had been the first room Pamela and her husband redid after moving into their fixer-upper house. They hadn't planned on a new baby and a new house in the same year. But settling into their own permanent nest had resulted in a surprise visit from the stork.

Penny had never asked to have her room redecorated, so the pale blue wallpaper with tight little pink rosebuds had remained, along with the white eyelet curtains and the glossy white-painted dresser that matched the woodwork. A simple white desk and chair had been added when Penny started school. The wallpaper was partly hidden now by samples of Penny's art.

Pamela surveyed the walls with pleasure. She'd always been proud of her daughter's artistic skill, inherited perhaps more from Penny's father than from a mother whose creative urge was satisfied by knitting. Penny's output had been diverse: oil on canvas still lifes of flowers and fruit produced in high-school art classes, Arborville scenes dating from a period when she roamed abroad with sketch pad and pencil, and recent portraits of family and friends, including one of Pamela. Pamela wasn't sure her forehead was quite that smooth or her lips quite that full, but Penny had somehow captured a determined look that Pamela felt mirrored her inner self.

Dust bunnies lurking where the baseboard met the floor would need to be banished, and the rag rugs taken outside for a good shake. And she'd need to take a dust cloth to the dresser and desk. But first she made the bed up with fresh sheets, enjoying the fragrance they'd absorbed from the sachet of lavender buds hanging inside the linen closet. She added a down comforter. The final touch was to replace the patchwork quilt Pamela's grandmother had made for her when Pamela was a little girl.

Penny's room finished and the upstairs bathroom scrubbed, Pamela turned her attention to the living room. She fluffed the pillows and arranged them in a neat row across the back of the sofa, and she dusted the coffee table and straightened the stacks of magazines. Then she made her way methodically around the edges of the room, lifting each thrift-store treasure and tag-sale find, dusting it and the shelf, cabinet, or table it sat on, and returning it to its place.

All that remained was to vacuum, and then she'd

be off on her errands. But as she ran the vacuum along the base of the sofa, it began to gasp. A staccato clicking sound, like a frantic hiccup, issued from its lower regions. Was this how a vacuum cleaner died? She'd bought it soon after she'd gotten married. It was quite old in vacuum years.

She pushed the button to turn it off and stepped backward to guide it out from between the sofa and the coffee table. Then she pushed the button again. With a whoosh, it started up, but without the desperate sounds. Perhaps it would last for a few more years. She resumed vacuuming, pushing it smoothly along the other side of the coffee table. She'd do an extra-thorough job and pull the coffee table aside to access the often-overlooked patch of carpet underneath.

That was when she noticed the glint of silver against the dark blues, greens, and burgundys of her rug. Bisecting a stylized flower bud on a long, undulating stalk was a metal knitting needle. The vacuum cleaner had picked it up, struggled with it in a hiccupping fit, and let it go again when she switched off the power. She carried it to the window to examine it more closely. It had to be the twin of the knitting needle she had found in the sofa cushion and tried to return to Karen. That needle had been silver and—she hefted it in her hand as if beginning to knit—definitely the same length, a good length for the first scarf project Karen had contemplated.

Relieved, she put it in her knitting bag, to be returned to Karen at next Tuesday's Knit and Nibble session—though there wouldn't be a pair for Roland until Detective Clayborn returned the one Bettina had given him. Just in time for Thanksgiving, here was something additional to be grateful for. If both her knitting needles were accounted for, sweet little Karen Dowling couldn't be Amy's killer.

She had to call Bettina.

"So who does that leave?" Bettina asked upon hearing the news.

"Bob Randolph," Pamela said decisively.

"But not Dorrie Morgan," Bettina answered. "Or Chad."

"Maybe the woman at Wendelstaff College who was passed over for promotion when Amy was hired. And the student leading the protests there."

"You said they both had alibis."

"But each one was the other one's alibi," Pamela said.

"The police must have looked into their alibis pretty thoroughly," Bettina said. "The people at Wendelstaff are just about the most obvious suspects."

"Let's not forget the yarn woman with the ticking biological clock."

"We don't know her biological clock is ticking."

"I wouldn't completely discount the vicuña fertility ritual angle," Pamela said. "That mystery yarn is definitely from a cuddly animal. Did you notice how Roland said it made him want to pet it? I think vicuñas are cuddly."

As she hung up from talking to Bettina, Pamela's stomach told her it was lunch time. There was just enough cheese left for a grilled cheese sandwich. She buttered two slices of bread, laid one on her griddle, buttered side down, and arranged every last morsel of cheese on it. She topped it with the other slice of bread, buttered side up. Then she watched, carefully lifting the edges of the sandwich to check as the bread turned from pale to golden to toasty brown. When the melting cheese began to emerge from between the crusts, it was time to transfer the sandwich to a plate. She ate it while glancing again at the morning paper she'd hurried through in her rush to start cleaning.

Pamela had already listed cheese on her shopping list for her Co-Op errand, along with the ingredients for the pecan pie. Now she pondered what to have on hand for Penny's visit. The next day would be the Thanksgiving feast with friends, but they could start the morning with scrambled eggs. Penny had always loved spaghetti with meat sauce. She'd make a big batch of that this evening. And she'd get yogurt and orange juice, and maybe deli sliced ham for sandwiches. And they could have a pizza delivered from When in Rome on Saturday, or eat out.

She collected her canvas grocery bags, pulled on her jacket, wrapped her violet mohair scarf around her neck, and set out.

The empty cat-food dish sat squarely in the middle of the doormat. Was that a thank-you, or a reproach? In addition to her usual evening visit, Catrina sometimes showed up for a handout first thing in the morning. Pamela had been bustling about upstairs and then running the vacuum cleaner downstairs, possibly missing the plaintive meow or the eyes peering over the bottom edge of the oval window in the front door. But with Catrina not in evidence at the moment, she didn't want to invite the raccoons to a cat-food feast on the front porch, so she moved the empty dish to a less conspicuous spot and went on her way. Overnight, crisp weather had turned to cold. A blustery wind made her pause to readjust her scarf so it skimmed the top of her head and covered her ears. But the wind had also banished clouds, and the sky was a dazzling shade of blue.

Half an hour later Pamela was heading along Arborville Avenue toward home, wishing she'd used her car for her Co-Op errand. The canvas bags were heavier than usual, with food for two and pie ingredients as well. She reached the stately brick apartment building at her corner and turned onto Orchard Street. Weighed down though she was by her parcels, she couldn't resist a tiny detour to peek behind the wooden fence that hid the trash cans. Who knew what treasures people cleaning for the upcoming holiday might have discarded?

The trash cans were lined up neatly as usual. Mr. Gilly might be a gossip, but he was a conscientious super. Piled between the trash cans and the fence were several black plastic bags, apparently filled to capacity and tied securely at the top. But tucked among the bags was what looked like a very nice fur jacket, a dark lustrous fur like one saw in the newspaper ads for Manhattan furriers. Pamela had never owned a fur, and the sudden mental image of herself strutting into the Co-Op wearing a fur jacket made her laugh. But someone might want a fur jacket. It shouldn't just go out with the trash.

She set her grocery bags down, balancing them against the fence to keep the contents from tumbling out, and stepped gingerly over the nearest plastic bag. Except her foot didn't make contact with the ground. Something was down there, something not exactly hard but not exactly soft. She retreated, then grabbed the plastic bag by the tails of the plastic tie that cinched its neck. She tugged it out from between the fence and the trash can at the near end of the row. It rattled as it dragged along the ground, but she only noticed that for a second.

After that, all her attention was focused on what had been under the bag. The scene was imprinted on her mind as if frozen by a sudden flashbulb going off. She was staring at two feet, one of them wearing only a sheer stocking, the other wearing a casual shoe, like an expensive loafer. Linking the feet to the lustrous jacket were a pair of legs clad in wool slacks, dark like the fur. The person wearing the slacks and jacket was positioned on her side, facing the brick wall of the apartment building.

Pamela felt her throat tighten. Was there a head? She pulled at another bag. Later she would ask herself why she didn't instantly summon Mr. Gilly to call the police—she'd gone out without her own phone. But perhaps she needed to satisfy herself that there was indeed a head, lest the vision of a headless woman in the trash become the stuff of nightmares for years to come.

As she drew yet a third bag out from behind the fence, the fur jacket began to shift. Suddenly, with a dull thump, the body (as she now thought of it) rolled onto its back, and the fur jacket slipped open.

Underneath the fur jacket was a sweater, not a handknit sweater but a fine-gauge wool—or maybe cashmere—turtleneck in a subtle shade of peach. And above the turtleneck, a face was now visible, a fourth bag having slid to the side as the body moved. But Pamela barely registered the fact that the body was in fact not headless. Her eyes were drawn to the dark stain that marred the left side of the sweater.

She bent to look closer. The stain radiated outward from a neat slit that interrupted the even rows of knitting. The slit was right about where Pamela imagined one would find a person's heart if one could peer through layers of skin, muscle, and bone.

It was a slit, not a hole, and there was no knitting needle protruding from this victim's chest. But there was no question that the dark stain, a deep brownish maroon, was blood.

Pamela realized that she was shaking—shaking so violently that she had to steady herself against the fence as she backed out of the trash can enclosure. She clung to the post that marked the end of the fence and tried to tame the thoughts that were swirling in her mind like random shouts from a restless crowd.

She didn't have her phone, because she never brought it on her walks, but she was at the corner of her own street. She could run the half block to her own house and call the police from there. Or she could hurry around to the front of the apartment building, push random bells until someone buzzed her in, and knock on the first door she came to. She could hail a passing car. She could search for Mr. Gilly in his basement lair.

But she was saved from having to choose among these alternatives.

"Doing my work for me today?" a genial voice called. Mr. Gilly came loping around the corner from Arborville Avenue. In deference to the weather, he'd tucked a muffler into the neck of his quilted utility jacket and pulled a knit cap halfway down over his bony forehead. "Nothing goes out to the curb today. They won't be picking up on Thanksgiving."

Pamela opened her mouth but no sound came out. Finally, when he was about ten feet away, she managed, "Something awful has happened." She backed shakily away from the fence post she'd been clinging to and nodded toward her recent discovery.

"Not those blasted raccoons again." Mr. Gilly hurried to her side and bent his lean frame to look around the edge of the fence. Then he froze. "Son of a gun," he said. "Somebody's grandmother. I'd better get the cops out here." He scurried toward the door in the back of the building.

The woman could even have been someone's *great*-grandmother, Pamela realized, since she herself was almost old enough to be a grandmother. The clothes could have been worn by any stylish woman of any age, and the hair was a soft light brown, but the face, though pleasant, was the face of someone who had already lived much of her life. And it looked familiar. But where had Pamela seen this woman before? If the outfit was typical, it couldn't have been in Arborville. Aside from Jean Worthington, few women in Arborville dressed with particular attention to current fashion or shopped at the mall anchored by Saks Fifth Avenue and Nordstrom. And for a woman of this age, Nell Bascomb's look was much more typical.

"You better stay," Mr. Gilly said, rejoining Pamela. "They asked me was I the one that found the body and I had to say no." He unzipped his quilted jacket and felt around for his cigarettes. "Need one of these?" he said, offering her the pack. Pamela shook her head no. "Do you want to sit down or anything?"

he asked. "You look a little shaky. We could go inside. Or I could bring a chair out."

But Orchard Street was barely five blocks from Arborville's center, where the police station, fire department, rec center, and library all clustered around the town's park. Pamela barely had time to assure Mr. Gilly that she was feeling okay now when they heard the rising and falling squeal of a siren. A police car swung around the corner and swerved into the apartment building's parking lot. Both doors opened at once. Officer Sanchez, the woman officer with the sweet, heart-shaped face, emerged from one, and a male officer emerged from the other. Pamela wasn't sure whether he was the same one who had come the night Amy was killed or not.

Mr. Gilly took over, leading the officers to the fence that hid the trash cans and directing them to the opening at the end. Officer Sanchez approached Pamela and pulled a small notebook from a pocket in her padded navy blue jacket.

"Was it you who found the body?" she asked. Pamela nodded. "The murder last week occurred in your front yard," she added. Pamela nodded again. Officer Sanchez wrote something on the notepad. "Do you know *this* individual?" The emphasis on the word "this" made it clear that Officer Sanchez remembered all the details of her conversation with Pamela on that sad night.

"No," Pamela said, nodding decisively. She didn't add that there was something oddly familiar about the woman. She had wanted to ask Mr. Gilly if the woman lived in the building, but the chance for private conversation with him had come and gone.

A ribbon of yellow crime-scene tape now stretched across the opening in the fence and all along the fence's length, and the other officer was talking to Mr. Gilly and making notes on his own small notepad.

There wasn't much more to talk about once it was established that Pamela had no idea who the victim was and had only looked behind the fence because people sometimes threw away interesting things. "And Mr. Gilly will tell you I stop by here and take a look almost every day," she added.

The look on Officer Sanchez's face suggested that rummaging in other people's trash struck her as an eccentric thing for someone who lived on such a nice street to do.

Officer Sanchez explained that Detective Clayborn would be arriving soon and that he would want to talk to Pamela about her discovery of the body. But first he would want to make sure the crime scene was secured. She looked closely at Pamela, whose teeth had begun to chatter from cold and nervousness. The wail of a siren announced that a second police car was rounding the corner, and a minute later it pulled up next to the first one. The siren subsided into a groan, then was abruptly quiet.

"You live just down the street," Officer Sanchez said. Pamela nodded. "Detective Clayborn can talk to you at your house. I'll drive you home and wait there with you till he arrives."

Officer Sanchez explained to her partner and the other officers where they were going, and they were on their way. After less than a minute, Officer Sanchez veered toward the curb and braked. Pamela's nerves were so on edge that she turned to Officer Sanchez in alarm. The young woman touched Pamela's arm reassuringly.

"Were those your grocery bags leaning against the fence?" she asked.

"Oh, yes!" Pamela clapped her hands. "Thank you."

Groceries retrieved, they made their way down the street again. At home, Pamela settled Officer Sanchez in a chair at the kitchen table while she put away her groceries. It seemed ages ago that she'd been browsing happily along the aisles of the Co-Op, deciding what size bag of pecans to buy, choosing an assortment of yogurts, and standing at the deli counter sampling a slice of ham before placing her order. Now she handled the items like souvenirs from another life.

"Shall I make coffee?" she asked.

"No, thank you," came the answer. Perhaps police weren't allowed to accept food from people they were interviewing about crimes. Maybe Bettina would know if that was true, because she'd gotten to know them from talking to them for the *Advocate*.

When the doorbell rang, they both hurried toward the kitchen door, nearly colliding. "I'll let him in," Pamela said. "Please have a seat in the living room, or . . . do you need to stay?"

But Officer Sanchez had continued on ahead, carrying her padded navy blue jacket. When Pamela reached the entry, Detective Clayborn was already stepping through the front door. He conferred briefly with Officer Sanchez, both talking in such low voices that Pamela couldn't make out anything they were saying. Then Officer Sanchez was on her way.

"There was a cat out there," Detective Clayborn

said, the faintest smile tugging at his lips. "But it ran away. Is it yours?"

"Sort of," Pamela said.

He offered his hand. "Detective Clayborn."

"I remember," Pamela said. She also remembered his face, comforting in its homeliness, like a faithful spaniel.

He unwrapped a scarf from his neck and peeled off a bulky three-quarter-length coat. The outfit underneath struck Pamela as identical to the one he'd worn the last time, even to the green tie with the pattern of brown squiggles. She reached for the coat and scarf and laid them on a chair in the entry.

He stepped toward the living room. "There's a better chair," Pamela exclaimed, flustered. She remembered how the rummage-sale chair with the carved wooden back and needlepoint seat had squeaked in protest the week before as he shifted from side to side. She gestured toward a substantial armchair.

"I'll be going over some of the things you told Officer Sanchez," he said, settling into it and producing a notepad and pen.

That was what he had said the last time. Perhaps it was a script they learned in detective school.

"It was you who found the body?"

"Yes."

"Why did you look behind the fence?"

"I sometimes find interesting things back there. You'd be amazed what people throw away." Pamela pointed toward the shelves, cabinets, and tabletops that held her treasures.

He nodded, as if this was a sufficient explanation.

"Two people have been killed on your street within a little over a week."

Pamela nodded.

"You knew the first victim."

"Amy Morgan," Pamela whispered.

"Did you know this individual?" She'd already answered that question for Officer Sanchez. But this was probably part of what they did—ask the same questions to see if they got the same answers. If she said no, would he be able to tell that she was holding something back, the fact that the woman had looked so vexingly familiar?

"Am I a suspect?" Pamela's heart began to thump, so loud she was sure Detective Clayborn could hear it. "She wasn't killed with a knitting needle."

Something tightened around his eyes, and he didn't look so homely anymore. He wonders how I know that, Pamela realized with alarm. Maybe his faithful spaniel expression was just an act, a way to make people open up and not feel threatened. "There was a slit in her sweater," she added. "Like from a knife. Anybody would have noticed it."

He nodded and wrote something on his little notepad, then he looked back up, but didn't say anything.

"She looked familiar." Pamela said it in a resigned way, as if confessing to something she'd given up trying to hide. "But I have no idea why. She's not somebody I knew from town, and she wasn't dressed the way most women her age dress in Arborville. So it's just a mystery." She paused. "Did she live in that building?"

The look on his face said she should have known he couldn't answer that even if he knew. Pamela went on. "If she did, she must have just moved in recently." His expression didn't change. "That was

Amy Morgan's building," Pamela said, watching his face closely for any hint he thought the crimes were related.

The interview veered off to topics less close to home, like how well Pamela knew Mr. Gilly and what the garbage collection schedule was like on Orchard Street. "Oh, yes," Pamela murmured. "Maybe the killer thought the body would be undisturbed there and he could take it away later and hide it someplace where nobody would ever find it." Detective Clayborn wrote something on his notepad.

At last he put the notepad and pen away and rose. Pamela led him to the entry, handed him his coat and scarf, and saw him out the door. On the porch she looked for Catrina, longing for contact with any comforting presence, even a skittish cat. But there was no sign of her. Nor were there any cars in Bettina's driveway. She'd have to wait to confer with her friend about this latest development.

Chapter Seventeen

Pamela was thankful she still had chores to do. Her mother's solution to any problem had been to find something that needed cleaning and clean it, and over the years Pamela had been grateful for her mother's example. But the house was already clean. There was cooking to do though—meat sauce for tonight's spaghetti and the pecan pie for Thanksgiving.

She was sitting at the kitchen table comparing pecan pie recipes in three different cookbooks when the doorbell rang. Not Detective Clayborn again, she prayed, and please not reporters clamoring to interview the person who found the body. She edged toward the kitchen door and peeked around into the entry. Through the lace that curtained the oval window in the front door she could make out a silhouette that was not tall enough to be a man, so it wasn't the detective. A face loomed close to the glass. The face was topped by a reddish-orange cap or . . . red hair. It was Bettina.

She hurried to the door, pulled it open, and swept Bettina up in a hug.

"Uh-oh," Bettina said when Pamela had let her go. Her forehead wrinkled with concern. "I was going to tell you something's happening at the corner—police cars, an ambulance, and people swarming all over. But I suspect you already know."

"I do." Pamela led her friend to the kitchen and took her coat. "Shall I make coffee?" she asked.

"I'll do it," Bettina said. "You sit down and tell me what's going on."

While Bettina busied herself at the counter, Pamela described checking behind the fence for cast-off treasures and coming upon the body.

"I suppose you've talked to Clayborn." Pamela nodded, though Bettina couldn't see her, because at that moment Bettina was opening cupboard doors looking for coffee beans.

"Above the stove," Pamela said.

Bettina turned.

"Yes, I talked to him," Pamela said. "I suppose you'll be talking to him too, for the *Advocate*."

"Probably not for a few days though," Bettina said. "He's a busy guy, and when you write for the weekly throwaway there isn't a big rush to be first with the hot story."

"That reporter from the *County Register* will probably be ringing the bell any minute. The *Register* tracked me down first thing the morning after Amy was killed."

As if on cue, the doorbell rang, and Pamela opened the door to discover that the *County Register* reporter had indeed arrived. It was the same reporter who had come the previous week, the energetic young woman with sparkling eyes and bright lipstick. Pamela stepped out onto the porch, coatless, and pulled the door closed behind her, hoping that this ploy would confine the reporter to only the most basic questions.

She described once again how she happened to find the body, and was surprised to get an approving nod when she explained about looking for treasures in the apartment building's trash. She acknowledged that, yes, she was the same person who found Amy Morgan's body and that Amy's murder had happened right out there in the front yard. She confirmed that Amy had been an old friend.

"Was this most recent victim also an old friend?" the reporter asked.

"Absolutely not," Pamela said. Then she hugged herself, muttered "brrrr" a few times, and escaped back into the house, before the reporter could inquire whether she had recognized the victim at all.

When she got back to the kitchen, Bettina had coffee ready and two wedding china cups and saucers set out on the table, along with two pieces of toast spread with jam.

"This was the best I could do in the way of goodies," she said, "but I thought you might need a bite of something."

Pamela gratefully ate a piece of toast and sipped at her coffee. "That dead woman looked familiar," she said after the two friends had sat in companionable silence for a few minutes.

"Like somebody from Arborville?" Bettina asked.

"No . . . she was wearing a fur jacket and just didn't have an Arborville look."

"Here's the obvious question," Bettina said. "Did the same person kill her as killed Amy? You said it looked like she'd been stabbed right through the front of her sweater."

"But with a knife or something, not a knitting needle. Not even an ice pick. Though there was that chisel thing Dorrie was waving around." She grimaced.

"Well, we already know Dorrie Morgan isn't our killer—at least if her tale about the ice sculpture for the bachelor party is true."

"And who could make something like that up?" Pamela said.

Bettina went on. "And would Karen Dowling switch over to a knife? Or Olivia Wiggens or that knitting protester? And anyway, what would this new murder victim have to do with Wendelstaff?" She turned her coffee cup this way and that on her saucer and studied its pattern. "Of course, maybe the two murders aren't related at all."

Pamela jumped up. "Wait!" She ran to the living room, returned with her knitting bag, and pulled out the knitting needle she'd found in the carpet that morning.

Bettina reached for it. "That's a relief," she said. "I like sweet little Karen."

"I do too." Pamela took the knitting needle back and set it on the table. "If the murders *are* related, this new one probably lets out that woman at the store in Brooklyn."

"The one you thought wanted the mystery yarn back to use in fertility rituals?"

Pamela laughed, the first time she'd laughed all day. "That was a bit far-fetched, wasn't it? And even if it wasn't, this fur-jacket woman would have had to have her own batch of the mystery yarn in order to make her a target."

"And you said the fur-jacket woman was older."

"Quite old—as old as Nell, probably."

"So that lets out Bob Randolph," Bettina said. "That is, if we were thinking his motive was unrequited love. But it's odd her body ended up outside his and Amy's apartment building."

"He could have had some other motive," Pamela said. "Like maybe he thought this woman somehow knew he killed Amy and so he had to kill her too."

They sipped their coffee, and Bettina got up and refilled both cups.

"That woman looked so familiar," Pamela said with a sigh. "But I just can't think from where."

"Where have you been lately, besides Arborville?" Bettina asked.

Pamela shrugged. "The funeral?"

Bettina nodded. "Maybe that's it. I don't remember any fur jackets, but it wasn't that cold a day. Those people definitely looked like a fur-jacket sort of crowd."

"But what would she have been doing in Arborville?"

"And who was she? I'll see if I can get in to talk to Clayborn on Friday. Or the *Register* will cover the story tomorrow. Maybe that reporter who tracked you down will have gotten an ID on the body from the Arborville police."

Pamela's favorite old mixing bowl stood at the ready, heavy pottery glazed a creamy caramel color with three white stripes circling it near the rim. A pastry cloth had been smoothed out on the kitchen table. She measured out a cupful of flour, added half a teaspoon of salt, and sifted the mixture into the waiting bowl. Rummaging in her silverware drawer for knives to cut in the shortening reminded her of the scene she was trying to forget. She closed the drawer and used her fingers instead, scooping up fingerfuls of flour, pinching off bits from the lump of shortening she'd deposited in the midst of the sifted flour, and rubbing until the result was, as the pie crust recipe she'd memorized long ago had put it, the consistency of coarse sand.

She sprinkled the mixture with a few tablespoons of cold water, tossed it with a fork, and pressed it into a rough ball with her hands. Soon she'd rolled out an uneven circle on the floured pastry cloth, maneuvered it into the speckled pie pan, and used the thumb of one hand and two fingers of the other to mold a gently scalloped pie-crust rim around the edge.

The question now was, did she have any rum? The three recipes she'd studied differed from one another only in a few particulars. There was disagreement about the number of eggs required. Three? Or four? But perhaps the recipe with the more generous egg allotment dated from an era when eggs, like almost everything else, were smaller. And how much sugar was really necessary if a cup of dark corn syrup had already been added?

The only difference that seemed significant was that one of the recipes called for rum, three tablespoons. Pamela prided herself on being an inventive cook and surprising people with twists on tried-and-true dishes. A little rum in the pecan pie could be just the thing to provoke delighted exclamations when the pie was sampled.

Pamela's liquor collection, such as it was, shared space with other bottled things, like vinegar and soy sauce, on the shelf above the stove where she also stored coffee and tea. Craning her neck, she moved bottles this way and that, clearing a path to forgotten items at the very back of the shelf. Indeed, she had rum, in a tall brown bottle with a tropical scene on the label—a long-ago gift, perhaps, from someone returning from a Caribbean vacation. She reached it down. Very little had been drunk. If rum proved to lift pecan pie to new levels of scrumptiousness, she would be able to get many many repeats of today's pie out of this one bottle.

Mixing the filling went quickly. Instead of chopping the pecan halves like the rum recipe suggested, she left them as they were. She liked the abstract patterns the small ovals made on the surface of the custard mixture, like a coppery mosaic. She stirred the pecan halves into the ingredients that waited in the caramel-colored bowl, gently coaxed the mixture into the prepared pie shell with her favorite spatula, and slid the pie pan into the oven. She'd wait until the pie was done before she started on the sauce for that evening's spaghetti.

As she'd moved around her kitchen working on the pie, the sky had gradually darkened. On these late-fall evenings night came even before six p.m., and it was getting on toward six thirty. Penny wasn't likely to arrive for an hour or more, but Pamela certainly didn't want her showing up to an unwelcoming house. She'd put the porch light on now just in case.

In fact, the whole house was dark. She switched on a light in the entry and detoured into the living room to click on a lamp. As she returned to the entry, a faint sound reached her ears. It was a familiar sound, and she smiled in anticipation. Sure enough, she flipped the switch that banished the darkness from the front porch, and a tiny pair of eyes met hers through the lace that curtained the oval window in the front door.

"Yes, it's dinnertime," she murmured, and she hurried back to the kitchen to prepare a dish of cat food.

Out on the porch, she stepped toward the spot near the porch railing where Catrina retreated to wait for her meals. Usually the cat retreated still further as Pamela approached, and she ventured toward the dish only after Pamela had disappeared and the front door had closed securely. But tonight the cat seemed braver. As Pamela stooped to slide the dish into place, she held her ground, and she began to eat without even a glance to see whether she was alone. Pamela watched her for a minute, enjoying the enthusiasm with which the tiny creature tackled what, in comparison with her own size, must have seemed unimaginable bounty.

She looked up to survey the street. And that was when she noticed the sleek silver Audi parked in front of her house. Bob Randolph's car, or one very like it. Why would he park here when he lived just down the street, and in a building with a perfectly adequate parking lot? But wait—she eased her way down the front steps and partway along the walk. He—or someone—was sitting in the car. She eased a bit closer. The driver's profile was outlined against the backdrop of Bettina's house, which glowed faintly in the light from the streetlamp. It was the profile of a young man with smoothly groomed hair, and—as a flash of headlights from a passing car revealed—it was definitely Bob Randolph.

It was getting on toward seven p.m. and he wasn't at work. Did that mean his shift in the emergency room didn't start until later? If so, he had no alibi for the night Amy was killed—whether he worked Tuesday nights or not.

And what was he doing in front of her house now?

Pamela retreated to the porch, ducking behind a porch column. Behind her, the cat-food dish scraped against the porch floor as Catrina pursued the last morsels. A twinge of fear tightened something inside her. Bob Randolph had made that comment about too many people in the world having nothing to do but mind other people's business. He had sounded angry. And she *had* been nosy—she had to admit that. If he was the person who killed Amy, he might have decided such a nosy person was a potential danger to him—a danger that had to be eliminated.

She peeked out from behind the column. He was still sitting in the car. As she explored the possibility that she might be in danger, new and alarming vistas opened before her. She moaned aloud. She'd left the front door ajar when she stepped out with the dish of cat food. Now she backed quickly into the house and slammed it behind her.

It was she who had found the body hidden by the trash cans. What if Bob Randolph *was* responsible for that murder? Here was nosy Pamela Paterson getting involved again. Her mind bounced back and forth. Maybe he wouldn't know she was the one who found the body. Bounce. He would though. It would be in the newspapers. Bounce. But the story wouldn't appear until tomorrow—and he was sitting in front of her house right now.

Oh, no—she moaned again. Mr. Gilly could have

told him. Mr. Gilly was a notorious gossip, and Bob Randolph had had firsthand experience of that. "It's never a good idea to discuss anything with him unless you want the world to know it," he had said.

She backed toward the chair in the corner of the entry and perched on its edge, hugging herself and shivering with fear. What could she do? Call the police and tell them a man was sitting in his car in front of her house? But the man was Bob Randolph, a respectable emergency room physician, in his silver Audi. Suppose she actually did figure out something important about Amy's death. She'd want the police to treat her like a rational, concerned citizen, not like a nut who was scared of her own shadow.

Pamela ventured back toward the front door and put her face up close to the lace curtain to look out. Penny would be coming soon, and Bob Randolph was still lurking in his car. Or at least his car was still there. She couldn't quite tell from inside the house whether anyone was behind the steering wheel or not. She didn't want to venture outside again, at least not to just *stand* there. As soon as a car pulled up and Penny got out, she'd rush out and hurry Penny into the house.

The awkward angle at which she was holding her head had begun to make her neck hurt, and the curtain was dusty enough to make her nose itch. She made a mental note to add it to her next batch of laundry. The sugary smells floating in from the kitchen as the pie baked would normally have given her the sense that all was right with the world. But all wasn't right. She strained her eyes trying to make out whether there was or was not a person sitting in the driver's seat of Bob Randolph's silver Audi.

Headlights flashed on the shrubs along Bettina's driveway, and a small car coming from the direction of the church swung in front of Bob Randolph's car and pulled up at the curb. Both doors opened, and Penny hopped out of the passenger side. Inside the house, Pamela fumbled with the doorknob, forgetting whether she'd locked the door behind her when she retreated inside. She rushed down the front walk. A tall and sturdy young man was hefting a suitcase out of the trunk of the car.

She glanced toward the Audi, relieved to see that Bob Randolph was no longer behind the steering wheel. Then it occurred to her that perhaps he had taken up a position in the shrubbery. He'd been waiting there to go after her with a knitting needle or some other sharp tool but had been put off by the prospect of a three-against-one struggle. Pamela thought of herself as an independent woman, but the fact that one of the three would have been a tall and sturdy young man was comforting nonetheless.

A quick introduction made her acquainted with Penny's friend, Kyle Logan, and the casual way Penny thanked him and said goodbye made it clear that he was indeed just a friend. He didn't have time for coffee or a snack, he said. His own parents were waiting for him a few towns over.

Pamela waited until he drove away to fold her daughter in a warm hug. She rolled the suitcase up the front walk, and Penny followed with a small bag. Together they boosted the suitcase up the steps.

"It's full of dirty laundry, Mom," Penny explained

when Pamela laughingly groaned at the weight. Then, as they stepped into the house, "Is that a pecan pie I smell?"

"Yes! I almost forgot." All thoughts of Bob Randolph were banished. Pamela dashed for the kitchen and jerked the oven door open. She was just in time. The scalloped rim of crust was a perfect golden brown, glazed with a buttery sheen, and the pecan-studded custard was the color of burnished copper.

Penny had followed her to the kitchen, shedding her jacket somewhere along the way. She watched as Pamela carefully transferred the pie from the oven to a trivet on the kitchen table. Satisfied that dessert was assured for the Thanksgiving feast, she surveyed her daughter with a long gaze.

"Do I look so different?" Penny asked with a laugh.

No. She was still Pamela's little girl, with the dark curls and the quick smile she'd inherited from her father. Pamela had been nearly the same height as her husband, and she'd liked the way that fact underlined the equality of their union. Pamela had friends whose children, girls as well as boys, had outstripped their mothers in height starting even in middle school. But Penny had taken after the Paterson side of the family, and Pamela was a good six inches taller than her daughter.

Under the bright kitchen light, Penny's face shifted from happiness to concern. "Are you okay, Mom?" she asked. "About Amy, I mean."

"I'm okay." Pamela nodded. She'd have to figure out when to tell Penny that there'd been a second murder on Orchard Street. And how much to reveal about her digging into the mystery of Amy's death.

But first Penny had to be made comfortable in her old room, and there was a spaghetti dinner to cook. "I'll leave that suitcase down here," Penny called as she headed for the stairs with the small bag. "I've got to do laundry tomorrow, or I'll be wearing these same jeans the whole time I'm home." Pamela followed her up the stairs and fussed over towels while Penny retrieved pajamas and a toothbrush from her small bag.

Back in the kitchen Pamela set water boiling for the pasta, chopped an onion for the sauce, and minced a clove of garlic. As she was working, she remembered the last time she had made spaghetti. Bettina and Wilfred had come for dinner, bearing three bottles of red wine, and it had been a merry night. Two of the bottles had produced sufficient merriment, and, as she recalled, the third had ended up in her pantry. If today wasn't the sort of day that should be topped off with a glass of wine, she wasn't sure what kind of day would be.

The wine was lurking behind the molasses, not far from where she had found the rum. She rummaged among her strainers, potato mashers, and special cooking spoons for the corkscrew. Though Pamela wasn't a wine connoisseur, serving wine gave her the opportunity to bring out one of her favorite garage-sale finds, a delicate set of stemmed glasses with a tracing of grape vines etched around their rims.

When Penny joined her, she was tending the sautéing onions and garlic with a big wooden spoon and sipping a glass of wine.

"Wine, Mom?" Penny said.

"Bettina and Wilfred brought it one night. It's good with spaghetti."

Penny picked up the bottle. "How about sharing?"

"I'm just having this one glass," Pamela said, "and you're—"

"*Mom* . . . I'm in *college*."

Pamela laughed. "The glasses are in that cupboard to the right of the sink. And while you're home I hope you'll resume your duties as the salad chef." She pushed the onions and garlic here and there, assessing whether it was time to add the ground meat. "We'll eat in the dining room," she added. "With candles."

As it turned out, the whole bottle got drunk. Between bites of spaghetti and salad, and sips of wine, Penny filled in the picture that her phone calls and emails had only sketched. Her roommate was sweet. The professors were brilliant. The campus was beautiful. The mother in Pamela was reassured, and she tried to paint an equally reassuring picture for Penny. Yes, Amy's murder was a horrible shock (and when *would* she find a way to tell Penny that there had been another horrible shock, that very day?). But the magazine was doing well, and she had plenty of work. The knitting club was lively as ever. She'd finished the Icelandic sweater and had only to sew the pieces together.

Penny set down her wineglass and fixed her eyes on Pamela's. In the flickering candlelight, her face was serious. "Is there any other . . . social life," she asked, "besides the knitting club?"

Pamela set her own glass down. "Do you mean . . . like dates?"

"Yes, Mom. I do mean like dates." She leaned into the candle's glow. "It's really okay. I *want* you to. Even when I was still at home, it would have been okay."

"No," Pamela said. "There aren't dates. And I'm not sure I want there to be."

An hour later Pamela and Penny were sitting on the sofa in the living room feeling well fed, content, and just a tiny bit tipsy. Pamela was almost dozing, her head lolling back against the sofa cushions, when Penny suddenly sat upright. "Do you hear that?" she said urgently. "That noise?"

"What?" Pamela was jolted awake. "What kind of a noise?" She could feel her pulse as a rapid thud in her ears.

"*Listen!*" Penny whispered.

It was coming from outside, from the street, a gurgling sound, high-pitched and musical. Threads of sound overlapped others like a chorus, then trailed off. And it was becoming louder.

Penny jumped up. "I have to see what this is," she said, moving toward the door.

"No!" Pamela shouted, grabbing her arm.

"Mom, what's wrong with you?" Penny turned and looked at her in confusion. "It's a funny noise in the street. That's all." She pulled away. "I'll just open the door a crack," she added soothingly.

Pamela followed her to the entry. The sound was louder yet, and Penny was right. It was indeed a funny noise.

Without switching the entry light on, Penny twisted the doorknob and the door creaked open. Then she screamed and jumped back in alarm. A tiny black shape streaked across the dim floor and disappeared in the direction of the kitchen. "Eeek! Mom! What was that?" Penny squealed.

Pamela was laughing so hard she couldn't answer for a minute. "We have a cat," she sputtered at last. Then she gathered her daughter up in a hug.

But the gurgling chorus was still coming from outside. Pamela kept hold of Penny's hand as she edged toward the door. She pulled the door back a few more inches and peeked out. A curious spectacle greeted her. She drew in her breath, let the door swing back, and pulled Penny to the open doorway.

A procession of remarkable creatures was making its way down Orchard Street. Their bodies swung from side to side, supported by pairs of spindly legs, while their tiny heads jerked this way and that on long necks. Some walked two by two. Others straggled behind in single file. They were just then passing under the streetlamp at the edge of Pamela's driveway. The light rippled along their backs in iridescent streaks. The chorus of melodic gurgles continued.

Penny slipped past Pamela and hurried down the steps. "They're turkeys," she called. "Wild turkeys. They have them in Massachusetts."

Pamela joined her as she walked toward the curb. "I've never seen them here before," she said, "but they must come up from the woods."

A swath of undeveloped land to the west separated Arborville from the next town over. Deer were known to live there, and as summer wore on they sometimes ventured across busy County Road at the bottom of the block to graze on lawns kept green by sprinkler systems.

Pamela sighed. In an odd way, the turkeys were beautiful. The air was still and cold, infused with smoke from a wood fire burning in a nearby fireplace and the soundtrack of the gurgles. They'd run outside without coats. Soon they'd have to retreat indoors.

From the neighboring yard came a voice. "Yes," the voice said. "They're wild turkeys. Quite a sight, aren't they?"

Pamela looked over. A torso was looming over the hedge that edged her driveway.

"I'm Richard Larkin," the voice added. "Your new neighbor."

He proceeded along the hedge toward the sidewalk, then hesitated as if waiting for an invitation to step onto her driveway.

With the streetlamp behind him and his face in shadow, Pamela couldn't tell much about him except that he was tall—very tall—and he had a lot of hair. She tilted her head. "Hello," she said. "I'm Pamela Paterson."

"I know," he said. "The note about the garbage."

"Thank you for cleaning it up."

"I'm not used to the suburbs," he added. "I know about wild turkeys, but not raccoons, and my job has been running me ragged." Not too ragged to have girlfriends, said a voice in Pamela's head. No wonder, the voice added, unbidden. He has a nice voice.

"I wouldn't have known they were turkeys," Pamela said. "They don't look like the typical Thanksgiving turkey. These ones are kind of . . . sleek." She remembered the turkeys Penny had made in preschool, pine cones with construction-paper tail feathers fanning out behind and twisted red pipe cleaners for those odd dangly things turkeys had at their necks.

"Turkeys only puff themselves up like Thanksgiving turkeys when they're courting," Richard Larkin said. "And only the male turkeys. This isn't the season—at least for turkeys."

Chapter Eighteen

Penny had gradually moved along the curb, following the turkeys as they made their slow progress toward the lower end of the block. Pamela was starting to feel the cold, and she turned away from Richard Larkin to head back into the house. Suddenly Penny was at her side.

"Your daughter?" Richard asked.

Before Pamela could answer, Penny's sweet voice cut in. "Penny Paterson," she said, facing him, her head tipped back as if regarding a larger-than-life-sized statue. But he was still looking at Pamela.

"You're shivering. Would you like some coffee? Or a drink?"

"I live right here," Pamela said with a laugh.

"That's right." He chuckled. "We're neighbors."

Pamela turned away again. "So I'll just—"

But Penny cut in. "Coffee sounds great."

"Done." He clapped his hands together and set off up the sidewalk. Penny followed. Pamela caught up with her and whispered, "What have you done? He has girlfriends your age."

"*Mo-o-om!*" Penny stopped walking and grabbed Pamela's arm. "He was looking at you the whole time." The gobbling chorus of the turkeys echoed faintly from down the street.

"How could you tell?" Pamela whispered back. "It's dark out here."

"I haven't had a chance to do too much with the place," Richard said as he ushered them into the living room that Pamela still thought of as Miranda Bonham's. But gone were Miranda's burgundy sofa and love seat, her mahogany coffee table, and the large seascape she'd hung over the fireplace. The walls were still pale peach, but the furniture was all black leather and glass and chrome. A rug that appeared to be the skin of a Holstein cow lay sprawled in the center of Miranda's peach-colored broadloom.

"All this pink has got to go," he added. "And you should see the kitchen. Bright yellow."

"My kitchen is yellow," Pamela murmured. "I find it cheerful in the morning."

He blinked a few times and clapped his hands again. "Well! I'll make the coffee. Please sit down."

Pamela and Penny took seats on the black leather sofa and waited in silence as they listened to the sounds of coffee being made in the kitchen. Soon Richard stepped around the corner bearing two mugs. "Milk or sugar?" he said.

"Just black," Pamela said, and Penny's voice overlapped with "Milk and sugar, please." He returned to the kitchen.

The bustle of getting everyone settled with their

coffee subsided, and Richard folded his lanky frame into one of the chrome and leather creations that flanked the chrome and glass coffee table. He did have a lot of hair, shaggy and blondish. Was it a fashion statement, Pamela wondered, or had he just been too busy to go to the barber's? His face was long, and bony, with a strong nose. But his mouth was surprisingly gentle.

"Big doings up at the corner today," he said. "Crime-scene tape all over the place. A guy waiting at the bus stop said there had been a murder."

"Mom!" Penny twisted toward Pamela, a horrified expression on her face. "What's happening around here? Why didn't you tell me?"

"I was going to. You just got home."

"First Amy, right in our front yard. And now . . . what was this one?"

Pamela set her coffee down, took both of Penny's hands in her own, and gazed into her eyes. "I'll tell you when we get home." She looked over at Richard. "It will all be in the paper tomorrow, I'm sure."

"I shouldn't have brought it up," he said. "Not very cheerful conversation for a first meeting—especially since there was that other . . . last week."

Pamela nodded and reached for her coffee.

When neither Richard nor Penny leapt into the conversational breech, Pamela gave a mental sigh, arranged her lips in what she thought of as her social smile, and said, "What brings you to Arborville?"

"Manhattan real-estate prices."

"So . . . no previous familiarity with raccoons, but you know about wild turkeys."

"I have a . . . thing . . . in Maine sometimes."

Pamela frowned. "They don't have raccoons in Maine?"

"I don't cook for myself when I'm there," Richard said.

Pamela was about to ask what the thing in Maine was when Penny cut in. "Where were you living before?"

"Manhattan," he said. "But my wife and I split up. I ended up in a studio, not much room for anybody but me. So . . ." He gestured around the pink living room. "My job is in the city. Arborville is close enough to get there."

They chatted a bit about the challenges of a daily commute to the city. "I only go there sometimes," Pamela said. "That's where my job is, but I sit at my computer at home most days."

"What do you do?" He asked as if he was genuinely curious.

She described *Fiber Craft* and added, "I've learned a lot—about making yurts out of yak hair, fertility rituals involving vicuñas, all kinds of things. We've got a magazine to fill twelve times a year." He nodded but didn't say anything, so Pamela shaped her lips into the social smile once again and said, "I think you're an architect?"

"Is it that conspicuous?" he asked with a laugh.

But Pamela explained. "I've been getting your mail. The carrier is new. Or something. I give it back to the post office. Sometimes I put it in your box."

He nodded. "My firm is just finishing up a huge job, and with the moving and all . . ." He rubbed his face.

"You're tired," Pamela said. Her coffee cup was almost empty, and she set it gently on the glass surface of the coffee table. She started to rise, and he sprang from the chair. She started toward the door.

"Oh—" he said with an embarrassed smile, looking down as if surprised he was on his feet. "I'm sorry. I wasn't trying to hurry you out."

"We have to go, really." Pamela made a shepherding gesture toward Penny. "Tomorrow's a big day."

"For me too. My daughters are coming here to cook for me."

"Daughters?"

"I have two. In college in the city. But I wanted a place big enough that they could come and go."

"I think I've seen them," Pamela said. *Because you spend too much time staring out your kitchen window*, added a voice in her head.

"You're in a big house for two people."

"One, now," Pamela said. "Penny is in college too. So I'm alone."

"Miranda Bonham told me. She said Arborville wasn't all couples."

They had reached the door. Richard started to say something, then stopped, smiled, and started again. "You wouldn't . . . if you're free tomorrow . . . there will be so much food." He smiled again. "But you probably have plans."

"We do," Pamela said. "Old friends of my husband's and mine."

"I knew your kitchen was yellow," Richard said as he reached for the doorknob. "I've seen you at your window when the light is on inside."

So, Pamela said to herself as she and Penny hurried along the sidewalk to the warmth of their own house, those were his *daughters*. He's not a lothario after all.

She glanced over at the curb. The silver Audi was gone.

As Pamela was checking that doors were locked and lights were off, Penny came downstairs in her pajamas. "I think he's interested in you, Mom," she said. "Maybe you should get to know him."

"Not a chance," Pamela said. "Those days are behind me now."

Before she went up to bed, Pamela put a few scoops of cat food in the cat-food dish and set it in the middle of the kitchen floor.

In the morning the cat-food dish was empty. It had been pushed into the corner where one set of cabinets made a right angle with another set. Pamela stooped for the dish, dropped it in the sink, and gave it a swoosh of hot water and soap. If Catrina was now to be an indoor cat, she'd need more than food. Pamela had sand in the garage for when the sidewalk was slippery. She'd put a bit in a shallow box and set it in the back hall. But first came coffee and the newspaper. She set the kettle to boil and headed for the porch to retrieve the *Register*. As she opened the front door, she heard Penny's feet on the stairs.

"Don't people sleep all day when they come home from college?" Pamela asked.

"I've got mountains of laundry to do," Penny said. "And we're going to the Nordlings' this afternoon and I have to wash my hair and find something in my closet that isn't jeans and a sweater." She grabbed the handle of the suitcase that had been parked in the entry overnight and began rolling it toward the kitchen and the laundry room beyond.

"There will be coffee soon," Pamela said, and she stepped out onto the porch, where an unaccustomed sight met her eyes.

Bettina, usually the most carefully groomed of people, was running across the street in her bathrobe and fuzzy slippers. An unfolded section of newspaper flapped in her hand.

"Pamela!" she called, clearing the curb with an extra-large step and bounding up the front walk. "That woman lived in Amy's building. It's all in the *Register.*"

"I guess they scooped the *Advocate,*" Pamela said as Bettina stood panting at the bottom of the porch steps.

"Well, when you only publish once a week . . ." Bettina said between pants. "But this is important. You have to read it right now." She hoisted the trailing hem of her bathrobe and mounted the steps. Pamela collected her own copy of the *Register* and gave Bettina a gentle pat on the back to usher her through the door. In the kitchen, Bettina spread her newspaper on the kitchen table.

"Look—it's all right here!" She flipped back to the first page, which was dominated by a color photograph of the crime scene, angled to show the wooden fence with its garnish of crime-scene tape, a few trash cans and plastic bags, and a police car. The caption read, "Arborville Police Stumped by Second Murder on Orchard Street."

"And *here*"—paper rustled as Bettina turned to an inner page—"it says 'According to building superintendent Thomas R. Gilly, the murdered woman had recently moved into the building. He was able to identify her as Phyllis Hagstrom, but said he did not handle the details of apartment rentals and referred police to the building's owner, who was not available for comment before press time.'" Bettina ran a finger down the column of newsprint, then paused. "And here's the interview with you, and then, 'The murder weapon, an inexpensive carving knife, was recovered from one of the trash cans. Apparently the killer had been wearing gloves, because police later reported that they were not able to retrieve fingerprints.'" She looked up at Pamela. "You *said* it looked like she'd been killed with a knife."

Penny had been at the counter slipping bread into the toaster when Bettina swept in. She'd swiveled around to watch as Bettina began her summary of the news report, and when she got to the part about the interview with Pamela her eyes had grown wide. Now she let out a squeal that modulated into a moan.

"*Mom!*" Behind her the toast popped up with a metallic click. "You said you'd tell me, and you didn't. Were you the one who found this person too? How can this be happening?" She stared at Pamela with a look both accusing and concerned.

Bettina circled the table. "Penny! I didn't even say hello." She put her hands on Penny's shoulders. "Look at the college girl. So great to have you home, sweetie." She pulled Penny to her in a hug.

Over Bettina's shoulder Penny continued to stare at her mother.

"I was going to tell you," Pamela said, "but it's so good to have you here. And I just wanted you to enjoy being home for a little while before I gave you something to worry about."

"And actually there is *nothing* to worry about,"

Bettina said firmly as she stepped back, her hands still on Penny's shoulders. "Besides, your mother is turning out to be quite the detective."

"'Quite the detective'?" Penny shook loose from Bettina and stepped toward the table that separated her from Pamela. "What on earth are you doing, Mom?"

"We've been following up all kinds of clues," Bettina cut in. "And now, since this . . . Phyllis Hagstrom . . . lived in the same building, there's probably a connection between her and Amy that will become really obvious as soon as we think about it a little bit."

The look on Penny's face had changed to outright horror, eyes wide and mouth stretched into a grimace. "Isn't that what the police are for?" she asked in a small voice.

"Police don't always ask the right questions," Pamela replied calmly. She'd lain awake a bit longer than usual after she climbed into bed the previous night, knowing she wouldn't be able to hide what she was up to from Penny and wondering how she'd explain. She'd finally decided to just be matter-of-fact. "I'll make some coffee," she said, and stepped toward the counter. "Shall I make a cup for you, Bettina?"

Bettina looked down at herself. "Oh, gracious," she said. "I can't believe I'm even out like this." She gathered the sheets of newsprint and folded them into a compact bundle. "I've got to get the turkey stuffed and into the oven. The children are bringing everything else, and Wilfred is making chili, of course."

Pamela followed her to the entry and out onto the porch. "I'll track Clayborn down tomorrow," Bettina whispered, even though Penny was all the way back in the kitchen.

Pamela nodded and whispered, "We've got to find out more about that woman and . . ." She paused while a new and interesting thought formed in her mind. "I wonder if I could even talk to Mr. Gilly today. It *is* Thanksgiving, but he lives in the building. Down in that basement lair."

"He doesn't know anything about her except what was in the article," Bettina said.

"Did the article say what apartment she moved into?" Pamela abandoned the whisper in her excitement. "What if it's Amy's old apartment? That could mean something."

"*Marked for Death in Apartment 3A*," Bettina said with a mock shudder. "It sounds like a nineteen forties movie."

Penny's face appeared in the partly open door. "Are you coming back?" she asked in a woebegone voice.

"Of course," Pamela said as Bettina headed down the steps. "I'll make that coffee and we'll have toast."

When they reached the kitchen, Pamela saw that the kitchen table was once again covered with newspapers. The first section of the *Register* was open to the inner page where the continuation of the "Murder on Orchard Street" article appeared.

"You don't have to tell me what happened," Penny said. "I know all about it now."

They drank their coffee and, because Pamela hated to waste food, ate the toast that had grown cold in the toaster. Pamela doggedly steered the conversation toward Penny's fledgling college career, and Penny gradually relaxed. When they'd finished a second round of toast and drained the last drops of coffee, Pamela stood up and said brightly, "Shall we get dressed?"

As they talked she'd glanced from time to time at the pecan pie waiting on the counter for its journey to the feast. She'd pictured it being sliced and placed on serving plates, where it looked somehow . . . *bare*. A walk uptown could supply ice cream. On food-related holidays—and really, what holiday wasn't?— the Co-Op opened for a few hours in the morning so forgetful cooks could pick up forgotten items.

Besides, a walk to the Co-Op would take her right past the stately brick apartment building at the corner, where Mr. Gilly might not yet have left for whatever Thanksgiving feast he had on his schedule. That's the real reason you decided the pie needs ice cream, said a voice in her mind. Perhaps so, she replied.

Upstairs Pamela made her bed, arranging her collection of vintage lace pillows against the head-board. She stepped into yesterday's jeans and pulled on yesterday's sweater. She'd change into a more festive outfit before they left for the feast. Back downstairs she retrieved her jacket, scarf, hat, and gloves from the closet. She bundled herself up, grabbed her purse and a canvas bag, and reached for the door-knob. Only then did she call out to Penny that she was running uptown on a quick grocery errand. Her plan to visit Mr. Gilly would be ruined if Penny tagged along.

Penny appeared in the kitchen doorway. "Where's the laundry soap?" she asked.

"In the closet across from the washer," Pamela said and set out on her errand.

The trees were completely bare now and most of the fallen leaves swept away by the town. The only color in people's yards came from evergreens, ivy, an occasional chrysanthemum, and the ornamental cabbages that Pamela had always thought would look more at home on a kitchen counter. As she climbed the slight hill to the corner, each exhalation released a cloud of frozen breath.

The crime-scene tape was still in place, bright yellow against the weathered wood of the fence that hid the trash cans. Pamela hurried across the asphalt of the parking lot without letting her eyes stray toward the gap that allowed a glimpse of the cans themselves. She focused only on the door that led to Mr. Gilly's basement lair. A small plaque mounted in the doorframe read "Thomas R. Gilly—Building Superintendent." Above it was a small round button.

She was just aiming her gloved finger toward it when the door opened. Mr. Gilly had been transformed. An elegant wool paisley scarf was tucked into the collar of a smoothly tailored wool coat that reached to his knees. Below were sharply creased trousers and sleek leather shoes polished to a high gloss.

"How nice you look!" Pamela exclaimed, then hoped the amazement in her voice hadn't implied a stereotypical view of apartment supers.

But Mr. Gilly smiled and said, "Going to my daughter's. Fancy house up in Timberley. Can't embarrass her in front of the in-laws. People leave all kinds of nice stuff behind when they move out." He stroked the soft wool of the coat. "But you know that."

He pulled the door closed behind him. "Caught me just in time. What's on your mind?"

"That woman who was killed—" Pamela waved a hand in the direction of the trash cans without turning to look at them. "The *Register* says she lived in this building."

Mr. Gilly nodded. "I told the cops, then I told that reporter. Boy, was *she* something—more questions than the cops."

"What I'm wondering is, what apartment did she live in?"

"Are you working for the newspapers too?" Mr. Gilly pushed back his coat sleeve to consult his watch. "I've got to be on my way real soon."

"*Please*," Pamela said. "That's all I want to know. I'll walk to your car with you."

Mr. Gilly gave her a tolerant smile and took a few steps toward a row of cars along the fence at the edge of the parking lot. "She moved into a two-bedroom on the first floor last week. Amy Morgan, since I guess that's why you're asking, lived in a one-bedroom on the third floor." He continued walking, and Pamela trailed along at his side. "But I'll tell you something I didn't tell the cops or that reporter—" They had reached a parking spot with a "Reserved for Super" sign posted at its head.

Pamela felt a shiver of excitement. Mr. Gilly pulled a set of keys from his pocket. "She knew Amy. But she didn't know this was where Amy had lived—"

Pamela cut in. "What happened? How did she find out? What did she say?"

Mr. Gilly finished his sentence, his voice tinged with embarrassment. "—until I told her." He shrugged. "She heard some people talking in the elevator about

Amy being dead and all, and when she asked them how they knew Amy, they got real quiet. I guess they thought it didn't sound good to be rehashing all the details of something so gruesome in front of a new tenant. So she came to me."

"Did she tell you how she knew Amy?"

"She knew the parents. She was at the funeral."

Ahhh. Pamela gave a mental sigh of satisfaction. So that was why Phyllis Hagstrom had looked familiar. She'd been one of the elegantly dressed older women at the reception.

Mr. Gilly selected a key from his key chain and inserted it in the lock on his car door. "I've got to go," he said. "Happy Thanksgiving."

As soon as Pamela stepped into her house, bearing a half gallon of French vanilla ice cream, she realized dramatic things had happened in her absence. "Mo-o-om!" wailed a voice from the kitchen, and at that exact moment a tiny black shape emerged from under the mail table, streaked across the entry, and disappeared under the living room sofa. Still bundled in her outdoor clothes, Pamela headed toward the source of the wail.

Penny was sitting at the kitchen table. "This is part of it all, isn't it?" she said. Her face wore the same look it had worn earlier that day, accusation mingled with concern. Propped against the wall at the far end of the table was the portrait of Amy Morgan with the disfiguring slash from forehead to chin.

"I didn't mean for you to find it," Pamela said weakly.

"It was in the closet with the laundry soap." Penny gazed at Pamela, hands folded on the table in front of her. "I remember what Amy looked like." The pose and the expression on Penny's face reminded Pamela of the few times in her life she'd been called to account by an authority figure. "Whoever this person is, it's a dangerous person. And I'd like to have one parent at least who's still alive."

Pamela's throat tightened. She felt a prickling of tears and closed her eyes. She was about to say she'd be careful. But what came out was, "Okay. I'll stop."

"By the way . . . I figured out where the cat has been hiding." A tiny hint of smile softened the stern line Penny's lips had assumed. "Under the washing machine. She was a little startled when it came on."

"She's under the sofa now," Pamela said. "We'll put out some food before we leave for the feast."

Chapter Nineteen

The Nordlings had a stream in their front yard. It trickled down from the forested hill behind their house and through a landscape thickly planted with azaleas and rhododendrons. The slate path to the front door was interrupted by a small bridge that crossed the stream. The house itself was a rambling structure built of stone and topped with a sharply peaked roof.

Pamela carried the pie, carefully wrapped in foil, and Penny followed with the ice cream in one of Pamela's canvas grocery bags. The front door opened just as they were stepping onto the porch. "Hello, hello, hello!" Jud Nordling sang out. "Happy Thanksgiving! I heard your car drive up."

He was a jovial man whose pink cheeks and less than svelte figure signaled his love of food and drink. He wore a "King of the Kitchen" apron over an outfit of khakis, starched shirt, and V-necked sweater. His wife Beth, as slender as he was portly, joined him and reached for the pie as Pamela approached the door.

"Thank you," she said. "Jud has been talking about your pecan pies all week."

"We've got ice cream too." Pamela took the canvas bag from Penny.

"I'll pop the goodies in the kitchen," Beth said. "Jud—help them with their coats." The house was warm and smelled of roasting turkey.

Pamela slipped out of her good coat, seldom worn and a decade old. Under the coat, she wore the only dress in her closet, a pale green sheath bought long ago for a wedding. Penny had rushed upstairs to get dressed at the last minute, and she had rushed back down and pulled on her coat while Pamela was in the kitchen getting the pie ready to travel. Pamela gave a tiny gasp now as Penny handed her coat to Jud Nordling. She'd retrieved from her closet the deep red dress Pamela had bought her for a Christmas party the previous year. But her dark hair was up in a twist and her feet sported what Pamela recognized as her own high heels, long neglected in her own closet. The dress had been transformed from the garment of a flirty teenager into that of an elegant young woman. How many years would it be, Pamela wondered, until she was truly all by herself in her big house?

"I see college agrees with you," Beth said, stepping in from the kitchen. "I want to hear all about it."

"Do you drink wine now?" Jud asked Penny. Without waiting for an answer, he added, "The bar is in here." Penny followed him toward the dining room, and Pamela started after them, but Beth touched her arm.

"Are you okay?" she said, her eyes looking as concerned as her voice sounded. "We were so shocked to hear about Amy's murder. Jud knew her, of course, and to think that it happened in your yard . . . and now this other thing. I could hardly believe it when I opened the *Register* this morning."

Pamela shrugged. "I'm trying not to think about it, for today at least. It's great to have Penny home, and it's great to be here with you and Jud."

In the dining room, wineglasses and an open bottle of red wine in a silver wine caddy were waiting on the sideboard. The table had been spread with an antique lace tablecloth and decorated with a collection of gourds, nuts, and corn husks. Beth's English bone china was arrayed in all its glory amid the gourds and nuts, but only four places were set.

Jud filled four glasses and proposed a toast: "To family, absent and present."

"We have to share Frankie and Sara with their in-laws," Beth explained. "We get Christmas this year."

"It's back to work for me," Jud said. He took a swallow of his wine, pronounced it perfect, and headed for the kitchen, wineglass in hand.

"Shall we?" Beth led the way to the living room, where a low fire burned in the grand stone fireplace. Twin sofas upholstered in flowered chintz flanked the coffee table. They chatted about Penny's college adventures and mutual friends as they sipped their wine.

"And speaking of mutual friends," Beth said, "I know Arborville isn't terribly large. I wonder whether you've met Richard Larkin yet?"

"Yes, we have." Penny spoke up before Pamela could answer. "He lives right next door and he seems very nice."

"He's had an unusual career," Beth said.

Penny glanced at Pamela and leaned forward as if

waiting for a storyteller to go on with a promising tale. But Pamela was just as glad when Jud appeared in the doorway and announced that dinner was served. Beth wasn't the matchmaker type—at least Pamela didn't think so. But you never knew what people would get up to. The impulse to match things up could be impossible to resist. Pamela herself often pitied the sad remnants of once-complete sets of glassware or dishes she encountered at tag sales.

Jud was in his element. He brought out dish after dish: scalloped oysters, baked onions, brussels sprouts glazed with brown sugar, a yam soufflé flavored with a touch of orange juice, rolls baked from scratch—and, of course turkey, a free-range turkey. He'd driven nearly to the Delaware Water Gap to select it from among its gobbling confreres, then waited while it was slaughtered and cleaned.

After dinner, they adjourned to the living room to stare at one another in amiable somnolence, then returned to the table for the pecan pie. Jud arranged generous slices on the dessert plates that matched Beth's bone china and topped them with scoops of French vanilla ice cream. The heady smell of freshly ground coffee drifted in from the kitchen.

"You've outdone yourself, sweetheart," Beth said as Jud finished serving coffee and settled back into his place at the head of the table.

"You certainly have," Pamela added, and Penny smiled and nodded.

"My turn to catch up with our guests," Jud said. He turned to Pamela. "Last week I ran into a guy my firm collaborates with sometimes. Richard Larkin. He said he's moved to Arborville."

"We covered that already," Beth said, "while you

were slaving in the kitchen. He actually lives right next door to them."

Penny spoke up. "You said he'd had an unusual career."

Jud laughed and looked across the table at Beth. "You told them about the tree house?"

Beth shook her head. "I didn't know a tree house was part of it."

Penny was leaning forward again, waiting for the rest of the story. "What about the tree house?" she asked Jud. "He said he had a thing in Maine. Is that the tree house?"

"We barely know him," Pamela said, trying to catch Penny's eye. "If he wants us to know about the tree house, I'm sure he'll tell us at some point."

"He probably won't talk about it," Jud said. "He's a very modest guy."

"Now you've got me curious too." Beth leaned into the candlelight. It had grown dark since they sat down to eat. Through the huge window that looked out on the forested hill behind the house, the bare trees were visible only as darker sketches against a shadowy ground.

"It was how the whole thing started," Jud said. He turned to Pamela. "You've been up to Maine, haven't you? Those towns where houses are half trailer and half shack?" Pamela nodded. "Rick dropped out of architecture school one summer and moved up to Maine to think about things. He built himself a tree house out of materials he scavenged from construction sites. He just did it for fun. But then he started noticing how people around there were living, and things took off. He set up a program where contractors unload stuff from buildings being demolished and volunteer architects and contractors help people repair and upgrade their houses with all this free material."

"That sounds very noble," Pamela said. Penny had arranged her face in what Pamela supposed was meant to be a meaningful look. But she wasn't sure what meaning was intended.

In the car on the way home they didn't talk about Richard Larkin. Instead Penny insisted that Pamela swear she would henceforth leave everything having to do with the two Arborville murders to the police. "No more detecting, Mom," she said firmly.

When they got home, Penny crept into the dark living room and stooped to peer under the sofa. "Catrina's not here," she reported in a whisper.

"Probably back under the washer," Pamela said. "We'll leave some food out and see if it disappears."

Chapter Twenty

Bettina had exciting news to communicate the next morning, but she didn't arrive in bathrobe and slippers. When Pamela opened the door to admit her, she was her usual well-groomed self. Her bright red bangs peeked out from under a brown felt beret adjusted to a jaunty angle, her hazel eyes had been enhanced with a touch of green shadow, and her carefully applied lipstick exactly matched the deep rust scarf she'd snuggled up to her chin.

"I've just come from talking to Clayborn," she said before even taking off her coat, "and if you have any coffee left I'd love a cup."

Pamela raised a finger to her lips and whispered, "Shh." She pointed toward Penny, who was lounging on the sofa communing with her smartphone. In her pajamas and with her hair still tousled from sleep, she had transformed from the sophisticated woman of the previous night back into her eighteen-year-old self.

Bettina draped her coat on the chair in the entry and followed Pamela to the kitchen. "What's up with Penny?" she asked.

"I'll explain," Pamela said, "but meanwhile, here's coffee." She poured a cup as Bettina settled at the table. "And how about some pancakes? I made a special breakfast in honor of Penny's visit, and there's plenty of that maple syrup you brought me from Vermont."

"I will never eat again." To emphasize the point, Bettina pushed the sugar bowl across the table. "The children outdid themselves—I've never seen so much food. And of course Wilfred would have been crushed if we hadn't done justice to his chili."

Pamela topped off her own coffee and sat down. She leaned toward Bettina and, as if anticipating a confidence, Bettina leaned toward Pamela. "Penny is afraid something will happen to me," she whispered. "She found the slashed painting, and it scared her, even more than hearing you and me talk about our detecting yesterday. She made me promise I'd leave it to the police to figure out who killed Amy and Phyllis Hagstrom."

"Well, *I* didn't promise," Bettina whispered back, "and you can at least *listen*, can't you? You have to hear what I found out from Clayborn."

"Maybe nothing I don't already know," Pamela said. "I talked to Mr. Gilly yesterday." At Bettina's chiding look, she hastily added, "Before Penny found the painting. Anyway, we already knew Phyllis Hagstrom lived in Amy's building. What I found out was that she moved in *recently*."

"Not into the apartment Amy had just vacated, I hope." Bettina shuddered. "That would be gruesome. I wonder how long they'll wait until they rent Amy's apartment out again—or Phyllis Hagstrom's, for that matter."

Pamela went on. "She actually knew Amy's parents, but when she moved into that building she had no idea it was the same building where Amy had lived. Our guess about why I thought she looked familiar was right—she was one of those elegant women milling around with champagne glasses in their hands at the reception."

Bettina leaned closer. "But here's something you *don't* already know—and it could be very important. Phyllis Hagstrom lived right there in Maple Branch— until she moved to Arborville just last week. She's recently widowed and wanted to be closer to New York City and her children and grandchildren, who live in the city."

"Someone has it in for people from Maple Branch?" Pamela said.

Bettina nodded. "That could be the common thread." She picked up her coffee cup, took a sip, and grimaced. "Warm this up a little?" She held up her cup.

"I'll make more," Pamela said. "I'd like a refill too."

A minute later she turned from the counter to discover that Penny had joined them. "Look, Mom," she said, holding out her smartphone. "He's really famous."

"Who's really famous?"

"Him." Penny nodded toward the window. "Next door." She turned to Bettina. "We met him, Wednesday night. He was out looking at the wild turkeys. He's really nice."

Pamela reached for the phone.

"Wilfred said something about the turkeys," Bettina said. "Funny they came around right at Thanksgiving." The kettle began to hoot, and Bettina jumped up. She busied herself at the counter while Pamela stared at the phone. The image on the screen was small, but recognizable.

"It's an article about him in a Maine newspaper," Penny said, sounding impressed. "His program is called the 'Recycle, Renew Project.'"

It was definitely Richard Larkin, looking even more in need of a trip to the barber's than he had the other night. The jeans that sheathed his long legs were faded and torn in a way that suggested either hard wear and much washing or a SoHo boutique and a breathtaking price tag. They were topped with a bright green T-shirt either purposely form-fitting or woefully shrunken. It proclaimed, "New lives for old things." In the background of the picture random doors and windows leaned against a chain-link fence.

Bettina had left the coffee to drip and was standing at her elbow. "He *is* nice-looking," she said.

"Mom's friends, the Nordlings, know all about him," Penny chimed in. "He started this heroic program up in Maine to help poor people renovate their houses."

"That settles it." Bettina raised her hands with a flourish and then clasped them to her breast. "Nice-looking, heroic, and he's right next door."

"Don't be silly," Pamela said. "He's much too young for me, and he's not my type at all. The tight jeans and the shaggy hair and all that. And he doesn't like yellow kitchens."

"Those little differences can be worked out," Bettina said.

After Bettina left, Pamela conferred with Penny about dinner. They agreed salmon with brown rice and fresh spinach would be a nice contrast with the rich meal they'd eaten the previous night. Penny was going to spend the afternoon with her friend Lorie Hopkins, who was also home for Thanksgiving. They were longing to go to the mall, and Pamela was happy to oblige with the loan of her car. Penny announced she was changing out of her pajamas. When the Penny who descended the stairs ready for her outing was the familiar jeans-and-sweater Penny, Pamela decided time was not hurtling forward quite as fast as she had feared.

A check of the pantry revealed plenty of brown rice on hand. But salmon would have to be fetched, as well as fresh spinach. The day looked so bright and the sky so blue that Pamela would have walked in some direction or other just for the sake of walking. The destination today, however, would be the Co-Op Grocery.

She had no sooner turned the corner at the end of her block than she almost bumped into Bob Randolph. Some impulse made her glance down at his ankles to check if he was wearing the argyle socks that had first put him on her list of suspects. But in deference to the weather, he was wearing hiking boots—though they seemed too elegant for an actual hike—and an expensive-looking down jacket like something from a high-end skiwear catalogue.

He uttered a yelp of surprise and jumped back.

"Excuse me!" Pamela reached out as if to steady him.

He nodded, though it was hard to know whether the nod was curt or friendly. "You take your walks on a predictable schedule," he said, "but we've got to stop meeting like this."

"Why were you parked in front of my house the night before last?" Pamela asked.

Confusion disrupted the harmony of his handsome features. His green eyes widened. "Is that where you live?"

"You must know it is," she said. "The report of Amy's murder in the newspapers mentioned my name and ran a photo of the house."

"Business at the church," he said, shifting from one foot to the other as if eager to be on his way.

"Are you usually free at seven in the evening?" As soon as the words left her mouth, Pamela wondered why she had said them.

"Sometimes," he said. "Not always."

"How about Tuesday nights?" Amy was killed on a Tuesday.

"As a matter of fact, yes. I am free on Tuesday nights. And since you're so interested in my schedule, I'm usually not free on Wednesday nights. Last night, however, I was helping prepare food for the Thanksgiving ministry to the homeless. That's why I had my car there. I usually walk. I like to walk, just like you do." He took a deep breath. "There. Is there anything else you'd like to know about me?"

Penny wouldn't have approved, but Penny was en route to the mall. "Have you ever lived in Maple Branch?" Pamela asked.

"What if I have?"

"Someone is killing people who live in this apartment building and are from Maple Branch."

"What is this?" Bob Randolph burst out laughing. "I know we've had two murders on this street, one of them in your yard, and both of the people lived in this building. And, unlike me, Mr. Gilly would just as soon talk as work. But I really don't think the police need your help."

Saturday morning the cat-food dish was empty, pushed into the corner where the cabinets that flanked the sink met the cabinets that flanked the stove. Catrina was eating regularly, and she'd discovered the temporary litter box. Perhaps it was time to set up a more permanent arrangement, with kitty litter and a real litter box from the hardware store.

Pamela busied herself making coffee. As if drawn downstairs by the aroma, Penny appeared in the kitchen doorway just as she was pouring the freshly ground coffee beans into the cone atop her drip carafe.

"I'm walking uptown soon," Pamela said. "What would you like for dinner? Or should we just order a pizza?"

"I know I'm just home for a few days," Penny said with an apologetic smile, "but would you mind if I didn't eat here tonight?"

"Of course not," Pamela said. "I'll have the rest of the salmon. What's up?"

"Lorie and I are going to the Golden Pagoda. I've been missing that taste the whole time I've been up in Massachusetts."

"They don't have Chinese food in Massachusetts?"

"It's not the same."

A cheerful voice hailed Pamela as she approached the corner. "Hey! How are you?" She glanced in the direction of the sound to see Bob Randolph getting out of his car at the edge of the parking lot behind the stately brick apartment building. It was truly uncanny how her routines seemed to mesh with his. At least he seemed friendly today. Having a laugh at her expense about her amateur detecting had apparently broken the ice.

He circled the car and opened the passenger door to reveal a pleasant-looking, elderly woman with gray hair worn in a smooth bob. She was holding a half-finished argyle sock in shades of navy blue, turquoise, rust, and cream, each color of yarn carefully wound onto its own bobbin. A sturdy knitting bag dangled from her arm. Pamela couldn't resist stepping closer for a better look at the sock.

"That's a very challenging project," she said admiringly. "And I love the colors."

"Why, thank you," the woman said.

Bob Randolph joined them. Pamela was introduced as "my neighbor from down the street," and she learned that the woman was his mother, visiting from Boston.

"Argyle socks are fun," Bob's mother said. "I already finished one pair—for Bob. These are for Bob's partner—well, soon-to-be husband—Andy." She looked up at Bob, who was blushing with pleasure. "You don't mind if I spill the beans, do you?"

Well, Pamela thought to herself as she continued on her way, this encounter had been instructive. If the notations in the knitting booklet retrieved from Amy's plastic bin were to be believed—notably "Love's labor's lost"—Amy had made argyle socks for someone, and that someone had been undeserving of the gift. But that someone hadn't been Bob Randolph, who now actually seemed to be a very

nice person with no reason to kill Amy Morgan—or
Phyllis Hagstrom—at all. But who did that really
leave? The yarn-shop woman? Olivia Wiggens or the
Wendelstaff student? And what did any of those
people have to do with Phyllis Hagstrom?

Back at home, after arranging the new litter box
in the back hall, Pamela served a quick lunch of fried
eggs on toast. She had work to do for the magazine
and Penny had reading to catch up with for school,
so they settled down for a quiet afternoon. Dark clouds
were blotting out the morning's sunny sky, and the
prospect of staying indoors seemed more a treat than
a privation.

Pamela stared at her computer screen, deep in
contemplation. People who knew a lot about fibers
didn't always know a lot about writing. Sometimes
they knew so little about writing that it was impossible to figure out what they meant. When she started
the job, she'd occasionally called authors up to ask
for clarification, but lately she just decided what she
wanted it to mean and rewrote accordingly. No one
had complained so far. But how a wall hanging could
express "desolation personified" she wasn't sure.
Perhaps she'd skip that part and come back to it
later.

The ringing telephone tugged her abruptly away
from "Contemporary Wall Hangings in the Busby
Collection." A voice responded to her startled "Hello?"
with a triumphant announcement: "I have your yarn."

Is this a threat? Pamela wondered momentarily.
My yarn has been taken hostage? But what yarn?

"Your yarn," the speaker repeated insistently. "The yarn you were asking about."

"What? Who?" Pamela stuttered. Then the editing challenge she'd been pondering yielded to the sudden recollection of her Brooklyn outing with Bettina. "Is this the Bedford store?" she asked.

"That Bedford Shop," the voice said crisply. "And I have your yarn. The yarn you wanted more of."

"I . . . oh, that's wonderful. Thank you for calling," Pamela said.

"So here's the deal—I have so much more that I'll trade you skein for skein for the ones you have and I'll toss in—for free—enough more to make a sweater."

"Why trade?" Pamela asked, puzzled. "You said it was more of the same yarn. Aren't all the skeins the same?"

"Yes and no," the voice said. "It's dog fur, those shaggy afghan hounds. Just the fur they shed, no shearing—that's why it's so rare. But the first batch was from Buster, *my* beloved afghan." The voice softened. "It took me ten years to collect it, and it was all I had left of him. He died last year. I'm embarrassed to say it really hit me hard."

"Was he sort of a gold color?" Pamela asked, picturing the yarn's mysterious glow.

"Oh, no—pure white. The unusual color comes from turmeric. All natural."

"It's balls now," Pamela said. "I unwound it and turned it into balls."

"Balls, skeins, it doesn't matter," the voice said. "As long as I have Buster back."

Pamela arranged to make the trade the following week. She'd ask Bettina if she felt like another outing

on Bedford Street. She closed her eyes and enjoyed
a few minutes daydreaming about what she'd do with
the yarn—that glowing color and the extra-soft texture. It would make such a special sweater for Penny.
She'd get busy right away and finish just in time for
Christmas.

Then she focused once again on her computer
screen and "Contemporary Wall Hangings in the
Busby Collection." She finished editing the article,
scrolled back to the problem sentence and decided
that maybe people who were interested in contemporary wall hangings would understand it just as it was,
and sent the file off to her editor. Then she hurried
downstairs to fetch Amy Morgan's plastic bin from
the laundry room.

Penny was stretched out on the sofa, head on one
arm, stockinged feet on the other. A book was balanced on her chest.

"I want to show you something," Pamela said,
perching on the edge of the sofa. She was smiling in
her excitement about the yarn and her plans for it.
She put the bin's lid aside and lifted out one of the
balls. "Isn't this color beautiful?" Penny closed the
book and lowered it to the floor. Pamela put the ball
of yarn on Penny's chest. "It's from a shop in Brooklyn,"
Pamela said. "I have four balls but I'm going to get
more. Feel how soft." She stroked the ball and Penny
touched it with a tentative finger. Pamela remembered Roland's comment the night she took the yarn
to Knit and Nibble at Jean's house—"It makes me
want to pet it." The words had amused her at the
time, but now they made a strange sort of sense.

"I'm going to make you a sweater—for Christmas,"

Pamela went on. "You'll let me know what style and I'll get busy and when you come home again . . ."

Penny squirmed into a sitting position. "Um . . . Mom . . ." Her gaze was focused downward, and her voice emerged as barely more than a whisper. In her lap she wrapped the fingers of one hand around the fingers of the other. "I don't wear the handknit things so much up there. It's kind of not what people wear in college now. So . . ." Her voice trailed off. For a minute there was silence.

Then she jumped to her feet. "What time is it? I've got to hurry out and meet Lorie." Pamela was still sitting on the sofa. Penny turned toward her. "I'm really sorry, Mom." She did look genuinely sorry.

"That's okay," Pamela said, trying to sound cheerful. "I'm glad you told me. I would have done a lot of work . . . for nothing."

Penny hurried up the stairs. Pamela slipped the ball of yarn back into the bin. She'd go to Brooklyn anyway. She might just as well give all the yarn back, especially now that she knew about Buster. You couldn't expect someone to wear something they didn't like just to spare your feelings.

After seeing Penny off to meet her friend, Pamela turned toward the living room. Amy's plastic bin with its odds and ends of variously colored yarn still sat open on the sofa, the ball of the golden yarn she'd pulled out to show Penny tucked in among them. She paused in the entry and stared. Something about the vision awakened the memory of a similar sight—a basket with a whole rainbow of yarn: red, blue, green,

violet . . . and gold. A second memory took its place—
champagne flutes, tasteful black ensembles, and
pearls . . . and a conversation about town doings.

Bettina had been there too. And the key detail in
Bettina's latest update on Phyllis Hagstrom's murder
suddenly seemed very relevant. They'd just been
pondering what that detail could mean when Penny
wandered into the kitchen with her smartphone.
The conversation had turned to Richard Larkin and
the moment had been lost.

Wilfred answered the door, dressed in his customary plaid shirt and bib overalls. "You're looking for
the boss, I guess," he said as he swung the door back
and ushered Pamela in. "Could I interest you in
some leftover turkey? Or anything else? The children
brought enough food for an army."

"Yes, yes," Bettina chimed in from the stairs. "Please
take some." She reached the landing and touched
Wilfred on the arm. "Wilfred—be a sweetheart and go
wrap some leftovers for her."

"Your wish is my command, dear wife," Wilfred said
cheerfully, and he set off for the kitchen.

"Just turkey is fine," Pamela called after him.

"Social call?" Bettina asked. She studied Pamela's
face for a minute. "I don't think so. You're up to something. Does Penny know?"

"Penny won't mind," Pamela said. "I just want to
verify a detail you mentioned."

"Okay. Let's verify." She led Pamela to the sofa.

"Phyllis Hagstrom moved here from Maple Branch."

"That's what Clayborn said."

"And we know Amy grew up in Maple Branch."
Bettina nodded. "Remember that conversation at
the reception after Amy's funeral—we were talking
to those women in the chic black outfits and the
pearls?"

Bettina nodded again. "I remember the crab
puffs too."

"Maple Branch must have a paper like the *Advocate*—
a weekly that really delves into town doings."

"The *Courier*."

"They must have online archives," Pamela said. "Is
your smartphone handy?"

She and Bettina huddled with the smartphone on
the sofa, heads together, the tiny screen casting a
pale green glow on their intent faces. They clicked
on link after link and became more and more excited. When Wilfred deposited a foil-wrapped parcel
on the coffee table they barely noticed.

At last Pamela stood up. She clasped her hands
purposefully. "I just have to check one more thing,"
she announced. "Then we can go to Detective Clayborn." She started for the door. "I think he'll be interested this time."

"The turkey!" Bettina followed her with the foil
parcel.

"I'll be right back."

"Take this." Bettina thrust her smartphone at her,
and Pamela was out the door.

Chapter Twenty-One

In the gathering dusk, Pamela hurried up the street toward Jean Worthington's house. A brisk wind was rising, and she squinted into it, feeling tears form against her lashes. Lamplight glowed behind curtains in the windows of houses she passed. Halfway up the block, she paused. Maybe she should double back and leave a note for Penny. But no, her errand would take ten minutes at most, and she didn't want Penny to know she was detecting again. Except this wasn't really detecting. She was just going to check something, and then she'd pass the information on to Detective Clayborn and that would be the end of it. She darted across the street and picked up her pace, excited to think that she was about to crack the mystery of Amy's murder.

The display of cornstalks, pumpkins, and chrysanthemums on Jean Worthington's porch had been augmented with extra chrysanthemums since the last Knit and Nibble meeting. Pots and pots of them were everywhere, in shades of rust, orange, and gold. Even Jean Worthington's doorbell was special. The button was brass and it was surrounded by an intricate brass filigree. Pamela took a deep breath and pressed twice.

Jean opened the door, gracious smile in place. "Why, Pamela," she said, surprised but cordial. "Whatever brings you out on such a chilly night? You look perfectly windblown." Jean was flawlessly groomed, as always, and was dressed as if for an evening out in a lustrous navy silk sheath that exactly matched her elegant narrow-heeled pumps. A pearl and diamond necklace accented the dress's graceful scooped neck.

"Phone problems—" Pamela launched into the speech she had rehearsed to herself as she hurried up the street. "Can you imagine the cell phone and landline both going out at the same time? I'm so sorry to burst in like this, but I'm desperate to know where you got those wonderful cookies you served when Knit and Nibble met here last week. They'll be perfect to send back to college with Penny—much cuter than anything I could make."

"Of course." Jean smiled. "I have the bakery's business card in the kitchen. But I love your baking. I wish I could do my own, but I'm just hopeless." She started toward the kitchen, then paused. "How *is* your daughter? I'm sorry I didn't have a chance to say hello to her."

"She's fine," Pamela said, struggling to control her eagerness to carry out her plan. "It was great to have her home, even if for so short a time."

"I'll just be a minute," Jean said. Ever the gracious hostess, she added, "Please have a seat." She waited while Pamela settled herself on the sofa. As soon as Jean disappeared down the hall that led to the kitchen, Pamela glanced toward the fireplace. She was relieved and pleased to see that Jean's knitting basket was exactly where it had been at the last meeting, tucked between a fancy wing chair and a lamp table at one side of the hearth.

She hurried to the basket, lifted it onto the chair, and raised its cover. Yes, inside was exactly what she recalled from the previous Knit and Nibble meeting. Jean had commented on the odds and ends of yarn left from various projects. To make the point, she'd displayed the jumbled contents of the basket, balls and twists of yarn in red, green, blue, purple, gold, and more. Pamela reached for the gold yarn now and tugged. Up came a whole skein exactly like the glowing mystery yarn in Amy's plastic bin. It was just what she'd expected to find. Now everything fit together.

The antique Persian hall runner had no doubt muffled the sound of Jean's high heels. Pamela was startled to hear a voice say, "What are you doing?"

Pamela turned. Jean was staring at the skein of yarn in Pamela's hand. The look on her face was polite, if slightly troubled. In her hand was a small piece of notepaper.

"I'd have opened the basket for you," Jean said. "You didn't have to help yourself." She stepped forward and held out the paper. "Here's the information about the bakery. I think they're even open on Sunday."

"This is very unusual yarn," Pamela said.

"Yes. Yes, it is, isn't it?" Jean smiled, perhaps a bit nervously, it seemed to Pamela.

Pamela gave the yarn a little shake. "It looks like the yarn I brought for show-and-tell on Tuesday."

Jean stepped forward, wobbling slightly in the

fancy shoes. "It *is* similar, isn't it?" She looked at Pamela curiously. "Is that why you're interested?"

Pamela returned her look. Jean reached for the yarn. Her hand was trembling slightly. In the gentle light cast by her artfully positioned lamps, her face looked more tragic than angry.

"It's more than just *similar*," Pamela said.

"No!" Jean pulled her hand back and clutched it with the other. "Lots of yarn looks alike." She studied Pamela's face. Then her own face crumpled, and she backed toward the entry hall. "You know," she whispered.

Jean continued backing up. She opened the drawer of a small table in the hall, and pulled out a pistol.

"I *do* know," Pamela said, feeling her pulse begin to quicken. "This yarn was in Amy Morgan's knitting bag, the bag you made away with after you stabbed her with a knitting needle and left her body in the hedge next to my house."

Jean's face changed again. She tipped her chin up, tightened her jaw, and narrowed her eyes.

"You had to kill her, didn't you? Because she knew who you really were—Tracy-Jean Slade, the borough clerk who embezzled half a million dollars from the taxpayers of Maple Branch and got away with it for ten years by changing her name and her appearance. Amy Morgan's parents befriended you and helped you get the job, and that's how you repaid them. The whole story is spelled out in the *Maple Branch Courier*. You discovered Amy had moved to Arborville and you were horrified, but you hoped you could avoid her. She recognized you outside the Co-Op and said hello, but you hurried away. Then you showed up for Knit and Nibble, and there she was heading toward my front door. You couldn't bear to think what would happen if she proceeded into the house, exclaimed how familiar you looked, and then figured out why."

"Yes, you're right," Jean said, advancing toward the arch between the entry hall and the living room. "I did kill her." Her throat tightened, and the words squeezed out. "But I needed that money to escape from being Tracy-Jean Slade, and I didn't want to become Tracy-Jean Slade again."

"Then you had to kill another person. She was a harmless empty nester, but she was from Maple Branch too, a member of the town council, like Amy's father."

"I saw her at the Co-Op. I knew she recognized me, so I followed her home, back to the parking lot behind her building. Luckily the Co-Op sells kitchen tools, so I bought a carving knife. And it was dark out." Jean paused for a moment as if collecting her thoughts. "Now you know. You know who I really am." She waved the pistol at Pamela. "Knitting needles don't make the best murder weapons. I was actually a little surprised that it worked. Carving knives are better, but not all that great. This will be perfect."

"Is your husband at home?" Pamela asked, trying to keep her voice steady. Maybe he didn't know about the other murders. Jean would have wanted to preserve her new identity with him above all. Maybe he'd come down the stairs any minute . . . and this nightmare would be over.

"He's at the skeet range. I made myself look and act rich, and then I married a rich man. But money doesn't just make itself, and he has to relax somehow. And now I realize these guns he collects can come in handy." She stepped closer to Pamela and glanced around the living room. For a moment her face relaxed and she was Jean Worthington, the proper suburban matron, once again. "All my pretty things," she said musingly. "I won't let them take me away from my pretty things." Her voice hardened. "Let's head out the back way so I don't get blood on my Kurdistan." She circled around Pamela and used the gun to motion her toward the entry hall. "It would be fun to drown you in the koi pond, but I think this gun will be more efficient. Besides, there's a dinner party on the calendar for this evening, and I don't want to spoil my dress."

Pamela was holding the handle of the knitting basket, but Jean didn't seem to notice or care.

Pamela backed up as Jean advanced. Jean herded her down the hall toward the back of the house, the pistol steady in her hand. They passed through Jean's kitchen with its soapstone counters, stainless-steel appliances, and splendid cabinets. From the kitchen they stepped into the breakfast room with its French doors and multipaned windows, curtained in country lace. Night was falling and the view was shadowy now, but Pamela knew from previous visits that the windows looked out on a well-manicured lawn and the koi pond, and that the French doors opened onto a slate patio.

"Open those doors," Jean said. Pamela reached for the brass lever on one door and pushed, edging her way through. She was still holding the knitting basket in the other hand.

"Hurry!" Jean shoved the other door aside and poked Pamela in the shoulder with the pistol. Together they stepped onto the slate patio. Light spilling from the breakfast room made the gray slabs silvery. The wind was even stronger now. Pamela shivered despite her coat, but Jean, in only her fancy silk dress, seemed oblivious to the cold. "Keep going," she said. "We're heading toward the garage." The garage loomed as a pale shape at the far corner of the property, linked to the patio by a slate path that ended at a door in the garage's side.

Pamela's pulse was thudding in her ears, and her eyes were watering from the wind. She had a lively imagination—too lively, she had sometimes thought. Now it leaped ahead to the probable outcome of this adventure. She could picture what was going to happen. Jean would herd her into the garage via the side door. The main door was conveniently closed, offering the privacy Jean would need to eliminate yet a third person who knew her story. Then perhaps Jean would wait until later, after the dinner party and maybe even a change of clothes, to drive Pamela's body somewhere and dispose of it. Pamela felt a pang as she imagined Penny waiting and waiting for her return, to no avail. What if she *had* left a note? Penny and her friend probably hadn't even started their meal yet. Any note would have been found much, much too late.

They had reached the edge of the patio, where a few steps led down to the lawn and the slate path. Pamela glanced at Jean, who motioned with the pistol for her to keep moving. She negotiated the steps. Jean followed, teetering with one foot still on the patio. "Damn," she said, pausing. "One of my damn heels is stuck in one of the damn joints between these damn slabs of slate."

Pamela had never heard Jean curse before. Apparently cleaning up her vocabulary was part of leaving

Tracy-Jean Slade behind. Jean continued to teeter. Even in the semidarkness it was clear she was holding the pistol steady. But suddenly Pamela had an idea. Evidently the combination of high heels and slate slabs was not one to assure good balance. She hefted the knitting basket in her hand.

Jean wiggled the foot with the trapped heel, alternating glances at Pamela and at the offending shoe, teetering dangerously but keeping the pistol leveled at Pamela. At last the heel came free. She bent her knee and twisted her head to peer down at the shoe. A bit of light from the breakfast room windows still reached them. "That's the end of these," she muttered. "The leather's a complete mess now." Then she steadied herself and stepped down onto the path. "Turn around," Jean growled, "and walk in front of me."

Pamela obeyed, alarmed to feel what could only be the pistol poking her between the shoulder blades. She picked up her pace a bit, moving easily along in her sensible everyday shoes. The slate path nearly blended into the shadowy gray of the lawn, but the slabs gleamed slightly in the moonlight. Pamela could tell she was getting ahead of Jean. The slight clicks Jean's heels made against the slate were growing fainter. Jean must have felt confident that the pistol gave her the upper hand though, because she didn't complain as Pamela increased the distance between them.

I could run across the grass, Pamela suddenly reflected, and Jean would be hopeless in those shoes. She paused for a split second and her eyes roved over the lawn.

"Don't even think of it." Jean's voice was low but it

carried through the chilly air. "I could shoot you right out here this minute and nobody would have a clue what was happening. People who live in privileged neighborhoods like this wouldn't even know that what they were hearing was a gunshot."

Reluctantly, Pamela continued on her way. The path curved to outline one edge of the koi pond. Pamela kept moving, more slowly now. The side door of the garage was only a few yards away. She had to do something.

Jean was catching up. Any second would come the order to open the door, and they'd step into the dark garage. Pamela glanced over her shoulder. Jean had nearly passed the koi pond. Pamela turned around. "Is the door locked?" she asked. Jean paused, confused, as if that wasn't a detail she'd thought of.

Then Pamela gave the knitting basket a mighty swing and let it go, aiming for Jean's knees. The second she felt it leave her hand, she swiveled toward the lawn and dove for the ground. Suddenly the yard was ablaze with light, the lawn Technicolor green, the chrysanthemums—yes, more pots of them, massed at one end of the koi pond—violent shades of rust, orange, and gold. The pistol discharged with an echoing pop, and Pamela, still lying on the ground, heard a terrific splash.

"Damn, damn, damn!" The word became more shrill with each repetition. Pamela wouldn't have imagined that Jean's voice could scale so many octaves.

She clambered to her knees and turned to see Jean splayed on her back in the koi pond. Her midsection was submerged, but her head and shoulders were above water, as were her feet in the elegant navy pumps, now thoroughly ruined. "Damn security lights," Jean said, squinting into the glare. "They thought you were a raccoon." She raised a wet hand to push aside a lily pad that was clinging to the side of her face. A crowd of fish huddled near an arrangement of ornamental rocks at the pond's edge.

The knitting basket lay on its side near the slate path, its vividly colored contents strewn here and there on the grass.

Pamela stood up, feeling a twinge as she straightened her back. She looked around, and her eyes caught a flash of silver in the grass. It was the pistol, lying near a potted chrysanthemum, orange. She darted forward and grabbed it as Jean squirmed to get out of the pond, fumbling at the sides to pull herself upright.

Then a voice that she didn't recognize as her own growled, "Stay right where you are." But it was her own. She waved the pistol at Jean with a delighted flourish, pulled Bettina's smartphone out of her pocket, and used her thumb to punch in 911.

Chapter Twenty-Two

Headlights flashed on the shrubbery along the Worthingtons' driveway, but no car appeared. Jean was still in the koi pond, struggling to pull herself to a sitting position. Pamela was watching her closely, holding the pistol at what she hoped was a threatening angle and wondering whether it had contained more than one bullet. She didn't think she would have the nerve to fire it anyway and was hoping the police would come very soon.

Now Jean was on her knees in the pond. She steadied herself with both hands on its edge and started to stand up. Her hair had become quite disarranged, clumps of sodden tendrils interrupting its smooth drifts of blond. She had to be cold, Pamela thought. The garage and the shrubbery provided a bit of shelter from the chilly wind, but not much.

"Will . . . you . . . help . . . me?" Jean gasped pitifully, lifting a wet hand from the grass.

Pamela was debating whether Jean had some trick in mind when both were distracted by a voice from the patio—a pleasant male voice calling, "Jeannie?"

Pamela looked toward the sound and recognized Douglas Worthington stepping through the French doors. He repeated the call, but this time with a note of alarm. Then he charged across the patio and down the steps, shouting, "Jeannie! What's going on?"

Still in the pond, but standing now, she turned toward him as he advanced along the slate path. "Douglas!" Her tone was despairing. "There are things about me you don't know." Pamela almost felt sorry for her, and she definitely felt sorry for Douglas Worthington, even though at that moment he was two feet away and reaching for the pistol. Pamela grasped it more tightly and tucked both hands behind her back.

"Jean? What has this woman done to you?" Douglas said. He looked more closely at Pamela. "Pamela Paterson? From down the street?" Pamela nodded. "Why is my wife in the koi pond?" He sounded more puzzled than menacing. Then his tone shifted. "Was that my pistol I saw in your hand?"

Many questions to answer, and Pamela wasn't sure where to start, or whether to run as fast as she could down the driveway and call 911 again.

But the sound of a siren rising and falling on the chilly air made the decision for her. "Your wife is a murderer," she said. "She killed Amy Morgan and that woman from the big apartment building at the corner, and she tried to kill me just now, with your pistol."

Douglas Worthington heard the siren too. He stepped toward his wife, lifted her out of the koi pond, and wrapped his arms around her. "Is that true?" he murmured into her wet hair.

Jean nodded against his coat front and said in a

small voice, "I wanted everything to stay just like it is. But people knew things about me."

Pamela wasn't sure what to do with the pistol. She knew you weren't supposed to point guns at people unless you were prepared to shoot them. It was possible that Douglas would lunge at her, but the police were on the way. The siren had grown louder and louder. Now its piercing wail softened to an angry moan and suddenly stopped.

Pamela backed toward the driveway, keeping an eye on Douglas and Jean. She could see the flashing lights of the police car at the driveway's end. She swiveled and ran toward the lights, the pistol dangling in her hand. "Back here," she called and paused to get her breath. "Back here," she repeated. "I'm the person who called." She was halfway to the street now. A figure swerved from the front walk and tore across the grass. Pamela recognized Officer Sanchez. Another officer emerged from the police car and started up the driveway.

"It's Jean Worthington by the koi pond," Pamela called. "She tried to kill me with her husband's pistol. She killed those other women too." She let the officers get ahead of her. Both were running with drawn guns. She stood on the driveway for a minute, panting shallow pants and struggling to fill her lungs with air. She was no longer frightened. In fact, she felt exhilarated, like the heroine of some great adventure.

She continued on to the backyard. Jean and Douglas Worthington were standing side by side, Jean wrapped in her husband's coat, his arm around her shoulder. In the glare of the security lights, they looked like actors on a movie set preparing for a retake of some particularly arduous scene. The varicolored balls of yarn scattered on the grass added an incongruous touch. The male officer was facing them, still with his gun drawn. "Where is the weapon now?" he asked.

"I have it," Pamela said. "She dropped it in the grass when I swung the knitting basket at her legs. But she fired it. You can see the bullet hole there in the door." Pamela laid the pistol across the palm of her other hand and offered it to Officer Sanchez, who was standing closer to her. From the street came the sound of another siren.

"We'll have some questions," Officer Sanchez said. "I'll drive you home."

Detective Clayborn showed up just as Officer Sanchez, seated on the delicate chair with the needlepoint seat, was tucking her notepad away. Pamela gave Detective Clayborn a sturdier seat and patiently went through the same details she had given Officer Sanchez. She started with the fact that she'd recognized in Jean's knitting basket a skein of the same rare yarn Dorrie Morgan had given her when she made a gift of her sister's knitting supplies.

Detective Clayborn's homely face creased in puzzlement. "Two people couldn't happen to buy the same yarn?" he asked.

"It was very rare yarn," Pamela said. "Made from dog hair and dyed with turmeric. Only a few skeins in existence."

Looking no less puzzled, he wrote something on his notepad.

There were more questions—many more questions. At last he stood up. "I guess it turned out okay," he said. "I'm glad nobody else got hurt. You took a big chance."

Pamela had no sooner seen Officer Sanchez and Detective Clayborn on their way than Bettina was at the door. "Did something happen?" she asked as she stepped into the entry. The look on her face mingled apprehension with excitement. "I heard the sirens and saw the police cars in front of Jean's house."

"A lot happened," Pamela said and led her friend to the kitchen. "And Jean Worthington isn't going to kill anyone else."

She had just described launching the knitting basket at Jean's knees, to Bettina's delighted clapping, when the doorbell rang.

"Penny has her own key," Pamela said. "And anyway, what time is it? Only about seven, I think. She's gone to dinner with a friend." Pamela had been amazed to check the clock when she got home. Scarcely more than an hour had elapsed between the time she left Bettina's for Jean's house and the time Officer Sanchez delivered her back home.

"I'll get it," Bettina said. "And then let's adjourn to my house. Wilfred is warming up some of his Thanksgiving chili."

Pamela waited at her kitchen table as Bettina hurried toward the entry. She heard the door open and then Bettina's voice saying, "*Hello!*" There was an indistinct reply, then Bettina's voice again. "Yes, it is me, Bettina from across the street. I'm her neighbor too. So nice to meet you at last."

Pamela frowned. Bettina sounded positively flirtatious.

Another indistinct reply, then Bettina said, "That was quite a commotion, wasn't it. But she's fine. And I'm sure she'd like to say hi."

The next thing she knew, Bettina was ushering Richard Larkin into her kitchen. He ducked coming through the door, as if—Pamela thought—a person as tall as he often risked bumping his head and he had learned to be careful.

"Ummm." He surveyed the room. "I like the yellow in here. It . . . works."

Bettina took over. "Richard saw the police cars at the corner and the police car bringing you home. He just wanted to see if you were okay or if you needed anything."

He smiled shyly, ducked his head again, and addressed Bettina. "It's Rick, actually. You can call me Rick." He glanced toward Pamela. "Both of you. Please." He shrugged and looked around the kitchen again. "Well . . . I'm glad you're okay. I just wanted to check. So . . ." He edged toward the door. He was wearing a pair of faded and patched jeans that could have been the same pair in the photo Penny had found online. A worn leather jacket completed the look.

"Do you have plans for dinner?" Bettina laid a hand on his arm.

"Ummm?"

"My husband is warming up a pot of his home-made chili. He always makes it for Thanksgiving.

Pamela is coming." Bettina flashed Pamela a huge smile. "And that reminds me, Pamela. I've still got that leftover turkey you were going to take home."

"Turkey?" Richard said with a smile. "I've got turkey too, and all the trimmings. I can't do chili tonight, but what if we all have a neighborly get-together tomorrow? We can pool our leftovers." He cast a hopeful glance at Pamela.

Pamela was just framing a refusal in her mind when a voice came from the entry. "That sounds like a lot of fun." The front door closed with a gentle thump, and a few seconds later, Penny stepped into the kitchen.

"My daughters will be there," Richard said, turning toward Penny. "I'd like you to meet them."

"I'd love to." Next to Richard's great height, Penny looked tinier than usual.

"So that settles it." Bettina gave a decisive nod.

"How about six?" Richard said. He and Bettina and Penny were all beaming at one another. Pamela was still sitting at the table, wondering how she could possibly veto a neighborhood potluck that had been so heartily endorsed by her daughter and her best friend.

Richard glanced around the room again, smile still in place. "So," he said, "tomorrow then." He started toward the entry.

Pamela jumped up. No point in being unmannerly, she said to herself. It had been kind of him to look in, and at least she could see him to the door. She'd have to think about the potluck though.

"There were turkeys again," Penny said suddenly. "In the street when I got home."

They all stepped out onto the porch together,

standing silently as their breath formed clouds in the chilly air, listening to the faint gobbling coming from the end of the block. "They're going away now," Penny said. "They were right in front of the church when I saw them."

"Grab your jacket and come on over," Bettina called as she set out across the street. "I'll tell Wilfred you're on your way."

"The mystery is solved," Pamela told Penny once they were back in the house. She ran through the details quickly, gave Penny a hug, and assured her that there would be no more detecting. Then she hurried across the street to eat chili with Wilfred and Bettina.

When she crossed the street again, the bright-eyed young woman from the *County Register* was sitting in her car at the curb waiting to do an interview.

"Mom?" Pamela opened her eyes. Her room was sunny. On these winter mornings she usually awoke when the sky was still the pale shade of dawn. Hinges creaked, and Penny spoke again. "Are you okay?"

Pamela raised herself on her elbow and looked toward the door. A sliver of Penny's face was visible in the crack between the door and the doorframe. Even with just one eye and the corner of her mouth visible, it was obvious Penny was concerned. "It's almost eleven," she said. "You don't usually sleep so late."

"Ummm." Pamela half sat up and wedged her pillow between her back and her bed's headboard.

She felt heavy and slow, as if every function of her body was operating at half speed.

"I made some coffee," Penny said, pushing the door open and stepping into the room. "I could bring you a cup."

"No," Pamela said, and her voice sounded faint, as if even uttering a monosyllable took more energy than she was capable of summoning. "I'll get up," she added, trying for a bit more liveliness.

It was over. The whole thing was over. She hadn't realized how caught up she'd been, asking questions, poking around, and then the sudden understanding yesterday—that the flash of gold she'd glimpsed in Jean Worthington's knitting basket was the same yarn she'd discovered in Amy's plastic bin, the strange golden yarn from the eccentric shop in Brooklyn.

She'd just been planning to make sure it was the same yarn, then tell Detective Clayborn what she'd discovered and hope he'd see what an important clue this was. But Jean had come back from the kitchen too soon and one thing had led to another and Jean had ended up in the koi pond and . . .

She closed her eyes, picturing Jean and Douglas standing on the lawn with the yarn scattered around them.

She was tired, and deservedly so. But she was happy too. Amy's killer wouldn't go unpunished. A frivolous thought intruded—that extra skein of the golden yarn. Who did it belong to, by rights? It had been Amy's, but Amy's sister had given all Amy's knitting supplies to Pamela. Maybe it should go back to the woman at the shop along with the rest of the golden yarn.

Pamela eased her legs around and lowered her feet to the floor. She pulled on her robe and headed downstairs.

Penny had brought the *County Register* in. It was the extra-large Sunday edition, but Arts and Lifestyle, Sports and Entertainment, and Business had been cast aside on the floor. The first section was on the kitchen table, open to a page that featured a photograph of Jean Worthington being led to a police car. Its backdrop was her grand house, including her porch with its carefully arranged cornstalks, pumpkins, and chrysanthemums.

"I read the article," Penny said. "A lot of it is about you." Was that just a touch of awe in Penny's voice? She jumped up. "Would you like toast?"

"Coffee first." Pamela helped herself to a cup at the counter.

"I put some food out for the cat after you went to bed," Penny said. "The dish was empty this morning."

"That's all we can do, I guess." Pamela slipped into the chair Penny had vacated and began to read the article.

Chapter Twenty-Three

Penny had plans to spend the afternoon with a friend. When she came downstairs dressed to go out, she was wearing one of the handknit sweaters Pamela had given her over the years. She was wearing it just to be kind, Pamela supposed, trying to make up for rejecting the proposed handknit Christmas gift.

Pamela decided that a long walk and a few hours catching up on work for the magazine would be just the prescription to bring her back down to earth after her dramatic adventure. Then there would be the potluck that evening and, Monday morning, the melancholy task of seeing Penny off to college once again.

Instead of heading up the block toward town, a route that would take her past Jean's house, Pamela set out down the block, toward County Road, the busy thoroughfare that separated Arborville from the woods where the turkeys roosted. Someday soon, she'd resume her old habits, shopping at the Co-Op and investigating the cast-off treasures behind the stately brick apartment building. But today she'd break with routine. Yesterday's wind had brought a still, bright day. It would be pleasant to meander along one of the paths that crisscrossed the little stand of woods, even though the trees were bare now. And perhaps she'd see a turkey.

Back at home an hour later, she ate a sandwich and settled in at her computer. She was not surprised to find that *Fiber Craft*'s editor in chief had barely taken any Thanksgiving break at all. Five articles were lined up for Pamela's attention, and she contentedly opened the first file and immersed herself in a discussion of vintage macramé handbags.

Soon she was yawning—not because the handbags weren't interesting, but because the walk had been wonderfully relaxing. She deserved to feel lazy, she told herself. And the articles weren't due back for a few days. Monday morning she'd declare vacation officially over.

She wandered back downstairs and eyed the sofa. She hadn't opened the living room curtains that morning, and the room was invitingly shadowy. Perhaps she'd just lie down for a bit. Pamela was too tall to stretch out fully on her sofa. Her head had to rest on the arm at one end and her ankles on the arm at the other end. She tugged the handknit throw off the sofa's back and smoothed it over her feet, pulling it up under her chin. Then she closed her eyes and felt herself sink into a welcoming darkness.

The next thing she knew, a face was hovering above her face and a lamp cast a pool of light on her feet at the other end of the sofa. "It's time to go to the potluck," Penny said. "Did you have a nice rest?"

"I guess I did," Pamela said, blinking a few times. "What time is it?"

"Five to six. Are you wearing what you're going to wear?"

"It's not a party, is it?" Pamela sat up and pushed the throw aside. She let her head loll against the sofa back and closed her eyes.

A light tapping on the front door drew their attention. A faint voice called, "We're on our way. Shall we wait for you?"

"Bettina and Wilfred," Penny said and hurried for the door. The next minute Bettina was standing in the middle of the living room gazing at Pamela with raised eyebrows and a tolerant smile. Wilfred stood in the arch between the living room and the entry holding a very large cardboard box.

"You're not wearing *that*?" Bettina said. Her voice mingled amusement and alarm.

Pamela shrugged and looked down at the jeans and sweater she'd put on that morning. "It's just a potluck."

"You go upstairs right now and put on something nice," Bettina said. "Richard Larkin is a very eligible man and he's obviously interested in you."

"I'm just not ready," Pamela said.

"Obviously." Bettina laughed. "Go upstairs and *get* ready. We'll tell him you're on the way."

"I mean, ready for *him*. Or anyone, for that matter."

From his post at the edge of the room, Wilfred caught Pamela's eye and flashed a sympathetic smile. He took a few steps toward Bettina. "Dear wife? This food is getting heavy. And cold."

"Go, all of you!" Pamela straightened her back and squared her shoulders, but she smiled to soften the command. "I'm sure you'll have a fine time without me."

"*Mo-o-om!*" Penny looked crestfallen. "I was looking forward to it."

"You go too," Pamela said. "All of you. I have a nap to finish."

Bettina retreated, but before she followed Wilfred and Penny out the door she darted back for a final comment. "You'll regret this when he finds someone else," she said, and the door closed behind her.

Pamela turned off the lamp at the end of the sofa, stretched out again, and pulled the throw up to her chin. An event was taking place at the church next door, and the lights illuminating the steeple cast a glow that reached her side window. Otherwise the room was dark. She closed her eyes.

She opened them again to the realization that she was not alone. She had no idea how much time had passed, but the lights were still on next door and Penny was still out. A soft warm something was resting on her chest, a very small something. She raised her head. In the faint light that came through the side window, she could make out a dark shape. She eased an arm from under the throw and let her fingers creep stealthily toward the shape. What they encountered was as soft and yielding as the mysterious yarn from Amy's plastic bin.

"Catrina?" she whispered. "Do you sleep on the sofa when you think you're alone down here?"

Feet tapped across the porch, the door opened, and light flooded in from the entry. Suddenly there was an empty spot on the throw and a flash of black fur darting across the rug.

"Was that the cat?" Penny said.

"I woke up and she was asleep on my chest. She must come out at night and curl up on the sofa."

Pamela tossed the throw aside and sat up. "How was it?"

"Oh, Mom!" Penny settled into the little chair with the carved wooden back and needlepoint seat. "His daughters are so nice. Laine—she's the oldest one— is just so *New York*. And I love her clothes and they're all vintage and she's going to take me thrifting with her when I come home for Christmas. And Sybil is majoring in art and they're both at NYU and that's why he bought this house, so they could visit him on weekends—" She paused for breath. "We all had wine, just a little. Bettina and Wilfred brought a bottle." She went on, still a bit breathlessly. "He was living in the city and they were living with their mother, but his apartment was really small and she got a job offer in San Francisco but they wanted to stay at NYU and they didn't want to leave New York, even though San Francisco could be fun too—"

Pamela smiled encouragingly. Penny's cheeks were rosy with excitement, and her eyes all the brighter blue in contrast.

"And they loved my sweater." Penny tugged her jacket open and traced the ripples of green, indigo, and violet that patterned the turtleneck Pamela had fashioned from ombre yarn. "They couldn't believe my mom had knit it, and then Bettina told them all about the knitting group." She took a deep breath and went on. "I brought some food back for you, out there." She gestured toward the entry. "You probably didn't eat."

At the mention of food, Pamela realized that indeed she was hungry. She stood up.

"It's in a bag on the table." Penny followed her as

she retrieved the bag and headed for the kitchen. "And, Mom?"

"Ummm?" Pamela unwrapped a turkey sandwich.

"I take back what I said about not wanting a sweater for Christmas. If you'd still do it, that is. With the golden yarn."

Pamela smiled to herself. She'd recruit Bettina and schedule that return visit to Brooklyn. Then she'd get started on the sweater.

"He isn't my boyfriend, you know." Penny addressed Pamela's back as Pamela stood at the kitchen counter layering Co-Op deli ham and cheese on whole-grain bread. Pamela had asked whether Kyle would like mustard on his.

"I know he isn't your boyfriend," Pamela said without turning. "I could tell by the way you told him goodbye. I just thought you might know whether he likes mustard."

"Well, I don't. Just make one with and one without, and if he doesn't like it I'll eat the mustard one."

Kyle Logan was due at ten a.m. to pick Penny up for the drive back to their college in Massachusetts. Penny's roller suitcase, packed with freshly laundered clothes, sat in the entry.

Pamela wrapped the sandwiches and slipped them into a canvas bag from her collection. She turned away from the counter. "Would he like an apple?" The antique wooden bowl that occupied a permanent spot at the end of the counter had been newly replenished with Co-Op apples.

Penny groaned, but the groan turned into a laugh.

"*Mo-o-om!* He's not my boyfriend. I don't know if he'd like an apple."

Pamela slipped two apples into the bag. She added another sandwich bag containing some of the Co-Op bakery's gingerbread cookies. Penny was dressed for the drive back to school in her usual jeans and a sweater, but she had finished the outfit off with a bright scarf that picked up the blue of her eyes. Pamela recognized it as Bettina's Christmas gift to Penny from the previous Christmas.

"I like the scarf that way," Pamela said. "And no, I don't think you're dressing up specially for Kyle Logan."

Penny fingered the complicated silken twist at her throat. "Laine was wearing a scarf tied like this," she said. "She showed me how to do it."

Just as the chimes from the church next door began to sound, the doorbell rang. "He's very punctual," Pamela said.

Penny scooted her chair back and jumped to her feet. "My other bag is upstairs," she said, and ran for the stairs.

The person at the door was not Kyle Logan. Pamela gave a start, trying to place this unexpected visitor. She had expected to greet a tall young man with a pleasant smile. Instead she was staring at a stocky woman with a nose like a carelessly molded lump of dough. Her eyes skimmed the baggy jeans and down jacket and traveled back up to the face.

The name she was searching for floated to the top of her mind, but before she could utter it, the visitor spoke.

"You thought *I* killed her, didn't you?" The tone of voice wasn't particularly threatening, but the unblinking gaze suggested this wasn't a social call. "That's why you tracked me down at the Haversack Wholesale Food Depot."

"Dorrie . . . I . . ." Pamela's voice trailed off. She hated to lie, and yes, of course, she *had* suspected that Dorrie Morgan killed her sister.

"The cops called me Saturday night. They said the killer had been arrested. And I saw the article in the *Register*." A faint smile rearranged the stern line of her lips. "You've got guts, I'll say that."

Pamela fingered the doorknob uncertainly. Maybe it *was* a social call? Should she invite Dorrie in for coffee?

From upstairs Penny called, "Tell him I'll be right down."

"My daughter," Pamela murmured. "Excuse me." At the bottom of the stairs she called back up, "It's not Kyle."

Returning to the doorway, she flung the door open. "Come in," she said. "We'll have coffee."

Dorrie seemed bent on confession. From her post at the kitchen table, she watched silently as Pamela ground beans and made a fresh pot of coffee. And as soon as Pamela set a steaming cup in front of her, along with a napkin and a plate of gingerbread cookies, she found her tongue. "Not that I wouldn't have liked to sometimes," she said. "Kill her, I mean." And she launched into a sad tale of sibling rivalry, in which Amy was the beautiful, favored sister and she, Dorrie, the ugly duckling.

Her voice grew more and more frantic, straining through a tightening throat as the story reached its climax. "And then," she said, "I thought I'd finally found someone who really loved me and then he met

Amy and he couldn't take his eyes off her and one thing led to another—" Her homely face had turned an unbecoming shade of pink. "And the thing of it was she didn't think he was anything special at all. And, yes, I did slash the painting. I suppose my parents might have wanted it . . . to remember her with. But when I saw it there in her apartment I was just so—"

Pamela reached across the table to grasp Dorrie's hand. "My friend and I heard the argument at the cemetery, back in there among the trees. I recognized your voice, but was the other voice your husband?" Dorrie nodded. "He's not really allergic to ragweed?"

Dorrie sniffed deeply. "He is, a little, but that's not why his eyes were red at the funeral."

Pamela heard footsteps on the stairs and looked toward the doorway to see Penny peeking around the doorframe.

The doorbell rang and this time it really was Kyle Logan. The voices from the entry roused Dorrie from her misery. She dabbed at her eyes with the napkin Pamela had supplied with the cup of coffee.

"Excuse me," Pamela said, standing up. "My daughter is leaving to go back to college and I want to see her off."

"Only one daughter?" Dorrie asked. Pamela nodded. "She's lucky," Dorrie said.

A few minutes later, Penny was out the door, roller suitcase bumping over the front walk, the elaborately knotted blue scarf peeking out from the neck of her jacket. Pamela followed along. At the curb, hugs were exchanged, calls and emails were promised, and the prospect of Christmas, less than a month away, was invoked. Kyle Logan exclaimed over the lunch and assured Pamela that he loved mustard, and apples, and gingerbread cookies. And then they were off.

Back inside, Pamela discovered that Dorrie had polished off all the gingerbread cookies on the plate. "Thank you," Dorrie said fervently.

Pamela wasn't sure whether the thanks were meant for the cookies or for Pamela's patient ear as Dorrie unburdened herself, but she offered a hearty "You're welcome."

"I'm not leaving him," Dorrie said. "He's sorry now, and maybe we can work things out. He never actually *did* anything with her, except for the paintings. We've had some good times, and we actually have a lot in common. And, honestly, I don't know who else would want him. *She* certainly didn't." She rose from her chair and slipped back into the puffy jacket. "And now," she said, "I have a gift for you. Grab your coat. It's out in my van."

At the curb, she twisted the lever that latched the van's back doors and swung them open. Pamela craned her neck to make out the contents of the dark interior, but all was shadowy. Dorrie edged around her, knelt on the lip of the opening, and clambered inside. "I'll push it out," she said, her voice echoing off the metal walls. "Whatever you do, don't let it slip past you."

As Pamela watched, a pale shape glided toward her, all angles, points, and jagged crevices. When it neared the open doors and emerged from shadow into sun, it began to glitter.

"Catch it," Dorrie called from deep within the van. "It's moving fast."

Pamela had already figured out what the curious object was composed of, but she was nonetheless startled when her bare hands encountered a freezing-cold surface, slicked with a bit of moisture.

Dorrie's head appeared beside the object. She flashed a satisfied grin and squeezed past it, managing a contortion that resulted in her landing on her feet right beside Pamela.

"What do you think of it?" she said.

"Very striking." Pamela braved its chilly surface to give it a pat. "I like all the points."

"It's you," Dorrie said. "My impression of you, so heroic." Perhaps noting the startled look on Pamela's face, she added. "An abstraction, of course. Though, as I told you, I do representational work as well. But abstraction can be so much more expressive."

"Well, it's lovely," Pamela said. "But I'm not sure my freezer—"

"Oh, it's not meant to last," Dorrie said cheerfully. "That's the nature of ice sculpture. Ephemeral, like life. But it's pretty cold out this time of year. You should get a couple days' worth at least. And I photographed it for my next show." She reached around the sculpture and coaxed it closer to the edge of the opening. "You grab one side, and I'll grab the other. It's okay to hold it by one of the points, but put your other hand underneath in case the point starts melting and gets slippery."

Pamela did as she was instructed, trying to ignore the fact that the sculpture's surface was very very cold.

"Where to, then?" Dorrie asked, once they had each gotten a grip on the unwieldy piece of ice.

"How about the backyard?" Pamela said. "It's much shadier back there."

They made their way slowly across the front yard to the driveway and along the side of the house, the ice sculpture balanced between them. Pamela tried to distract herself from the numbness that was over-taking both hands by focusing her eyes on the desti-nation she had in mind: the ivy patch sheltered by her prize rhododendron. The rhododendron was so old it was nearly a tree, and it kept its dark, oblong leaves all winter.

"We'll put it here," she said, nodding toward the huge plant. They veered toward the edge of the drive-way and gently deposited the ice sculpture on the ivy. Both stepped back, each rubbing her cold and wet hands together.

"I'll be off then," Dorrie said briskly. "Lots to do today." She reached for Pamela's hand, which was now tingling as if pricked by a million needles, and gave it a brief squeeze. "Thanks again, for everything," she called as she strode down the driveway toward her battered van.

Pamela had lots to do too. Upstairs, she stripped the sheets off the bed in Penny's room and replaced the comforter and the quilt her own grandmother had made for her long ago. Gradually the tingling in her hand subsided. She checked the closet to make sure Penny hadn't left anything crucial behind. The deep red dress that Penny had worn on Thanks-giving had been left where she found it—college social life these days apparently didn't include fancy occasions. On the closet floor were Pamela's own black high heels. She'd leave them there.

On her way downstairs she'd stop in the bathroom to collect the towels Penny had used, but first she glanced around the room one final time. Her eyes paused when they reached the drawing Penny had made of her, looking rather like the heroine of a romance novel, resolute but beautiful. She supposed her recent adventure had borne out that she could indeed be resolute when the occasion demanded, and Bettina wouldn't stop insisting that Richard Larkin was attracted to her.

"Too, too silly," she murmured to herself as she stepped out of the room and closed the door.

The batch of articles in need of editing waited on her computer. She finished the one about vintage macramé handbags, worked through a profile of a textile designer who had moved in the same circles as Frank Lloyd Wright, and took a break for a quick sandwich. By the time she attached the edited versions of all five to a message of her own and clicked "send," the view her office curtains hid was only darkness.

Holding the banister, she felt her way down the stairs into the dark entry. In the kitchen, she flipped on the light switch, blinking at the light that bounced off the glazed floor tiles and illuminated every corner of the room. It illuminated things that might have gone unnoticed when natural daylight was enough for most tasks—things like Catrina's dish. The little plastic dish lurked in the shadowy corner where one set of cabinets met another.

"Oh, no!" Pamela sighed. When had Catrina last eaten? She'd scurried from Pamela's chest the previous night when Penny came in from next door and switched on the light. And she'd been forgotten in the bustle as Penny described her newfound friendship with Richard Larkin's daughters. Then this morning there'd been a lunch to pack for Penny and

Kyle Logan, plus a surprise visit from Dorrie. Even if Pamela had remembered to fill the little plastic dish, all the coming and going would have assured that Catrina stayed out of sight.

Now Pamela stooped to retrieve the dish and gave it a quick wash at the sink. She took a fresh can of cat food from the cupboard and cranked the can-opener around its rim. She delicately picked the now-detached lid from the smooth surface of the pinkish mixture, wondering whether the strong fish odor was more appealing to cats than to humans. As she spooned a few tablespoons from the can into the plastic dish, she became aware of something brushing her ankle. The touch was as soft and whispery as if the skin exposed between jeans leg and shoe was being tickled with a skein of the golden yarn from Amy's plastic bin.

She looked down to see Catrina weaving this way and that, making figure eights as she rubbed her tiny body against Pamela's ankle. Her tail stood up stiffly with a little kink at the end, and the faintest of meows escaped from her throat. I have a cat, Pamela said to herself. It's time to call the vet and make sure this little creature is healthy.

Chapter Twenty-Four

Pamela and Bettina were the first to arrive. The tastefully modern living room was ready to welcome guests, but as they settled themselves on the low-slung sofa, a cupboard door slammed in the kitchen, followed by the sound of glass shattering. Then a masculine voice uttered a muffled curse. Roland DeCamp's wife smiled a serene smile. "He wants to do all the refreshments himself," she said as she perched on a sleek chair in the same deep turquoise color as the sofa. Melanie DeCamp was quite sleek herself, with her blond hair pulled into a high pony-tail and her well-exercised legs clad in smooth black leggings.

The DeCamps lived in a section of Arborville referred to as "The Farm," though it had ceased being a farm twenty years earlier when a developer bought the land. Against a backdrop of much grumbling from the Arborville old-timers, he created a community of nearly identical split-level houses. They were huge places, with more bathrooms than anyone could need, though—in the minds of many—no charm at all. A bit of charm had been gained as the spindly twigs planted in the new development grew into substantial trees, but many of the old-timers still hadn't forgiven the Van Ripers for trading their generations-old farmland for mere money.

Another cupboard door slammed in the kitchen and another curse followed. Footsteps thudded in the hallway, and then came Roland's exasperated voice. "I can't find the coffee grinder. What have you done with it, Melanie?"

"It's right on the kitchen table," his wife said sweetly. "You put it there yourself." Roland mumbled something unintelligible and the footsteps retreated. Melanie turned her attention back to Pamela. "He loves the group so much," she said. "And the knitting is really helping him relax. He's been so much calmer." The doorbell chimed three descending notes, and Melanie hurried to greet the next arrival.

"Here's our local hero," Nell Bascomb exclaimed, white hair adrift around her cheerful face as she stepped into the living room and caught sight of Pamela. "How *are* you, dear?" She deposited her knitting bag at the end of the sofa and bent over Pamela, grasping her hands. Melanie DeCamp followed with Nell's ancient coat draped over her arm.

"Fine," Pamela said with a modest smile. "Just trying to forget the whole thing, really."

"And I guess our group has lost a member," Nell said. She eyed the low-slung sofa warily and started to sit.

Melanie DeCamp intervened. "Nell—here—" She touched Nell's arm and guided her to a substantial armchair. "Roland and I can barely pull ourselves up from that sofa anymore. Only the dog really likes it."

Clicking toenails on the hallway floor announced the arrival of the DeCamps' dachshund, Ramona. "She knows when people are talking about her," Melanie said. "Yes, sweetie," she added, turning toward the dog. "I'll take you out in just a few minutes."

Pamela doubted that Melanie DeCamp, with her well-exercised legs, actually had trouble rising from the sofa, but Bettina chimed in, "I'm not sure *I'll* be able to pull myself up," she said, "but I can see why that short-legged little doggy likes it."

"Poor Jean Worthington," Nell said after she'd retrieved her knitting bag from the sofa and begun extracting needles, yarn, and a half-finished elephant.

"How on earth can you say 'poor'?" Bettina leaned forward as best she could, given the dramatic pitch of the sofa. "She killed two people and almost killed Pamela. Not to mention that she stole all that money from the people of Maple Branch."

"Misguided, for sure," Nell said. "But she started out in more desperate circumstances than any of us can imagine, and she thought she'd reached her goal. Jeff Morgan hired her out of a women's shelter—that little detail was in the *Register*. If those two people from Maple Branch hadn't moved to Arborville, we'd be having Knit and Nibble meetings at that fancy house and eating gourmet cookies forever. Or at least until somebody from Maple Branch eventually *did* move here, unless everybody was old enough at that point that nobody recognized anybody anymore."

The doorbell chimed again and Melanie hurried to answer it, followed by Ramona. The front door opened, and a sweet voice came from the hallway. "Am I late?"

"It's Karen," Nell said, "and that reminds me— Dave has a job offer. I ran into him at the Co-Op this afternoon."

"Congratulations," Pamela and Bettina said in chorus as Karen stepped into the living room.

"What for?" Karen's cheeks were already pink from the cold, but Pamela thought their color deepened.

"The Arborville grapevine," Nell explained. "I saw Dave at the Co-Op."

"Will you be staying in town now?" Pamela asked.

Karen gave a delighted gasp and her lips curved into a huge smile, as if she had just realized the implications of her husband's job offer. "Yes," she said. "Yes, we definitely will. The job is at Carradine State, a little further drive for him, but not much, and they want him to develop some new courses. That will mean a raise—more money for the home improvements." She took a seat next to Bettina on the turquoise sofa.

In the kitchen, Roland cursed, and there was a reverberating thump, like an oven door swinging open and bouncing on its hinges. The slight smell of burned sugar that Pamela had begun to notice while Karen was being welcomed intensified.

"Oh, my!" Melanie raised her pretty hands to her pretty face. "I'd better check on things. He's making something he found online—a dump cake." She hurried toward the kitchen, where Roland's gruff complaints gradually yielded to his wife's soothing encouragement. Pamela caught the words "I think you noticed in time" and "That's what ice cream is for," and a few minutes later, Roland strode around the corner beaming with satisfaction. The leather briefcase he used for his knitting supplies was dangling from his hand.

"Shall we get started with our knitting?" he said. "Refreshments at eight."

A few excited barks came from down the hallway. Pamela heard the jangle of a leash and the click of toenails, and Melanie and Ramona appeared at the entrance to the living room. "I'm taking her out now," Melanie said, catching Roland's eye. "Good luck with all your projects." She smiled at the group. Melanie was bundled in a lambskin coat, with a fuzzy hat that matched the creamy fur of the coat's wide collar. Ramona was dressed for the chilly night as well, in a doggy sweater. As Melanie bent to fasten the leash to her collar, Ramona broke away and scampered into the living room. She rushed from person to person, tail wagging furiously and licking any hands that reached out to give her a pat.

Something about Ramona's sweater looked familiar. It was knit from thick yarn in a natural off-white shade, and it covered the dachshund's long back from her neck to nearly her frantic tail. Wide bands of elastic held it in place. An erratic welt of raised stitches meandered here and there on its otherwise smooth surface, like a cable that had lost its course.

Bettina suppressed a giggle. "Is that what became of the cable-knit sweater you were making, Roland?"

In the entry, Melanie grimaced delicately and waved a hand in a subtle warning gesture.

Roland's face assumed a vaguely menacing expression no doubt familiar to his legal opponents. "She needed something to keep her warm on these cold nights," he said, in a voice that suggested no further comment would be forthcoming on that topic.

A thought was struggling to take shape in Pamela's mind, details hovering just at the edge of her memory—some errand she'd wanted to combine with her attendance at Knit and Nibble tonight. As soon as she opened her knitting bag, she realized what it was. Atop her supplies rested a lone knitting needle, slender and metallic.

"Karen," she exclaimed, brandishing it aloft. "Look what I found—or rather, what my vacuum found."

"Thank you!" Karen said. "I knew the other one had to be somewhere."

Bettina pulled its mate out of her own knitting bag. She leaned toward Pamela's ear and whispered, "Got it back from Clayborn."

Karen reached out a hand for the needles. "Maybe I *can* get the hang of using these. Or maybe . . . Roland?" She looked toward where Roland sat on the sleek turquoise chair that matched the sofa. He raised his head from a knitting needle with a few inches of freshly cast-on yarn. "Those metal needles turned up. Are you still interested?"

"I bought my own." He held out his newly begun project, and the needles glinted in the lamplight.

"Do you have a particular project in mind?" Nell asked. "Or could I recruit you to do an elephant?" Dangling from her needles was a nubby yellow oval with a smaller oval head and the beginnings of legs.

"I'll make an elephant," Pamela said. She'd come to the meeting with that very aim in mind. Her next serious creation would be the Christmas sweater for Penny, but the trip to Brooklyn would have to be scheduled first. She'd trade the golden yarn made from the hair of Buster the afghan for the substitute golden yarn promised by the proprietor of That Bedford Shop—identical but for its pedigree. And she'd come away with enough skeins to make sure of not running out of yarn midway through.

Pamela pushed herself up from the low-slung sofa and slid a small hassock next to the armchair where Nell sat. She extracted from her knitting bag a ball of orange mohair yarn that Nell pronounced to be "just enough" for an elephant, and the right color too. Under Nell's tutelage, she was soon engrossed in her new project, picking up stitches at the end of each row to shape the curve of the elephant's back.

Conversation ebbed and flowed as people traded ideas for using Thanksgiving leftovers and agreed that going to the malls on Black Friday might be good for bargain hunters but was not worth the aggravation.

"Anyway," Karen Dowling said, "Dave and I have agreed that his job offer is the best Christmas present we could ever have, and we'll save our money to spend fixing up the house."

"What about gifts for relatives?" Bettina asked.

"I buy little things all year and put them away," Karen said.

"I do too," Nell said. "Rummage sales. Everything doesn't always have to be new."

"Rummage sales?" Roland looked up with a horrified expression on his face. "I don't think Melanie would be happy with a gift from a rummage sale."

"I might." Melanie's voice floated in from the hallway, accompanied by the jangle of a leash. Ramona dashed past the living room doorway. Melanie paused in the opening, still bundled in her lambskin coat and the creamy wool hat. "I didn't just marry you for your money, you silly man."

Looking pleased with himself in an embarrassed way, Roland turned back to his knitting. In a few minutes, Melanie was back, without the coat and hat but wearing an apron that covered her from chest to knees. "I'll help serve the refreshments," she said. "Are you ready for a break?"

"It's called a dump cake," Roland said as people inspected the tray Melanie had deposited on the dining room table. The tray held six dessert plates, each bearing a square of cake topped with a scoop of ice cream.

"I cut them from the middle," Pamela heard Melanie whisper to Roland. "It was only the edges that got overdone." She turned to the group. "I'm taking orders for tea or coffee. Coffee's made, and I've got water going for tea."

"This looks delicious!" Bettina inspected her square of cake. "Are those walnuts?" Roland nodded. "And peaches? This time of year?"

"From a can. Two cans, really. Then you spread cake mix on top, right out of the package. Nuts if you want them, and you bake it and it all turns into a cake."

Back in the living room, people concentrated on their cake and ice cream for a few minutes, punctuated only by Nell's comment that the cake could be made with fresh fruit and it would be a lot healthier.

"Well, I think it's delicious," Bettina said. "And the recipe sounds like just my kind of cooking—easy. I'm dying to try it."

Pamela waited until forks had been deposited on empty plates and all offers of second helpings had been refused. "We have some club business to discuss," she said.

"In that case . . ." Melanie rose and began collecting plates and forks.

"You can stay," Pamela said. "We're not a secret society—but at this point we're down to five members. So if anybody knows anybody who likes to knit . . ." She surveyed them—sweet little Karen Dowling; Nell Bascomb, with her gentle face and her do-good projects; Roland DeCamp, still as tightly wound as ever, despite the knitting; and her faithful best friend, Bettina. "We'll be meeting next week, of course, so be thinking and ask around."

Nell's eyes widened and she gave an exasperated sigh. "It's my turn to host, isn't it?"

"I think so," Bettina said.

"Workmen are coming. It was the only time I could schedule them, and the dining room ceiling is just about to come down on our heads." She smiled sadly. "The joys of an old house."

"We can meet at my house," Pamela said.

The people facing her looked at one another in alarm. Finally Bettina spoke up. "I don't know, Pamela," she said. "At your house knitting is, well, murder."

KNIT

The Frugal Knitter's Scarf: Bohemian Chic

If you've never knitted, it's easier to learn the basics by watching than by reading. The Internet abounds with tutorials that show the process clearly. Just search "how to knit."

You only need to learn the basic knitting stitch. Don't worry about "purl." That's used in alternating rows to create the stockinette stitch—the stitch you see, for example, in a typical sweater. If you use "knit" on every row, you will end up with the stitch called the garter stitch. The garter stitch is actually better for making a scarf, because the knitted piece won't have a tendency to roll up at the edges, as happens with stockinette, and it won't have a "wrong" side. It will look the same on both sides.

To knit a scarf you will need at least 200 yards of yarn—more if you want it to be longer or wider. A typical skein of medium-weight acrylic yarn from the hobby store contains 170 yards. The fun of the Bohemian Chic scarf, however, is that it's made from random bits of this and that. If you're a knitter, you probably have many interesting yarn remnants left from other projects. Another source of yarn is tag sales. It's not unusual to come upon a whole stash of leftover yarn at a tag sale—especially if it's one of those sales in which a whole house is being emptied.

Collect your yarn, the more colors the better. If you have different textures—like angora, mohair, or bouclé—consider using them too, alternating them with smoother yarns. For this project, use medium-weight yarn and medium-gauge needles (size 8, 9, or 10).

Casting on 40 stitches will make your scarf ten inches wide. If you want it to be narrower or wider, cast on fewer stitches, or more. Use the simple slip-knot cast-on process or the more complicated "long tail" process. Either works fine. "How to knit" tutorials usually include casting on, or you can search "how to cast on." Now pick your first color and knit an inch or so, which will come out to five or six rows. Then graft on another color. To do this, just cut off the strand of yarn for your first color, leaving a tail of at least three inches, and tie the end of your new color to it, also leaving a tail of three inches beyond the knot. When your scarf is finished, you will weave these tails into the knitted fabric to hide them. If you cut the yarn off right at the knot, the knot can loosen, and then stitches will unravel. Keep knitting, adding new colors every inch or so, occasionally returning to a previous color. If you want a really random look, you can change color in the middle of a row.

If you don't have a lot of different colors, you can use the alternating-color idea at both ends of the scarf and buy a skein in a coordinating color to knit a long one-color stretch in the middle. A scarf can be as long as two yards, but take into account how you want to wear it, and measure scarves you have and like for reference.

When the scarf reaches the length you want, cast off. The instructions for this process are usually part of a "how to knit" tutorial as well, or you can search "how to cast off." Leave a tail of about three inches after you cast off the last stitch.

Now it's time to hide your tails. Use a yarn needle—a large needle with a large eye and a blunt end. Thread the needle with your first tail and work the needle in and out of the knitted fabric for an inch or so. Pull the yarn through and cut off the shorter tail that's left. For the striped parts, hide the tails in the knitted sections that correspond to their colors.

For a picture of a finished Bohemian Chic scarf, visit PeggyEhrhart.com.

NIBBLE

Autumn Apple Cake

Use crisp, slightly tart apples; even Granny Smith or other green apples will work.

Ingredients:

    3 large or 4 medium apples
    2 cups sugar
    3 cups flour
    1 teaspoon baking soda
    1 teaspoon salt
    1 teaspoon cinnamon
    1 teaspoon nutmeg
    1 cup vegetable oil
    2 eggs, slightly beaten
    1 teaspoon vanilla
    1 cup chopped walnuts
    Powdered sugar

Core and peel the apples. To do this easily, quarter them first, then slice the cores out and peel the quarters. Chop or coarsely grate the apples. You want about 4 cups' worth. Place the apples in a small bowl, add the sugar, and let the mixture sit for an hour. Sift the flour, baking soda, salt, and spices into a large bowl. Using a beater, mix in the oil, eggs, and vanilla, and then stir in the apples and sugar, and the walnuts, by hand.

Turn the mixture into a greased tube pan and bake for one hour at 350 degrees. Let the cake cool, then invert it onto a serving plate. Sprinkle it with powdered sugar. To do this evenly, put the powdered sugar in a small sieve and shake it over the cake. Cover the edges of the serving plate first to protect it from the powdered sugar. If you like, you can offer whipped cream or vanilla ice cream when you serve the cake.

For a picture of the finished cake,
visit PeggyEhrhart.com.

Connect with Us

Visit us online at
KensingtonBooks.com
to read more from your favorite authors, see books
by series, view reading group guides, and more.

Join us on social media

for sneak peeks, chances to win books and prize packs,
and to share your thoughts with other readers.

facebook.com/kensingtonpublishing
twitter.com/kensingtonbooks

Tell us what you think!

To share your thoughts, submit a review,
or sign up for our eNewsletters, please visit:
KensingtonBooks.com/TellUs.